BRING ME FLESH, I'LL BRING HELL

BRING ME FLESH, I'LL BRING HELL

MARTIN ROSE

Talos Press

Talos books may be purchased in bulk at special discounts for sales promotion, corporate gifts, fund-raising, or educational purposes. Special editions can also be created to specifications. For details, contact the Special Sales Department, Skyhorse Publishing, 307 West 36th Street, 11th Floor, New York, NY 10018 or info@skyhorsepublishing.com.

Talos® and Talos Press® are registered trademarks of Skyhorse Publishing, Inc.®, a Delaware corporation.

Visit our website at www.skyhorsepublishing.com.

10 9 8 7 6 5 4 3 2 1

Library of Congress Cataloging-in-Publication Data is available on file.

Cover design by Anthony Morais
Cover photo credit by ThinkStock

Print ISBN: 978-1-940456-09-6
Ebook ISBN: 978-1-940456-15-7

Printed in the United States of America

"Everyone sees what you appear to be, few really know what you are."

—*The Prince,* Nicolo Machiavelli

"It is not the well-fed long-haired man I fear, but the pale and the hungry looking."

—Julius Caesar

PART 1

LAZAR HOUSE BLUES

Rain is hell on rotting flesh.

Rain dripped from the brim of my hat in rivulets while I waited for someone to answer the door, stabbing the button with one hand and clutching my jawbone in the other. Bleached bone protruded through thin, moldy flaps of skin. Bundled in a trench coat and a wide-brimmed fedora, I looked like a Sam Spade cliché ten years dead. A scarf concealed the lower half of my destroyed face until the rain and the wind conspired to tear it away and leave my tongue and the inner workings of my lower mouth exposed to the moist air.

My jawbone broke off an hour ago. Brushing my teeth in front of the bathroom mirror. A swift jerk of the toothbrush and my jaw came unhinged, fell into the sink, wet and ringed with toothpaste foam. I had stared a long moment, digesting this new, uncomfortable experience. I may be dead, but I was determined to take excellent care of my pearly whites. It was the unintended consequences I was having trouble with.

When a body part inexplicably breaks off, most people seek a doctor.

I apologize, that's not true—first the screaming, then the doctor. If you're a high-functioning corpse, however, medical plans are limited. Death qualifies as a pre-existing condition, so insurance companies loathe me and doctors don't like me because they're not sure how to bill a corpse. I exist in a gray netherland of loopholes.

So who does a zombie go to when he starts falling apart?

Not the sort of question I thought I'd be asking myself at the age of thirty, when I expected my biggest worries were going to be how to keep the lawn watered and how to send my son to college. Staring at my jaw at the bottom of the sink opened up a new world of questions that shook me in uncomfortable ways.

Better get used to this, Vitus. You've been dead ten years now. What's going to start falling off you when you're twenty years dead?

I thought of my son as I picked up my jawbone, balanced it on my palm with a long sigh. Molars embedded in the black gum line, the peeling flesh. These were the same teeth I used to tear my family apart with coyote hunger, with wolf appetite.

When a zombie falls apart, he goes to see a mortician, of course.

✳

Niko cracked open the door through the rain streaming from the gutter. I stepped back, startled. I had not expected her.

A moon-shaped face peered out, tired blue circles beneath the eyes, pale skin. Dyed black hair. Bangs squaring her face in a Bettie Page pantomime. Goth-scene chick fixing up corpses for food money. How did a cute thing like her end up at Pleasant Hills Funeral Home playing nursemaid to rotting corpses?

A jaw is helpful when speaking. Without one, I could hardly use my charming wiles on her, so I brought something more persuasive with me.

I pulled out a Glock 19.

The barrel cut a black line through the pouring rain and she froze. A breath hissed through her clenched teeth.

"What—"

I thrust a note into her face, distracting her from the gun. Her hands were small and coated with enough rings to double as brass knuckles. Dainty fingers with the nails painted black. She took the note from me and held it in the squall until ink smeared down the page.

I am falling apart and I need you to put me back together.

She peered over the edge of the paper and stared in the dark space where my eyes should be, swallowed in the shadow of the hat. If she was looking for my features, she would make out little to nothing, and that was the way it was supposed to be, the way I engineered it.

I held my breath until the steam ran out, funneling between us.

Memory flickered behind her eyes. With it, a small part of me blazed brighter. Then her expression turned opaque along with the feeling behind it, and what I took for recognition was only fear and nothing else.

I was relieved. She didn't recognize me.

"This isn't a doctor's office, or a hospital, we don't have those kind of—"

I ripped the note out of her hand and it pounded flat to the pavement beneath the rain. I fished into my pocket, bringing forth my jawbone into the light.

I thrust it into her hand.

She cried out and dropped it onto the cement. It played dead like a raw pork chop swimming in a pool of water.

I groaned through the scarf, hot breath in the cold.

How could she be so careless, dammit? That was a piece of *me*.

I lifted my gun, jerking the muzzle from the jawbone then back to her, making it clear that she should pick it up.

I appreciated that the gun had not driven her into hysterics, and she bent in the downpour to retrieve the rotten piece of flesh from the ground. She hesitated and then her fingers closed on it. The second she had it, I wasted no time and hustled her over the threshold and into the building. Ensconced in the dry warmth of the ventilated air, I motioned for her to keep going down the hall stretching out before us. Obediently, she backed before the muzzle of the gun. Her pleasing hour glass figure led the way, a curl of hair hugging the swell of her breasts.

I cursed myself for noticing it and wished I were still alive—wished I were that errant curl of hair nestled against her warm flesh. My salivary glands kicked in, churning my mouth into a cut-open tomato's wet, pulpy center.

Through a second door and we were in a room filled with gurneys, tables, and funeral home equipment—formaldehyde, fungicides, mentholated germicides, pump machines to siphon blood out and embalming fluid in, glues and tools too numerous to mention. Drain holes in the floor like sharp-set mouths with metal teeth. Florescent light reflected stark white walls.

Cold light fell upon me and I shrank in on myself—my grisly appearance made me self-conscious in the unforgiving CFLs—reduced to an insect examined under stadium lighting. How much could she see, now that we were out of the drizzle and in the arctic florescence? With my jaw in her dainty fingers, the resemblance to Bettie Page became even more striking as she tracked me with diamond-cut eyes.

I held the gun away from her and set it aside on one of the metal tables, the muzzle pointed at the concrete wall. Her shoulders fell, visibly relaxed.

Let's see how long that lasts, I thought grimly, and unwound the scarf from my face.

To her credit, she did not scream, but took one tottering step back.

I removed the fedora, setting it beside the Glock.

And waited.

The world seemed to have stopped. The room, the building, embedded in oceanic silence. I knew if I arrived in the early morning hours I could catch her alone, doing preparatory work for upcoming burials. Corpses lay out beneath their shrouds in an orderly line from gurney to gurney, the impression of their noses and mouths and closed eyes casting deep shadows beneath. They bespoke an eternity I tasted but could not remember. The bodies made the room heavier with unmeasured gravity and my collar itched with discomfort. I was a trespasser in the natural habitat of the dead; and hushed, the quiet amplified and added to her vulnerable beauty.

Without my jaw, my tongue hung and dangled down into empty space like a pink necktie. My upper lip, purple-toned, and grotesque gaps revealed deeper tissue into the bone beneath. The light cast me in wretched hues as she studied me with eyes as big as paper lanterns.

I took a deep breath.

She could run, fight me, refuse me. I waited for her to decide my fate with a look or a word. Or a scream.

And then, she set the jaw on a stainless steel countertop and opened a rattling drawer where they kept surgical wires for use on corpses who needed heavy work to make them look normal—accident victims, chain saw oopsies, and other unforeseen massacres.

She picked up a scalpel, the wiring, and my jaw in her tiny hands, and turned to me, drawing closer—closer than she wanted to be. I tilted my head into the light, struggling to be still and keep my homeless tongue hanging in place.

"Will this hurt you?" she asked.

I shook my head. My tongue followed in an obscene pendulum swing.

She took a step forward and my back found the wall. Tiled surfaces, linoleum, and sterile smells conspired to close in on me and dizzy my senses. I could not remember the last time someone had touched me without intending to kill me.

"Brace yourself," she whispered.

I closed my milky eyes. Her warm fingers pressed against my ravaged face, and then she drove the wire in.

★

Three hours.

Three hours of broken skin and vile fluid, of Niko turning aside to wretch. She wore lipstick rendered in a pornographic red and when she finished she stepped back to admire her handiwork, head tilted beneath a cascade of black curls.

I opened my mouth, working the jaw. Metal clicked deep in my bones, but the fit was comfortable and it did the job.

I withdrew a battered pack of cigarettes and stuck a coffin nail between my rotted lips, dipped the end into the lighter flame, and breathed fire into my lungs.

"Are you going to kill me?" she asked.

"No."

"Are you dead?"

"You ask a lot of questions for a scared mortician."

"Death doesn't scare me. You look like all the corpses, but the smell is what gives you away. You smell like them. You smell like dead meat on a butcher's table."

I sighed. This conversation was finished. I turned, swiping the Glock off the table and tucking it into my shoulder holster, where it disappeared into layers of fabric. I grabbed the fedora and the scarf and faced the long hall to the exit.

"Wait."

But I did not wait. I left, trailing a long curl of smoke behind me, thinking of the days when I would have stayed.

★

The long, sterile hall fed into a lobby, with plush carpet and soothing blooms of fake plastic flowers. My shoes left imprints, stamped into high-end Berber until I came to stand before a suit of armor.

A knight dominated a pedestal beneath a showcase light, cross-hatching long shadows down the metal plates. His presence was designed to offer a symbol of strength in a time of grief, a chivalrous, noble sentiment, or maybe just an expensive museum piece to give the funeral home a posher atmosphere. A long, black slit divided his visor, and I stared into the emptiness where eyes should be, transfixed. Even without substance, he pushed a sinister presence into the room, disapproving with his shield and his sword. Stained metal gone to rust at the edges. He looked ready to challenge me, to take me on.

I gave him a final resentful look and took my leave.

★

Finding work when you're minus a pulse and a heartbeat is difficult.

For this reason, I take on specialized clients through referrals. I'm a lone wolf kind of guy, even before Virus X, but Glock and I work together just fine—myself and several of his smaller, cordial friends. They're all the company I need, and all the company capable of tolerating me in turn.

This is how I came to be staring at the home security footage of two potential customers loitering on my front porch, ringing my doorbell at an ungodly hour of the morning. Morning itself wasn't my prevailing setback. Every hour of my unlife is ungodly, and being dead fixes problems you thought you had—like a need for sleep.

I used to waste my midnight hours in darkened bars in which most of the customers were packing metal where they shouldn't be or slinging dope; now I was left with the dubious comfort of an easy chair, watching black-and-white movies and silent films into the wee hours of the morning. These activities were punctuated by the chime of my digital watch, reminding me to swallow my dose of Atroxipine. Thanks to this handy drug, all that stands between me and a shambling, low-function, flesh-eating monster is a thin chemical veil activating key sectors of my brain in the frontal lobe, where the seat of forward thinking lives.

Occasionally, I do like to keep the odd bit of raw hamburger meat in the fridge for when I'm feeling under the weather. Other than that, I get by in a haunted house full of bad memories. It used to be full of family pictures—wife smiling, child playing, all the stereotypes that populate the beloved suburban dream I chased and chased until I woke up from the dream and found myself alone in a new nightmare. I burned the albums in the backyard when I'd had enough.

The pictures are gone, but the memories, those are harder to get at.

★

I dry swallowed my dose, two pills. My jawbone pinged a metal sound to follow the action, evidence of Niko's work. I smiled and touched the place where she drove the wire in to hinge the jaw, but sentiment didn't suit me. How long would my benevolent feeling toward her last with my brain's crumbling infrastructure dictating my emotional life? Better not to linger on her and confront the business at hand of the newcomers on my porch.

After attempting to make myself presentable—a challenge for a modern-day monster—a button-down shirt and a ragged pair of jeans later, I opened the front door.

A man and woman. He wore a pair of wire-rimmed glasses portraying his face as mousy and his eyes doubled in size, pushing forty with sandy hair graying at the temples. His sweater vest, his shoes, and his carefully creased khakis made him look like he stepped out of a catalog. The Dork Summer Fashion Line.

The woman wasn't any better, dyed red hair carefully coiffed, a long skirt down past her knees and to her ankles. Puritans had more flair.

We stood there, all three of us, frozen statues staring at a lone scarecrow in the doorway playing dress-up. I lifted an eyebrow and eyed them from the interior where the murk devoured my destroyed and rotted face. I removed all the lights in the house years ago, preferring the darkness both for myself and my customers. They didn't need to lose their lunch, and I didn't need the constant reminder that I should be six feet underground, not an extra from a Michael Jackson music video. Or Michael Jackson.

"Shut up," I began.

The woman, who had opened her mouth to speak, shut it, with a startled blink of her eyes. Like her husband, she resembled a pigeon, with the same degree of intelligence.

"I only take clients who have been referred. I don't know who you are. So before you say one word, I need to know how you got to my porch. Assuming you aren't here to hand out religious tracts."

The man cleared his throat and cast a nervous glance at his wife.

"Mr. Vitus, we got your number from Geoff Lafferty."

Geoff was an officer with the precinct. Sort of. He wrecked a cruiser and suffered paralysis as a result. When cops become disabled, arrangements are made—early retirement, disability, that sort of thing. But if you're only twenty-six, it's a tad young to be calling it quits, so they moved him to the evidence facility, where they store all the items from crime scenes. In a pinch, he was a quiet guy who could connect me to things the rest of the world had forgotten about, or even make inconvenient items disappear from a court case. A good guy to know in a state full of crooks.

"I'm listening."

"Aren't you going to invite us in?" the woman asked.

My hand fell away from the threshold, subsiding into the darkness. I turned my back on them, found a kitchen chair, and dragged it across the floor to perch before them. I offered them nothing. If I couldn't eat or drink, they wouldn't, either.

"Don't mind the smell. My dog died and I haven't buried him yet," I said acidly.

They came forward, and their faces twisted in unison as the smell hit them. I was going to have to get some air fresheners soon, I supposed. Couldn't have the neighbors calling the cops because there was a dead body in the house. Myself, I barely noticed the aroma of decay that wafted from my dry-rotted skin.

If I could describe the smell that pervaded in these dark rooms, the smell that oozed from my rotting flesh, I would have to say it was a cross between carrion, roadkill, and tuna salad.

Choking a little, the woman sat on the sofa, clutching her purse to her chest. She held her sleeve to her nose, watching her husband. She beat out a hesitant Morse code with every blink of her eyes: *Can we leave? Please?*

He cleared his throat before he began, but I believed he was choking on his previous meal.

"Mr. Vitus, we, ah," and I let him flounder a moment as he tried not to vomit. When he recovered himself, he tried again.

"Our son has gone missing. Geoff recommended that we contact you, said you were the best detective—"

I rolled my eyes at the word. *Detective* sounds ancient, right up there with *blacksmith*.

"—this side of the coast, and if there was anyone who could locate our son, it would be you."

"How old is your son?"

"Seventeen."

"The police couldn't help you?"

"No. They filed a missing persons report, and said they would keep us updated, but we weren't satisfied with that."

He didn't look upset that his son was missing. *Odd*, I thought. Odder still, his son was hardly a boy—a grown man, really. No wonder the police weren't worried; this couldn't be the first time the "boy" had skipped town. Not with fashion sense like his parents had.

"Did you dress him?"

"What?" the man asked.

"Never mind. How long has he been missing?"

"A week."

"Give me the facts. What's his name? When was he last seen?"

"Owen was staying after school to help with their activities. He helps other kids who need someone to talk to, kids who are feeling depressed, that sort of thing. We didn't see him after that. He was supposed to have been home in time for dinner, but he didn't show. Didn't think much of it—sometimes he spends time with friends, we thought maybe he was meeting a girl. And then he didn't show up later that night. No show the next morning."

I rolled my eyes. The kid ran away. Case closed.

I looked at my watch.

"I have his picture," the wife said, opening her purse with a *snap!* She rummaged through random objects with her elbow held at an odd angle, as though she were afraid something inside the bag would bite her. Her face was forgettable and ordinary. This common ugliness in her features would have been forgivable if not for her equally forgettable and ordinary personality. When she spoke, it was in monotone.

She found the picture and held it out to me, leaning forward on the couch.

A sense of claustrophobia flirted with me. The housewife I'd taken as marginally intelligent was playing with me and wanted me to draw closer to her and there was nothing I could do to avoid it. She lifted the photo.

I gritted my teeth until the metal clicked and approached her.

Lazy, I thought, swiping the picture from her hand and retreating into the darkness before ambient daylight could reveal my monstrous features. The last thing I needed was a hysterical couple screaming, "Oh my god, what happened to your face!"

Wouldn't be the first time, I sighed.

I looked down at the picture.

Rotten breath deflated my lungs. My throat closed and my fist clenched around the photograph. A boy stared up at me, liquid eyes all brown and soft lines of tender youth. We all begin this young, this untouched, but his innocence was not what moved me.

"I thought you said he was seventeen," I barked. The hand holding the photograph shook. My fingertips turned white beneath black mold. "This is a young child. A toddler."

Mrs. Rogers clucked her tongue as though to chide herself for her mistake and fanned her hand out in exasperation over her chest. There was another quick rummage and she offered me a card deck of photos—passionless school portraits of a boy moving through awkward adolescence—but I did not take them, so she was left offering them to the thin air.

"These are all we have. Will you take the case?"

"I burned this picture years ago," I whispered, closing my eyes. My boy, my son, Clayton Adamson. I moved my thumb across his face in the photo, as though I could touch him still. I was supposed to buy him a sheriff's badge when I got back from the service. When I returned from Kosovo. He still had his baby fat, still had his baby teeth and his round, teacup eyes.

I promised him.

And he's dead now.

How did they get his picture?

"What were your names?" I asked, turning with the photograph in my hand as though it were an ace in a winning streak—I dared not let it go.

"Oh, I'm Suzanne Rogers," she said. "My husband is Rick."

I looked down at the face of my dead son, searching for a trick, an explanation in the picture itself.

"Mr. and Mrs. Rogers, eh?"

In a better mood, I may have found that information hilarious, but faced with a picture stolen from my past, I found nothing funny.

Someone in this room was lying.

"And you say this boy in this photo is alive and well, by the name of Owen Rogers?"

"Well, yes, and we'd very much like to know where he is and have him safe at home again. Will you help us?"

Mrs. Rogers had a set of brown eyes rapidly spilling tears like an overfilled glass. I reached for the other photos and kept them before me, consumed their glossy stills with my eyes while she fumbled with a tissue, dabbing at her face so she wouldn't smear her carefully applied mascara. Once, she must have been gorgeous. He, too, once upon a time, must have been her Prince Charming, but he had the look of a man starving himself to keep his youthful shape—a receding hairline, sagging skin necklacing his throat.

"Well," I said, and smiled, allowing the grin to consume my face, stretching from broken tooth to broken tooth. Metal clicked inside my mouth, like the sound a hammer on a .38 revolver makes. "I've got a soft spot for kids."

I have a lot of soft spots. But that's beside the point.

★

I watched them as they left, standing from my porch in shadow, watching the video feed from my security camera as they linked hands and descended the steps to their sensible wood-grain station wagon.

Owen's picture—the picture of the child once mine—remained on my desk, face down. I dared not look at it.

Call it a lack of courage. Monsters are not known for their bravery, after all. Here I was, a corpse in a glorified coffin I called a house, with not a single lightbulb in my lamps, for fear someone might turn them on and see me for what I really was, too petrified to look at the frozen image of my son. My smiling, blond-haired, brown-eyed, gap-toothed boy.

But it could not be my smiling, blond-haired, brown-eyed, gap-toothed boy. He'd be only twelve by now and this doppelgänger was older. What could explain away this schism?

I had no answer.

Beep-beep.

The sound of the digital wristwatch sang my personal lullaby, my siren song. I set logic aside to take my dose. I shook out a pill of Atroxipine from the orange bottle and pushed it through my decaying lips.

I'd died during the night and had forgotten to shave; now I would spend eternity with a five o'clock shadow that rasped like sandpaper every time I sucked down a pill. Parts of my face were missing, tears and striations of eaten-away flesh, gone with time and sorrow. I wandered over to the window, thinking about the boy I'd once had, the family we had once been. All over now.

Zzzzzt. Zzzzzzzzzt.

My lips curled away from my tombstone teeth, a grimace of disgust. A blue bottle fly buzzed against the window pane, throwing itself against the glass with vigor. His aggravated buzzing became a desperate wail.

There are few things the dead fear. If you lay down to sleep one night and wake up a shambling, decaying corpse the next day, the last thing on your mind is what your stamp collection will fetch in the fair market or how many points the stock market plunged. Fear of discovery? Perhaps.

One day, a guy riding high on one Romero film too many is apt to blow my head off with a shotgun, and double-tap for good measure, but when you join the army at eighteen you expect people to take shots at you. Injury poses no threat to me. Death is inevitable.

My secret fear?

Maggots.

Maggots can reduce the carcass of a deer to a pile of bones in twenty-four hours. To miss my dose of Atroxipine would be to resign myself to a likewise existence—mindlessly consuming flesh with no thought process, no consciousness of who or what I'd been before the moment I opened my jaws and shoved a living person inside. Naturally, the thought of being consumed by a cloud of insects as disgusting as fly larvae would give me nightmares—if I were capable of sleep. They would eat me from the inside out in miniscule bites, and who knows what would happen to them in return—would they carry on as undead flies, eating their own the way I am prone to eat my own?

Would they eat their wives? Their children?

In their reduced state, would they fail to heed their families' cries? Fail to recognize the pain they cause, see only what they once loved as a chance to satisfy this insatiable hunger that gnaws at the belly, craving a food that dare not be named?

I snapped, smashing the fly with a strike of my fist. His fat body popped like a blackberry against my skeletal hand, and the window shattered, fracturing in a spiderweb pattern. Blood spurted briefly from the resulting cut until the blood flow stopped without a valid heart to push more through.

I crushed the body of the fly with my boot, just to be sure.

We can't be having killer zombie flies, now can we?

★

I took the Rogers case, and I should have been working on it. Working on it like a dog, fighting against a cruel world that would kidnap children, attempting to assume the role of freakish superhero, without the tights. However, morals don't motivate me—they're as rotten as my fallen-apart flesh. And Mr. and Mrs.

Rogers had tears you could purchase at a Halloween store—manufactured and prepackaged with a money-back guarantee.

I tucked Owen's picture into my pocket, where it pressed against my dead flesh to the dead heart beneath. Beside it, I holstered my Glock, and then came the dressing ritual, a careful inventory to protect me from the prying eyes of the public. Camouflage become high fashion. My palette composed of dark blues and grays designed to fade me into the background at a moment's notice—coupled with a human tendency to ignore that which does not please the eye—and my transformation to a forgettable human version of myself was complete. Most work in this day and age can be conducted from home, freeing up the nighttime hours to roam in relative secrecy without too many people asking for my autograph and telling me I did great work in *Resident Evil*, and was Milla Jovovich nice?

Such are the risks when you're a corpse.

Sunglasses, check.

Atroxipine, check.

Hat, check.

Attitude, negotiable.

★

Pleasant Hills Funeral Home, aside from employing an attractive mortician who looked like Bettie Page, was adjacent to the town cemetery, which was bordered by wrought iron gates. I stopped at a street vendor a few blocks down, swapping a rumpled Andrew Jackson for a dozen roses, and passed through the gates unnoticed.

Two aisles, and then three to the left, and I was home.

Three graves in a line. The weather was pleasant, and I stood there like a suitor stood up by a prom date, recalling Jessica when she had been alive.

Jessica Adamson, Loving wife, b. Sept. 14, 1978, d. July 25, 1999.

Beside her, a marker with my name on it:

Vitus Adamson, Devoted Husband, b. Feb. 5, 1979, d. July 25, 1999.

A flag denoting I was a veteran waved halfheartedly in the wind.

The grave was empty.

Beside it, a smaller one with an engraving of a rosebud, broken in half; an old Victorian image symbolizing death before the deceased was given the chance to bloom. My son, the broken rose.

Clayton Adamson, Beloved Son, b. April 19, 1997, d. July 25, 1999.

I pulled out a single rose for him, setting it against his marker.

His grave was likewise empty, but for his bones.

I knew it because I oversaw their burial. There had been nothing left of him to bury by the time my brother realized his error and soldiers burst into my house on July 25, 1999.

I stooped to set down the roses against her stone.

"You shouldn't buy cheap roses from the street guy. We've got better ones inside."

Startled, I turned, pressing my fingers against the Glock.

Niko. Long, black dress hugging her skin in just the right places. Bedroom eyes studied me in full light, assessing me in this new place. She looked like she belonged in a music video for a gloomy band. She must be at least ten years younger than me, and with half the experience and bitterness that I carried.

"The street guy doesn't chitchat," I replied.

"You're a quiet guy."

I said nothing.

"You're also a zombie."

I cleared my throat. Was that a piece of my epiglottis stuck there? I swallowed it down.

"Pre-deceased," I corrected. "Zombie is so . . . inelegant."

She studied the tombstones. Polished quartz facades reflected the sun into her eyes, and she stepped closer to read them.

"They all died on the same day," she said.

Silence. The nice thing about death is tears become a thing of the past. My eyes are dry, desert stones pressed into my waxen face.

"No one left anything for him," she pointed out, gesturing to my headstone.

I decided that she was hot, but annoying.

"You know, if you need help with anything else, you should just ask. You don't have to come waving a gun around."

"Careful. I might take you up on that."

"Good. You need help. You're a fucking mess."

"Thanks. You dress like an expensive hooker."

"Thanks. You kiss your mother with that mouth, corpse-face?"

Pretty and demented. The only bad thing about this being dead gig was the lack of dating options and ability to act on them. I glanced at the headstone, *Jessica Adamson*, and wondered if it qualified as infidelity to flirt in front of your dead wife's grave.

Well, it was only good until death do us part, after all.

"No, I eat her with it."

Niko had nothing to say after that. She left, long strides in black combat boots through the grass, and I watched the sway of her hips a moment before letting my breath escape in a hiss.

Don't worry. My mother's alive and well in a nursing home in Lakehurst.

★

Being an investigator—or as most people think of it, a detective—is boring as shit.

The pay sucks; there's no vacation time. You work long hours watching people doing stupid things, like shop at a box store, pick up groceries, pick their noses, and cheat on their spouses. They all think they invented lying and they were the first to pull a fast one and no one will ever figure them out. There is nothing glamorous about toting a gun around and dropping bits of your flesh onto the pavement now and again.

The next few hours was exactly that.

I took a trip down to the high school, Westerly High. Everything was in proper order there: records showed an Owen Rogers in attendance, and as I thumbed through old report cards, tilting my head into shadow while the receptionist politely covered her nose with a tissue and wrestled her gorge back into place, I wondered if it were possible. Could my son have survived?

Everyone assumed I had eaten him.

They'd found his blood, they'd even found his bones . . . but the doubts began to multiply and creep in. My brother had been so desperate to sweep up the government's mess, they could have missed such a detail. After all, they'd found the bones of a little boy. That did not automatically make them my son's.

My thoughts were broken by the hiss of an air freshener. The receptionist shot a jet of Bayberry Dreams into the air, where it misted like car exhaust throughout the office.

Hint taken. I stink.

I handed her back the papers, and she waved me out eagerly. Niko might have been a smart-ass, but there was a girl used to smelling death on a daily basis. I realized I missed that kind of human interaction—you know, the sort that doesn't require an aerosol can.

★

By all accounts, Owen Rogers appeared to be a real person. He had a social security number, excelled in his biology classes, even dated a cheerleader. According to a pizza-faced senior in his class, a twitchy kid who fiddled with his glasses every other sentence, everyone loved Owen Rogers.

"But the parents? Sheesh. *Real* strict. Like, he went to party where everyone was invited to sleep over, and they came at three a.m. to pick him up once they found out where he was. Benny Tuttle made a joke that they keep him in a cage in the basement, and you know what the funny thing was? Owen didn't laugh. Those people are weird."

"Owen ever talk about it? About the parents?"

"He never talked much. He was the kind of guy who always listened a lot. Chicks like him, 'cause he would listen to their problems. You probably wouldn't find a person who didn't like him, but anyone who knew him, like, really knew him? Good luck, buddy."

"Thanks."

"Hey, Mr. Adamson?"

"What?"

"Could you sign my paper, here? I really loved *Zombieland*. Big fan."

"Sure kid, whatever."

★

My son.

I looked at the picture from inside the car, the dome light illuminating a young boy's face. I didn't take it out often, as though my touch were a poison that could stain the photo film.

In the high school, there had been other pictures of him. I'd torn out the page of the yearbook, and there was a much older Owen Rogers there. Seeing my own picture in the hands of the Rogers had enraged me, filled me with a demon energy I could not exorcise—I had come to accept the fact that my son had died and would never be a man, gotten used to the baby face, the terminally innocent brown eyes.

Now I had a picture of the becoming man.

He'd thinned out from the chubby toddler with the baby cheeks. Replaced youth with a long, angular face. Quick and scintillating eyes above a trained smile. I felt a swell of quiet pride. Handsome, well-liked, and irreproachable. Owen Rogers looked like I had at his age; the most damning proof of my imagined paternity.

He can't be your son.

And why not? There had never been a body. What if Jessica had been babysitting someone that day, what if Jessica had dropped Clay off at the neighbor's for a playdate, or left him with a caregiver to escape the frenzy of motherhood for a stolen moment, a moment the fates looked the other way? I rejected such flimsy logic in the next second. No such thing had happened and hadn't I tucked him into his crib myself? Still, I persisted in building fantasies in which a well-meaning emergency responder took Clay to the hospital, where the child fell into the social system, his origins forgotten, his slate wiped clean. I imagined alternate scenarios of those first minutes and hours in the aftermath of my turning, in which Clay simply toddled off onto the neighbor's lawn through throngs of frantic people, straight into a new home and a new life. Each fantasy more outrageous than the previous.

I turned over the possibilities.

Or someone was hoping I would fall into this trap; believe in what I wanted. Count on heartache to do the work of persuasion. Exploit the remains of my heart.

I tucked the pictures into my pocket and left the car.

★

I came to the Rogers' house unannounced. They had never given me their address, and Rogers populated the phone book in greater numbers than I had phone minutes to waste—the school proved useful in providing me what I needed from a list of dead-end addresses, and I stood before what appeared to be a burned-out shell of a building. Concrete foundation sketched a square embedded in derelict land.

No one lived here, if anyone ever had.

I entered the yard anyway. A sad, overgrown, neglected garden grew up through burnt timber and beams, vines snaking along the remains of a wooden frame. The ground blackened where the house fire had burned hot and long. If there had been furniture, items of personal nature, they were gone. Faded caution tape spiraled out into the wind and, beside me, the doors and windows of neighboring houses stayed closed. No one asked me my business and this was not unusual.

I poked through the thorny interior. The coastal wind shifted and spat a random paper at me that pressed against my leg until I snatched it up. A missing child flier for a boy called Marco Spitz who had been eight when fate snatched him away into the abyss of the world, never to be seen again. The flier was two years old. I crumpled it up and tossed it away. I inspected the walls, what was left of them, peering into their sandwiched insides. Rats and deer mice scattered from their nests, trailing insulation and black mold. Gossamer webs infested every wretched corner of broken joists and surviving studs.

In the backyard, the grass became a churning frontier land of thigh-high weeds. You would think that when your house burns down, you'd mention it, but I guess when you're busy summoning fake tears for the benefit of a fake stolen son, it's the last thing you think of.

While I pulled my shoe out of a sucking puddle of black mud, I followed the line of a chain link fence along the back that pointed like a rusting arrow to a dog house nestled in the corner of the property.

Somehow, they didn't strike me as the dog-loving type. I took them for cat people.

I advanced through the weeds. I wasn't a dog fan myself nowadays, as they tend to find me on the tasty side, like an overripe pork roll. I expected wildlife to dart out from the darkness as I bent down to peer in the hole. Gnats swarmed thick and heavy in a cloud, and I swatted at them until I gave up and breathed them in and out as though they were inconvenient elements of the air itself, like humidity.

I thrust my hand into spiderwebs, into moist, spongy wooden walls. My skeletal fingertips tapped against warped wooden boards as I searched the interior. No loose plywood, nothing questionable—

I passed over an object. Nails rattled and a board clattered loose and fell to the earthen floor in an expulsion of mold. Beneath this, pill bugs and carpenter ants sprinkled down through my seeking fingers until I encountered a ridge, gripped it, and pulled it out.

A journal.

A journal hidden in a dog house. Someone was keeping secrets, and I didn't think it was Rover.

★

I didn't dare open it on the property. I needed a place that was quiet, where I wouldn't be bothered, so I drove back the way I had come, to the darkened house of bad memories I called home.

How I wished I could still drink like I had when I was alive.

Beep-beep.

I reached for the orange prescription bottle, shaking out a fresh dose. With a metal click, my mouth closed over the pills and I savored the medicinal flavor. After each dose, I registered a subtle change as the medication hit my stomach lining, breaking apart and passing through the membrane in minutes. Chemicals lit up my neurons and receptors like fireworks, bringing my fading intellect back to life again, making logical human thought possible.

Without it, my memories otherwise were broken fragments, shuffled cards. I did not like to think of it. I understood the feral nature of my condition and was at home with it; what I did not suffer gladly was the loss of self-awareness and identity.

I did not read the journal right away. At my desk and with my hand over the warped cover, I lingered and thought of Clay, the boy as I remembered him. But I had as many memories as there were human remains of my boy: nothing.

Nothing at all.

I turned the first page.

★

There was a boy, and this boy had no earthly father.

This boy had guardians and watchers, men and women who wore the same outfits like uniforms, like khakis and sweater vests and ties and suits and long skirts. The guardians and watchers were made up of a thousand eyes, and they watched the boy every minute of every day.

The guardians and watchers kept the boy and sheltered him in house after house. This boy never had a home, just a thousand and one couches he was shuffled from, and sometimes when there were no couches in these dilapidated homes, there were only basement floors or attic rooms.

For the boy was a secret; a secret the guardians and watchers did not want others to know. And the boy was schooled in social manipulation, how never to give oneself away, and he understood without being asked he should bury his heart and his feelings and never be close; not to the fake parents who pretended to love him, or even to the schoolchildren who really did want to love him.

When the boy asked where his real parents were, he was told he had none. He was born into this world through Righteous Passage, conceived as Jesus was to Mary; and the boy was their holy son.

A thousand eyes watched the boy; but even eyes grow tired.

Guardians and watchers are people, and people sleep. So the boy learns to save himself, gather his energy for the night, when the guardians pretend they are an ordinary, average family. They go to separate bedrooms like in old 1950s sitcoms where no one ever has sex, even in a marital bed. And there, the guardians sleep.

The boy uses this time to stir, to come awake. He creeps across the floor and becomes expert in assessing a house the moment he enters it. He intuits the places where the floorboards are most likely to creak and give him away, knows where the shadows will be at their thickest in the midnight hour, so when the stray guardian awakens in the middle of the night to take a leak, he shrinks into the darkest corner and waits there, unnoticed, until they fall asleep once more.

He does not escape these clever prisons made of many people's homes, that do not look like prisons at all. Here, the bars are white picket fences, and garden gnomes in bright flowers stand guard with an air of menace. They have made it clear over time, with sinister suggestions, with strange weapons they keep in gun cabinets and stranger weapons like whips beneath their beds, that bad things will happen to him if he questions the life they have built for him.

He wants to escape. He dreams of empty fields and crowded streets where he fades from their thousand eyes, but he fears the consequences of failure. This is not why he sneaks like a weasel by moonlight. No, he lurks and haunts the nighttime hours so he can find books. They stack paperbacks and coffee table offerings in an effort to appear literary and intelligent, but the books are just a part of their masks. The boy teaches himself how to read complicated words, and from time to time he finds newspapers on the dinner table from the day before.

He studies everything he touches, so when he is done reading it, he puts it back in the exact position he moved it from. He does not want the guardians and watchers to know how intelligent he has become. If they knew, they might make a more complicated prison. Bad enough he knows that because he is young, no one will ever believe him, no adult or figure of authority will ever give his story credence.

The boy plays dumb at school. If he excels at a subject, he'll flunk the next test to bring the grade down. If he is too well-behaved, he'll pick a fight with the bully in the school yard. He helps with activities, not because he loves or enjoys them, because that is what is expected of him.

They speak too, in the evenings, of responsibility and they review the day's events. And one day—the boy cannot remember when—they speak of a Great Father.

Who? Asks the boy and they say, your father, the one who will come one day to claim you at last.

And at this, the boy experiences his first understanding of optimism and hope. That there might be a bright point in his life of reconciliation with a saturnine figure that has been missing from his youth. He conjures thoughts of wizened Merlins, of Odins, of Santa Clauses and Sitting Bulls, of old men with gray in their hair and long beards who will be both close and familiar and impart the discipline and sagacity he did not know he longed for until that moment. That he will meet this shadow figure they refer to in hushed and excited whispers and know at last, who he is, and what he was born for.

This Great Father has another name: Lord of the Flesh Eaters.

The boy has heard the guardians and watchers talk about the Lord of the Flesh Eaters. In hushed voices, they exchange words with guarded looks, as though they fear the Lord is nearby, listening.

The boy has known this presence, this overwhelming sense of Other, a darkness that follows him from house to house, from family to family, and finds him even when he awakens in the night to creep out of bed and read the dusty pulp novels of his latest guardian.

They are all afraid of the Lord.

In the meantime, the boy has become clever. He carries a knife in his pocket he bought from another boy in school. He's not violent—he has no need for a knife. His guardians provide him with everything he needs. But he knows the guardians and the watchers keep a cage in the basement. The cage is always empty, it is the sort of cage you might store a dog in, a dog roughly the boy's size. So he keeps the knife close. Just in case.

None of the guardians or watchers have ever hit him or touched him wrongly. The cage sits in a corner against the concrete slab floor, mute testament to what could happen if he begins to question, if he should demonstrate his defiance. He longs to leave these strange families that keep watch over him, isolating him from the rest of the world and shutting him away from any hope of help.

No one has ever said he is a prisoner, but he knows without having to be told that he is already in a cage.

★

They tell the boy that December 21 is his birthday—the longest night of the year, and that it marks his fourteenth year. He has never celebrated his birthday, without any real, earthly parents. He is awkward in his adolescence, listening to his guardians and watchers speak.

He does not believe it is his birthday; he thinks he might be younger than fourteen. But whatever the case, this must be a special occasion, because all of his guardians and watchers have taken the trouble to leave their homes and come to him where he is living now, and they are all wearing their long, dark robes, red as bricks.

They stand in the living room while he waits for what they will tell him.

He wonders if his mother will come; but she is the one who sent him to live with these strangers. It has been ten years since he saw her, knew her warmth and maternal embrace. The world begins and ends with her, and likewise do his memories. There was a place he used to live before, and he played in a green frontyard where he picked tulips out of the garden. That was when he met his new mother. She walked past the white fencing in a dark, long dress, the fabric gathered around her ankles like a stage curtain. He wanted to touch it, and she let him while he played at her feet. She asked if he wanted to walk, that she knew a place where they kept such pretty things, if he would walk with her. And his new life with his new mother begins thus, with a clasped hand, a furtive look back into the yard he is snatched from, their quick steps down the broken pavement.

Until the day his mother loses her face. After that day, she would not speak to him or suffer his presence, sending him to live with the watchers and guardians.

His heart broke without her, a fragile instrument of blood and flesh—destroyed and shuffled from one guardian to the next.

He knew they always went to "church" on Sunday. They never spoke of it, but they disappeared without him during the day, and with a few carefully placed questions he was able to discover that his watchers never go to church, not a real one, at least. He had friends whose parents attended the Lutheran church, the Protestant, the Catholic church, and none of them had ever seen any of his guardians or watchers there. So the boy knows something is going on; and he is a part of it, though he has never been there, and cannot say what it is they do when no one is about.

They tell the boy that he is special, unlike any other; in his blood runs a magic spark, a power. His red blood pumping through his veins is a blood designed to save the world; his body a host for a greater power.

The boy says: What?

Yes, *they say*. Yes, unbelievable, isn't it? But our king, our Lord of the Flesh Eaters, has been dead for centuries now. We have kept the faith in our God, and he has told us he has chosen you. He wants you to be the vessel for his holy spirit, and he is almost ready to ascend to this world.

The boy still does not understand. But they are crowding all around, and he can smell the sweat underneath their clothes, the excitement they can barely conceal in their shuffling feet, their nervous stares as they watch him with vacant eyes.

The boy gets up, clenching his hands into fists. He touches the knife he keeps in his pocket through the denim to reassure himself, but he is unprepared for this. They are too many, and he is too young, still trying to be a man in a boy's body.

Tension rises. He looks for an escape exit, anything, but the room is filled with red robes and his guardians.

The first one reaches out to touch him, gripping his shoulder with a hand. The boy does not wait—waiting is over. He snatches the knife out, slashing the man's hand. The guardian gives a startled cry, as though he has never seen blood before, and reels backward into the crowd which consumes him, swallows him up with a sigh.

The Lord speaks through the boy! *a woman shrieks, with a moan like sex; the display gets her off in a religious ecstasy.*

Get back, *the boy hisses.* The Lord says get back.

But they do not get back.

Hands and fists and claws all come for him, digging at him. He slashes, he brandishes his weapon, and blood flies from hands, from arms, from faces. Swatches of blood and red fabric litter the floor by the time it is all over, but he is no closer to the door when the fight is finished. They are clutching their damaged limbs, and the strong who overcome the boy carry him down the basement steps two by two in a thunder of rushing feet.

In the cool, damp air, they open the cage door and thrust him in.

Cramped and bent over, the boy waits until they are gone, and then he cries in the dark with the night divided between cold bars, hard concrete.

Happy Birthday, Owen.

★

I could have called my brother, Jamie.

Ah, Jamie. Golden son, favorite one.

Jamie always had contingency plans, what survivalists and military types like to call "redundancies." Backup plans for your back-up plans. He would have known what to do with this, how to fix this problem.

This is the sort of thing Jamie and I picked up in the military, but along the way, I picked up Virus X, Jamie's pet engineering project on behalf of Uncle Sam. Ever get a booster shot when you were a kid? That was the idea—a virus that would protect us, lengthen our lifespan.

Jamie encouraged me to be a test subject. Four others guys and myself had the honor. Twenty-four hours of observation, and we were still healthy as a stable of robust horses, young men making dirty jokes and wondering where our next beer was coming from. I traded stories with a soldier called Hearst, and we talked about how much we missed our wives, our sons.

When we were dismissed from our experiments, we went home and did all the things we said we would do when we got home. I told my son I would buy him a sheriff's badge. Shining gold to pin to his chest. An accessory to dreams. We kissed our children and played with them, we took our wives out to dinner and made love to them in the hot darkness.

And while we lay there, basking in the afterglow of skin like warm peaches, worms were eating their way into our centers. Virus X carved pathways to our hearts, where infection and rot would spread from our pulsing blood.

Into the witching hour, we soldiers awoke, miles apart in the darkness, suffering from a common affliction. We were dying.

You've known disease, infection, fever; sick-room days, lying on your back, shallow breaths as you try to wrestle your ghost into your body. You're not ready to die, you think. It can't be happening.

But it is happening, when you wake up with a 110-degree fever. Brains boil inside your skull and you stare into the ceiling, confused, dazed. What do you do? Do you get up, take some aspirin for this pounding hurt inside your brain? But the heat collapsed your reason in upon itself—so you continue to lie there, just like a dog panting and sweating through your clothes.

The wife wakes up. Jessica asks, *What is it, honey,* and then screams when she feels the heat baking off you. She's the mother of your child, your wife who waited for you through the war. She waited through Kosovo, through missions on foreign soils—she knows what you need.

Relief overwhelms. Of course Jessica knows what to do. I am saved.

She is so small—a tiny, five-foot, four-inch woman, she stops short of my larger, six-foot frame and lifts me from the bed. How she lifts two hundred pounds of dead weight, I don't know. And she carries me to the bathroom, where the bathtub overflows with cold water, with cubes of ice floating at the top.

I don't have time to protest. She dumps me in. The shock of the cold water should have brought my fever down. I melt the ice and the water comes to room temperature in minutes. I feel funny inside my chest where I press my fingers.

I remember her hands, gripping the edge of the tub. Her knuckles are white as she watches me, and she's got a thermometer in her hand. She tries to get my attention so she can slip it under my tongue.

"Honey," I said. "I can't feel my heart."

But the words come out in a whisper. She leans close.

It is so hard to make the words. Between the frigid bathtub and the last hour, it had become harder to concentrate, to piece together events in a linear time frame. And I hear her heart, but I can't hear mine. It pulses steady as a snare drum, and I smell her sweat, I inhale and taste the aroma that is uniquely my wife's—her blood smells like iron.

I open my mouth. Words stumble, stall, press slowly out.

A veil descends.

Nothing makes sense after that. Everything jitters into a series of out-of-order images, like a movie where the frames have been swapped and inter-stitched.

What I can piece together are only fragments of the last seconds of my humanity, and the new beginning of my monster life. I feel the turning in my blood.

I remember her wrist. I taste perfume in my mouth, the perfume she used to spray on her wrists every morning. I remember a flying curl of hair from a turning head. There are distorted sounds locked in my confused memories, and some of them are screams, hers and mine, in eerie harmony. I remember bloody bathwater. Ice cubes floating in coagulating red.

The rest is darkness.

★

In four other homes across the country, four soldiers were doing the same thing. The military disposed of them, sending out their elite to enter the suburban tracts, breaking down doors and gunning my comrades down.

The same fate was reserved for me. Death writ my appointment on his balance sheet and reaped with all fury; I should have been cut down with the same surgical precision as the others. I resented the special treatment Jamie took advantage of all through our lives to advance himself with promotions he had not earned; my brother chose to trade in hard work for the privilege of riding the coattails of our distinguished father. I was different. I lived to spite the old man, and from day one I made Jamie swear never to tell the wily gray fox of my whereabouts, and Jamie agreed with reluctance and disdain for my stubborn pride. He saw my desire to earn something on my own power and by my own intellect as infantile and naïve. The sort of fool Machiavellians like himself scoffed at.

You'll never settle it between you and the old man, will you? You could have had everything. Anything.

Fuck him, I cursed.

Jamie knew the score, knew I didn't take special favors. I started at the bottom in the infantry and I went to Kosovo without the magical shield of our affluent and well-placed father and survived. Until now.

My brother knew this; we had a deal. If I dangled above the mouth of trouble and the fates cut me loose, he should let me go.

And the bastard went back on his word. Jamie pulled strings he had no business pulling, he made calls to phone numbers that didn't exist, and, with diplomatic urging, planted the suggestion into the ears of the powerful that I had more value undead than permanently dead. I could better serve my country as an experimental subject than from six feet underground. He chivvied his agenda through lines of command in the Central Intelligence Agency and the National Security Agency and every acronym whose standing armies were composed of black-suited men with dead eyes.

He sold me like a pitch to a corporation. Jamie made me his mission. Restricted to a medical capacity, he tread dangerous waters by interfering on my behalf; he arrived at my house armed, prepared to turn against his own country and kill the mercenaries in tow if they dared lay a finger on me. The way he told it, he was not going to allow a few scared soldiers to put me down, but in my private moments between movie marathons and trash television, I asked myself if he didn't come there ready to bury me if the trouble outweighed his bottom line. Or if he just wanted to see and measure, in his own scientific fashion, the effects of a bullet on a determined corpse.

He was convinced I could be saved. The government bought his pitch and now they were invested in profiting from the fruits of this experiment—a soldier who cannot die is a valuable commodity, after all. In the end, they gave him permission to bring me back and continue "experimentation."

Jamie broke into the house and found me with their bloody carcasses, gnawing on their bones, my eyes blood red, covered in gore. If there was anyone who could say if my son had survived—if he had gotten away, it would be Jamie.

Or had Jamie lied? Had they found my son and whisked him away?

I pondered all these possibilities. Sometimes, the surest path to an answer is to ask the source directly.

★

Disguise is everything, not only because of my line of work, but because when pieces of your face fall off on a regular basis, it makes simple tasks, like going to a bank or discussing stock options, difficult.

The military base and its hospital was a half-hour from my secluded ranch in the suburbs. Conspiracy theorists joke about the black helicopters, but here they were an everyday reality and made their practice runs over barren pine lands and forgotten suburbs that collapsed with the economy.

I thought about taking my 2002 Ford Thunderbird onto the freeway and into an emergency room. A few blood tests would blow the lid off Jamie's pet project. They'd ask my status, and I would explain that I had died July 25, 1999. Did they have anything I could take for an acute case of death? It would amuse me, to shake the jar and watch my brother run in circles to keep the lid on.

The worst thing about the emergency room is they frown upon smoking.

I sighed and dialed 9-1-1.

★

Jamie showed up in an ambulance.

I sat on the porch steps, hat on my blistered, peeling skull. I never would have worn such a thing in my living life, but hats shield one's rotting corpse from the sun. So hat it is.

I kept my Glock in my holster, against my skin. Of all the people I did not trust in the world, the one I trusted the least was my brother.

Jamie pulled into the driveway in the ambulance, flashing lights dying in the hot sun. The box truck came to a stop, "Jersey Medical" emblazoned with red decals on the surface. After a long moment, while smoke rings wreathed the air between us, the door cracked open and my brother exited the truck.

Once, he'd been as thin and rakish as I was, my doppelgänger, so alike we were often mistaken for twins. But the resemblance had died the same time I had. I wondered, if I had continued living, would I have gone to seed, developed a softness that spoke of languorous meals and expensive living?

Light bounced off the Rolex on his wrist. He came dressed in his medical whites, lab coat and civilian clothes beneath. They looked rumpled, a man too lazy to iron. His late thirties, I decided, did not suit him, and I liked that. Very much.

"Vitus," he said.

His voice was heavy, my name fraught with meaning.

"Jamie," I returned. "Sit a spell beside a corpse, will you?"

"I prefer to stand," he said. He put one polished shoe on the front step. I studied it through a veil of smoke and considered the lack of scuff marks and the fresh tread and thought, *Here was the portrait of a man who never leaves his desk.*

Hard to believe that the man standing inches from me shared the same bloodline. Jamie had always been analytical, logical, dispassionate; I was his hot-blooded shadow. While he brought home awards and scholarships, I brought back broken noses and cuts on my face from punch-outs and knife fights. He went to college, I enlisted, and despite that divergence in paths, we still met at the center of this dirty military secret. Strung together by the old man, that gray fox. Reading Robert Greene's *The 48 Laws of Power* by the firelight until he got up and left the damn thing on his chair and I threw the book into the fire. *You'll have plenty of time to read in Hell, old man. May the Devil take you.*

We never saw the old gray fox anymore. Yet Jamie could return home to his wife and child. I could only visit the graves of my own, left to envy my brother's contented life from afar.

"How's the family?"

Jamie shrugged with a pull of his shoulders, a muscle in his jaw tightening.

"How old is that boy of yours, now? Must be graduating high school by now. Ames, I think his name is—"

"Amos. And he's interested in pursuing a military career."

"That must make his old man proud," I replied with a touch of acid.

"Actually," Jamie snapped, "it's because of you."

I quirked an eyebrow in his direction.

"You heard me right. When we held the funeral for . . ." he coughed, to fill the space for the names of my wife and child—names he could not bring himself to say. "When we held the funeral, he would not stop asking about you. He begged me to tell him again and again how his uncle was a soldier, so I spent every night for far too many years giving my son a bedtime story about a guy named Vitus and the sacrifice he made."

"It's only a sacrifice when you know you're giving it for the greater good, Jamie. I didn't exactly sign on for zombification to contribute to world peace."

I hadn't seen Jamie's child since the funeral, and all I found were blurry half-memories in the dim corridors of my mind. The event itself was difficult to remember, and I found trace images of Jamie's boy lurking in the background—we'd taken the boys to the beach once, and Clay ate sand while five-year-old Amos held him in his lap and tried to teach him how to make castles. I imagined what kind of impression that left in the mind of a child, to have a cousin living one second, dead the next.

I was uncomfortable with the idea of Jamie telling his child about me, as though the events of my life were on equal footing with a bastardized Grimm's fairytale. And now the boy thought I was a hero and wanted to follow in my footsteps—not his own father's.

That must rankle, I considered, staring at Jamie with a new assessment. He must have thought that by telling my sordid tale to his son he was paying penance for his scientific mistakes, his unbridled aspirations to meddle with a nature that refused to bend to his will and expectations.

Jamie sent me invites to barbecues, family reunions now and again. Our father never came and I didn't miss him. Before Kosovo, there was the mess of Sarajevo, and it was always between us. I never responded. I was left to imagine what kind of life our families might have enjoyed together—camping trips,

picnics, games. My son and his son together, in the same way he
and I had been as brothers before things became strained and our
father's presence provided an ever-widening gap, sowing rivalry.
Now Jamie's family only highlighted everything I had lost, and I
could not bear to face them.

"Is there something you need?" he cut into my thoughts.

"A brother can't call a brother for sentimental reasons?"

"I've had all the sentiment I can stand."

"Ah, ah, ah," I said, holding up a finger. "That's not very
nice. You turn me into a pre-deceased corpse with your military
cocktail, and this is how you repay me? You had your chance to
kill me then, and you refused."

I casually lifted the Glock from the holster, standing up to
hand it to him, butt-first. Sweat collected on his upper lip in
dirty droplets as he stared at the handle, silent and still.

"You know I can't do that."

"Because what you've done to me is so much better."

"What do you want, Vitus?"

"But that's your secret, Jamie. You can go home at night. The
sound of your heartbeat will lull you to sleep. I'll never hear that
sound again. What do you think an infant hears, the very first
sound in its insignificant life, as it sleeps in the womb?"

"A heartbeat."

"That's right," I smiled, reholstering the gun. "And when you
do go home and listen to your living heart, I'm not around. I'm
out of sight, out of mind. But I have to live with this every day of
my life—the constant reminder of the brother who doesn't have
the balls to kill me."

"What's stopping *you?*" he hissed.

"The fact that you brought me back in the first place is what
stops me. So I think you owe me some fucking respect, don't you?"

Cicadas droned in the overwhelming heat. August dog days
dragged on. He stared off to the side, as though something
fascinating was roosting in the bushes that demanded his attention.

"What if there was a way to return you to who you used to be?"

I snorted derisively and he continued relentlessly.

"Do you really think I enjoy watching you, my brother, suffer this long, slow death? Do you think our sibling rivalry extends so far that I will never, ever stop feeling broken over what happened? That I wouldn't give everything to reverse it?"

"Reverse it? And here I thought you might have learned a lesson in all your scientific dabbling. Come up with a cure, reverse my condition—I'd jump at the chance. But at what cost? You scramble to fix the mistakes of the past and everything you do has a consequence that destroys more than it repairs. It's not worth the risk, Jamie."

"You'll never forgive me, will you?"

"Is that why you think I called you here? Oh, Jamie. Ever the optimist. I wanted to ask you about July 25."

He flinched.

"I need to know about my son."

"This is ridiculous, Vitus. You need to lay them to rest."

"Did you find his remains?"

"We buried Clayton, Vitus. Buried him and Jessica."

"Are you sure about that?"

"How in the hell could I be sure!" he snapped, irritated. The heat was getting to him and the ocean humidity sent sweat down his face in slug trails. Breathing labored. "You don't want to know."

"No," I said, stepping closer to him.

He stepped back, keeping the distance between us.

"I don't *want* to know, Jamie. But I *have* to know. Are you sure that what you found in the house was my son? Are you 100 percent sure?"

He sighed. "There were . . . pieces everywhere. You know as well as I do there is no 100 percent without proper identification. We found scraps. Christ, Vitus, why are you asking?"

I exhaled smoke. I debated telling him the truth, but there was no point. My brother was a thirty-two-year-old ancient man who looked years away from a heart attack. Bags under his eyes suggested he slept as little as I did—his guilty conscience working overtime.

"Nothing, little brother," I said. "Go back to the hospital. And let Megan know I said hi. You hear from the old man at all?"

"We'll hear from him when he's damn good and ready. You know how he is. You'll never forgive him for Sarajevo, will you?"

I bared my teeth.

★

Beep-beep.

Time for candy. I dry swallowed the dose with an automated motion.

I took out the picture of Owen Rogers/Clay Adamson, gap-toothed, smiling boy, and stuck it on my empty fridge with a single magnet. I called the Rogers an hour ago, and for people living in a burned-out husk of a house, they were pleased as punch to hear from me. They didn't feel inclined to mention their real address, so I informed them I had some questions and information, would they kindly come by for a visit? I'd love to chat with them.

In the meantime, I pondered the picture in silence until I heard the sound of the car pulling into the driveway. With a sigh, I holstered the Glock, lit a fresh cigarette, and watched the couple exit the car; if I didn't know better, I would think they hadn't changed clothes from the last time I saw them.

Clearly, I didn't know better.

I chain-smoked with abandon and, when I heard their feet coming up the steps, I opened the door, throwing it wide. Early morning air heavy with dew flowed past my dead skin, and Mrs. Rogers smiled her tired, eerie smile as she came up the steps first, Mr. Rogers trudging behind her.

Then, her head was gone.

★

The cigarette in my mouth sizzled as Mrs. Rogers's blood and brain matter extinguished the glowing ember, my face slick with her fluids and pulverized skin. Her body stood bolt upright, ending abruptly at the neck, where parts of her fleshy throat remained, like a flower in bloom, pieces of her skeleton jutting out of the red center. Shattered bones.

Her legs continued to walk forward without the rest of her, like a chicken after execution. Her sensible pumps marched right on to my deck until, finally, the legs crumpled from under her just before she reached me, the body collapsing to the floor. Blood jetted onto the wood boards in a thickening pool.

Mere seconds elapsed. Mr. Rogers, who looked as though he had eaten urine-soaked cereal that morning, had not noticed. His gaze remained focused on his shoes as he came up the stairs.

I pulled out the Glock and jerked out the magazine from my side pocket. Urgency pressurized the air and I loaded the magazine with the echoing *thwack!* of metal into the dense polymer frame. First round chambered.

"Suzanne?" Mr. Rogers whispered, looking up for the first time and seeing his wife. The gap in his cognition as his senses gained parity with real time recalled me to ancient hurts when I had been standing in his blood-soaked shoes. I experienced a moment of regret for all my criticism and narrow judgments of before. The moment was brief. Was my sociopathy a function of my compromised brain matter or the collateral damage of the heart beneath, unable to feel after being tasked to feel far too much? There was no time to get existential about it and, in one second following another, I went from a sad bastard to just a mean bastard.

All color left his face, leaving him as white as a bleached bone. He stared at the body on the porch, frozen in his tracks.

"You'd better get up here *now*," I suggested, scanning the street.

I calculated the shooter's distance, his weapon, his plan of action. Nothing was visible out on this quiet, suburban drive where polite WASPs continued their business of tending their lawns and ignoring each other. For all they knew, they lived cheek to jowl with pedophiles and zombies and serial killers. As long as the lawns were mowed and kept, no one cared about moral integrity.

I reached forward to grab Mr. Rogers, who had no intention of moving anywhere. He continued to stand with bovine aplomb, all eyes and dumb expression, in his prim sweater vest and wire-rimmed glasses. Spots dotted the upper corner of his button-down shirt, peppered with bloody spinal fluid.

I was long past the ability to vomit, but bile collected in the back of my throat in a sad testament to memory, to the days when I could. Congealing like honey.

With a fistful of his sweater vest and my extinguished cigarette still clamped between my teeth, Mr. Rogers's head followed suit, exploding in a mist of blood and gore, bone fragments thrown into my face.

The sound of an expulsed shell from a distant gun ricocheted off hot pavement.

I twisted and zeroed in on the sound echoing through the cul-de-sac and bouncing off the eggshell sky. Mr. Rogers's headless body fell like a puppet as I released him, jetting blood like the Trevi Fountain. My deck became an abattoir, my shoes soaked in pooling crimson.

A shadow outlined against a house a hundred yards away. Between the manicured topiary, his silhouette formed a target against bleached vinyl siding, and I took aim, firing once, twice.

The sniper stumbled as one of the bullets hit home. His face veiled in a ski mask in the hot summer sun, the man snapped his arm toward me, adjusting his aim with a fistful of hot lead: he returned fire.

My hand exploded.

Two fingers evaporated into blood mist in the blast; their remains rolled across the porch like lollipop sticks and then were lost between slats of wood into darkness. I ducked. *Lucky shot,* I thought with grudging respect and irritation. Hunkering in the shade with my knees soaking in the Rogers' blood, I looked down through the porch boards as though my fingers were dropped change and I could make out one crooked nail on the edge of a severed fingertip. I kneeled in warm blood, stared at it, and fought the urge to reach down and lap it up, to pick up the fleshy fragments and eat them like a man at a barbecue roast. My mangled hand hung like a limp, wilted flower through my sleeve.

The pills could push my monster urges into the background, but they could not eradicate them. I would always be hungry for a food I forbade myself to feast upon.

When I looked up next, the shooter was gone. The yards and the lawns were empty. I waited a moment longer, to be sure the neighborhood was deserted. The nice thing about suburbia is that no one ever calls the police. Not for murder, not for Hitler, not for headless people on my porch. People moved here to be alone and to increase their isolation. They would fight to preserve it, even if it meant ignoring a fire fight in our own frontyards.

When you eat your wife, technically, the marriage is over.

I am a widower. Gone are the humble gatherings at the dinner table and gone the trappings of a well-feathered nest infused with the warm smell of apple pie, the feminine grace adding a softness to my days and a kindness to my heart.

I had a new girl now and she's harder and meaner; hot to the touch and never worries about her weight even though she eats lead and copper by the round. Though it's sad commentary to suggest my most trustworthy friend in the world is a firearm, I would rather have my hand blown to shreds than lose the last thing I loved the most.

His shot blew apart the butt of the gun, and the magazine inside, destroying the weapon. Fragments of broken synthetic plastic tore holes through my palm, fracturing my wrist and debriding parts of my hand. Flesh came away like a glove dragged over barbed wire, the skeletal structure visible beneath my tendons and ligaments. Two fingers gone. MIA. I would have to fish them out later to prevent infection to the local squirrel population.

My hand looked awful. I whisked away Mrs. Rogers's scarf, since she no longer needed it, and used the dry end to wrap it.

Only one person was capable of repairing this extensive damage, but I dreaded going back to her.

A hand can be replaced. But a good, reliable weapon? That was priceless. I felt naked without it.

I dragged the bodies into the trash barrels around the side of the house. You might be thinking, won't someone notice? What about all the blood, the gun shots, hell, what about the friendly garbage men who collect the trash?

Well, we have an automated service, a truck with a robotic arm that picks up the can and dumps the trash. The garbage man never leaves the cab while the process occurs. If they see anything, they don't talk about it.

Behind swatches of beige vinyl siding, people within cocoon themselves in the glow of computer screens and game systems, others medicated into their own versions of a brave new world. The conscious population does not care, and does not want to know about your personal business. Half of them are embezzling, laundering, smoking things the government doesn't want them to smoke, and growing them to boot. They don't want to notice you, because they don't want to be noticed in return; and the rest are sleepwalking through their lives, the twenty-first century path to better living.

I want to believe there was a time when people cared, when people paid attention, when someone would have noticed five gallons of blood bleeding from my porch like my own self-contained water park. I want to believe that it was not always like this. Someone would demand answers and justice for what occurred here.

But you don't ask a lot of questions from a pre-deceased corpse who likes to carry firearms, do you?

And anyway, the next-door neighbor had a power washer. I'm sure if I asked nicely, he'd let me use it to get the blood off the porch. Brings down property values, you know.

★

I waited until dark.

Pleasant Hills Cemetery.

Freshly watered grass soaked my boots and up into the fabric of my pants. Tombstones stood in the moonlight like upright fingers. My hand trailed the ragged, bloody edge of a scarf and held the last bits together with my congealing flesh.

I cased the building and attempted to light a cigarette with my maimed hand. The funeral home shut down for the evening and I could see Niko through the window, moving back and forth in a yellow square of light.

I'd gunned down a few nasty things in my life, but I was terrified of a petite, Bettie Page look-alike. That's the power of beauty—it shakes you deep within, but skin-deep wouldn't be strong enough to do that. Niko's volatility burned through to the outside like a foundry. A man, or a woman, for that matter, could be tempered by her fire and love every second of the burn.

Her silhouette disappeared, and then the back door opened and she stood in the threshold, blue-black hair illuminated by the orange street lamp.

"You should come inside. It's getting cold out."

I trudged through the grass, across the graves. Some might think it rude, but the only difference between me and the ones in the ground was that I was still ambulatory. Cigarette smoke trailed out in a ghostly line behind me.

"How'd you know?" I asked.

She smiled, holding the door open for me. Ripped denim at her knees with fishnets beneath revealed warm skin pulsing with blood. I found myself licking my lips and stopped, clamping the cigarette harder between my teeth.

"I saw the cigarette."

Her eyes fell to my destroyed hand as I reached out with my good one for the door. Still, I hesitated before entering, wary, and even guilty. I should leave her alone. I would only bring trouble here to find her. Trouble was all I knew.

"Bad day at the office," I explained.

"You get that a lot? Or let me guess—you brought roses for me, but the thorns were really, really big." She gestured at the bloody rag holding my hand together.

I smiled. "I'm a sucker for flowers. I liked them so much I kept them."

"Your wife must like that."

"I don't have a wife," I answered.

I stepped inside, and she led me into the building. We continued trading words back and forth. Her gait rolled onward, easy and weightless as we ducked inside the funeral home proper. We passed the empty knight on his pedestal. Though Niko commanded all my attention, I found myself wrenched away to stare into the blackness of his empty visor. To imagine him taking his first ringing step to the floor. Pulling out his sword. I manufactured the hiss of steel in my head. The sound of his gauntlet. Every strip of metal rattling to signal his approach.

I rushed past. The swinging door shut behind us and we left the knight behind. Mentholated smells of fungicide swept over me, the familiar drain holes in the middle of the floor. *I should have some installed on the porch*, I thought, taking in the newest corpses laid out on the tables. There were two; busy day in town.

"Divorced?"

I shrugged and when I turned to answer her again, she touched me. The instant took me aback as she grabbed me by the shoulder with one hand and pushed down on the center of my chest with the other. She forced me into a chair like a bull captivated by a matador. I did not resist. Her fingers were warm.

She turned away to gather a tray of surgical instruments, leaving me cold again.

"It's complicated," I said.

"Maybe you should tell me about it."

I puffed out smoke between my lips.

"You always have a thing for dead men?"

She turned back to me.

"Just you."

Blades and mortuary instruments glinted in the light, cold steel. She took hold of my intact wrist, waxen corpse flesh beneath the cotton of my shirt cuff. With a firm grip, she pulled the sleeve up, revealing gangrenous flesh, moldy skin. She stared at it a moment.

My rasping voice broke the silence.

"You can pretend all you want. But at the end of the day, I'm as rotten as the corpses you treat. And I'll never be human. Do you understand that?"

What little blood was left in her face flooded out, giving her flesh a subtle, blue note and her lips condensed into a thin line. She unwound the scarf from my blown-away hand, gentle, as though I still had any semblance of feeling, any sensation of pain. All that was over for me. I could sense when I was damaged, I knew parts of me had fallen off, but pain was a thing of the past. All that remained was discomfort and regret.

If in her tender, young heart, she was beginning to feel something for me, better that I crush it now. I sensed her burgeoning regard, a tension expanding the air between us each time our paths crossed. Barometric pressure inviting a storm. I regretted having come here in the first place. She could deny she felt anything, and the idea was preposterous—the last time I had a pulse, Britney Spears was a virgin.

Preposterous it might be, she had a way of looking aside from me, a blush that crept into her cheeks when she was as close to me as she was now, flustered and embarrassed.

"You understand, right?" I pressed her.

She laid my crippled hand bare on the table. Strange fluids oozed out, green and black and red. Half of the hand, from the palm up, was not even connected to the carpals; they would have to be pieced back together with other means.

But the hand was not important.

While she peeled back parts of the skin to assess the damage with a pair of tweezers, I used my good hand to touch her shoulder. She was so warm. I remembered life. I remembered the *thump-de-thump* of a heartbeat. I remembered blood and breath and intimate union.

I swallowed and my grip tightened until she stopped what she was doing and looked at me.

"It can never happen, do you understand? A kiss alone infects. There is no cure. I will never be alive, ever."

Her expression didn't change but her eyes shifted and she looked past me.

Before I could speak, a cleaver appeared in her hands, and in the next instant, my hand was gone.

★

Some butcher's paper, I thought, *and you could mistake it for a pig foot. If you discounted the blasted-apart fingers, that is.*

My severed hand lay on the table. I missed it, even though it was well past its useful life. I'd had it since birth, carried it with me through grammar school and into adulthood. I'd shot my weapon with it. I had a lot of good memories with that hand on many a long, Saturday night. I smiled, remembering that part of living—the gentle part.

"What are you smiling at?" she asked, turning toward me with a fresh hand.

"Oh, nothing. You keep leftover hands around all the time?"

"Maybe it's better that you don't know."

"You didn't take it from a corpse, did you?"

She said nothing, but plunked the hand on the table next to me and began to pull out a series of surgical wires. Enough injuries and I'd be made of metal more than flesh.

"Don't you think the relatives are going to notice dear old Dad is missing his hand?"

"No," she spoke casually, aligning the wrist to my own. "Closed casket. I'll throw yours in before they seal it up."

"So, you just roll over one day and decide you want to touch dead corpses for a career path? Why not something more genteel, like a realtor? I hear that's all the rage these days."

She snorted with derision. Instead of being pig-like, it sounded cute.

"Maybe I really do like dead men."

I hitched a breath in, taken aback, before I decided she was joking. Her sense of humor ran dark—real dark. I liked her.

"Seriously."

"Well," she said. "I was born on Hawaii, the Kalaupapa Peninsula. The island of Molokai."

"Truly?"

"Truly. And they offered some programs paid through the government, and one of them was mortician work. So I went for it. Most thought I was crazy, but I like being alone. What about you? You shoot yourself in the hand just to have an excuse to see me? I won't tell anyone."

"Like I said—no wife. No one to tell. And someone shot me."

"There are people who can help, you know."

She was pressing wires into my arm, through the moist stump of rotten flesh as she spoke. They stuck out on the end like antenna on Sputnik, a bizarre, artistic sculpture.

"Hospitals don't know what to do with me."

"No, not the hand. I mean, with your other condition."

"It's called death, Niko," I sighed, and pulled out a cigarette with my free hand as she began to connect the dead hand to my wired wrist.

"Yeah, that one."

I said nothing. It was sweet that she wanted to help, but entertaining such a notion was counterproductive. I breathed in smoke, the lit ember dancing before my eyes.

"I left family behind," she said. "They wanted me to stay, but there was no future for me. And I was not like them."

"And leave all this behind?" I gestured at the bodies displayed in the cold, flickering light.

She smiled. "I learned a useful thing or two from my people. I know what it is like to live in a world starved of human touch, Vitus."

I swallowed, and it sounded louder than I anticipated. As if to stress the words, her fingers pressed insistently over my exposed bone.

She stepped back from the table, extra wires clutched in her hand. "There, try it now."

I stood up from the chair, evading her gaze. Now, I felt awkward and naïve before her, afraid to look at her face framed in dark, fragrant hair. The mentholated aroma of fungicide permeated the air around us like a perfume. I lifted my hand and flexed it, clenching it into a fist and opening it again.

The flesh was new, smooth. Unbroken skin whose cells still radiated with a near-visible aura of vitality. As if my clenched fist could hold on to the phantasm of my past life, anima draining away with each passing second.

The former owner of this hand could have been anyone—a banker, a construction worker, a food server, a pencil pusher. Were his memories still buried in the skin I admired for my own? Did the flesh hold ghostly echoes of this man's meals, his typing habits, how he moved his fingers when he went fishing, if he did? I recalled a time when my hands had been so smooth, so young and untouched by the terrible vicissitudes of fate.

"You didn't have to do this," I told her. A mist of smoke and hospital smells permeated the air and I contributed to it with each exhale.

Niko startled me, reaching over the tray of tools on the table between us, and plucked my new hand out of the air, with the cigarette dangling between the fingers. She curled warm fingers around my new ones, bringing the back of my hand to her lips.

I hissed a breath in warning. The skin she pressed her lips to was unbroken, but no matter how smooth the new hand may have been, such contact was still a risk. I pulled back like I had touched a burning hot stove, her lips still pursed, beguiling, as she looked up at me.

"Don't do that," I whispered. "You're too young to be fooling around with monsters."

"Then stop coming," she challenged, throwing her head back like a boxer in a ring, ready for the next punch. "But we both know you'll be back."

Flicking ashes off my sleeve, I sucked in a lungful. Smoke outlined halos around us as I turned and left, hunched inside my trench coat.

She was right. I would be back.

★

Beep-beep.

Time for my dose. I dry swallowed a pair of pills like candy, forcing them down my sticky, decomposing throat.

When a client dies, the case is over.

I hung the picture of Owen on my fridge, the toddler picture and the high school picture side by side, and stood against my counter in the frigid dark with only cigarettes for company. I studied the two faces as though either could give me an answer about their identity, their circumstances. Mr. and Mrs. Rogers were dead, their story ended.

Clay's—Owen's—was just beginning.

★

When I arrived at my house, a vulture was perched on my porch.

Talons dug into the old, splintered wood, pig-like eyes sunk into wrinkled, lizard skin. His feathers looked like an old man's unwashed hair, stringy, thin.

"Quoth the raven, nevermore," I intoned ominously.

He was warming himself in the early morning sun breaking over the horizon. They sun themselves in solitude. None of this explained why he had chosen my porch. Other than a few gallons of blood soaked into the wood, there was no reason for him to be here. The garbage men had dutifully disposed of Mr. and Mrs. Rogers. There were plenty of pastel-colored houses in this neighborhood done in the style of the Levittown suburbs in which he could make his home. Abandoned McMansions made obsolete in the housing boom and bust.

"Shoo," I said, waving my new hand at him. He stared at me with an air of boredom. Clearly, I did not inspire feelings of fear or authority in the large bird. He smelled of ripe carrion. Then again, it was probably me.

"Fine."

I ignored the bird and he closed his beady, sphinx eyes as though he were exhausted with the effort of putting up with me.

Inside the darkness, I knew my home by memory, every step and bend. While most people raised in these urban environments are happy to go the rest of their lives without weaponry as a permanent fixture, I kept caches of weapons and ammo stored all over the house, a holdover from my military training. After a prolonged treasure hunt through my late wife's china cabinet, I withdrew a brand new Glock 19.

Old-style revolvers looked nice, but I preferred a weapon that had been updated since the invention of the wheel. I leaned toward semi-automatics. Nobody wants to load bullets into six chambers while a maniac is trying to cut your head off with a chainsaw just because the revolver looked "pretty." You'll be pretty dead with bullets in your hand.

I holstered the weapon and with it came a feeling of homecoming, as though I had been made whole where before had only been emptiness. It rode against my rotted flesh, and I approached the table where I had abandoned Owen's journal amidst a litter of crumpled paper, used-up pens, and bullets. My new hand was slightly larger than my old one, like an ill-fitting glove, and I sent the book to the floor in an aborted attempt to pick it up.

I cursed, hoping the grip would not affect my ability to wield the gun in the future as poorly as this, and managed to pick up the journal off the floor on the second try. The house was a mess, and I wondered what sort of maid service I could arrange. *Slightly undead guy, needs gentle house cleaning, formaldehyde. Doesn't like flies. Provide references.*

I snagged the journal by the spine and a paper spilled out from the pages.

"What a cliché," I muttered. "Let me guess, it's a napkin with a bar name conveniently stamped on it, or a phone number leading me to a smarmy villain intent on destroying all life on Earth as we know it, with a penchant for over-explaining his plans while he ties me up with poorly knotted rope."

I slid the paper off the floor, but it wasn't paper, and as far as clues go, true to life, it was piss poor. I enjoy movies, flickering black-and-white images of sleepy-eyed detectives and their hourglass dames, but rarely does life emulate the old films.

In real life, crime is a dirtier animal. People get away with murder more often than not, the femme fatales are definitely not shaped like Rita Hayworth. In fact, the men and women alike wear the scars of their ugly existence. If they are thieves or scoundrels driven by lives of poverty, they look twice as old as they are; if they are rich criminals, they look like well-kept thoroughbreds, rotting from the inside out.

Sometimes they're sloppy enough to follow movie clichés, like dropping matchbooks with names on them, which never happens.

What fell to the floor was none of these. A tarot card.

It's never something banal either. I couldn't get the Nine of Swords or the Prince of Wands, could I?

Death.

A cloaked skeleton, the classic medieval image of the plague. The scythe rested against his shoulder, a tired figure, in the midst of a field of grain. MORT was written in Old English script at the bottom, as though I needed instruction on the figure whom I shared so much with—we were practically long-lost brothers.

My dead wife used to keep plastic bags in the drawer, and though I had exterminated so many traces of her feminine mystery, her soft memories, the kitchen had never been my forté, and even less so now that I would never eat there again. I found one from my living years, and stuffed the card inside the plastic, slipping the "evidence" into my breast pocket.

From the corner of my eye, the vulture flew past the window, startled into flight and abandoning my porch. Reflex moved me in response, instinctual memory. Only when I looked down did I realize the firearm was in my hand, the first round chambered and held at the door, my jaw clenched, my milky eye aiming with ferocious focus.

Ding dong!

Two long shadows cast over my door, and I frowned, watching a moment before I holstered the weapon and came to see what fresh hell was this.

★

I opened the door, jangling the chain stretched taut across the threshold, giving us an inch to stare at each other.

They stood like chickens, with the same eager-to-please emptiness in their eyes. For a moment, I thought Mr. and Mrs. Rogers had been re-animated, put back together like sloppy puppets. A moment staring at their stretched smiles, their expectant faces, and I realized they were a different couple, but with the same haunting hallmarks—the man wore a sweater vest like Rick Rogers, and the woman beside him donned a long skirt down to her ankles, a look that echoed the previous Rogers.

Two seconds of a flat stare transmuted into confusion, and seconds more followed as their cognition overtook their senses— for them to recognize, at last, the smell wafting from me and the diamond-plate texture of my face. I was used to seeing the same insidious terror in Jamie's eyes. How do you keep a poker face when a corpse answers the door? How do you stare into his cloudy, milky gaze?

I had yet to find it in Niko's.

I pushed that uncomfortable thought away and addressed my new visitors.

"Who the fuck are you?"

The woman blinked as though I'd hammered her over her head with my fist. Her husband was remote and aloof, as though he were a foreigner who did not understand the language.

"I'm Mrs. Rogers!" she exclaimed and stuck out a hand in greeting.

Her enthusiasm took me aback. How many Rogers were there in this godforsaken town?

I slammed the door in her face, undid the chain, and opened it wide. Her hand still wavered in the air, and I offered her my cold, waxen corpse hand. She was good, but not good enough to conceal the shudder as she folded warm fingers into my spongy, moldy grip. Even the thick ringlets of her dyed red hair shook with her.

"Let me guess," I said, "Mr. Rogers, right?"

I offered him my hand. I haven't eaten in ten years, but sarcasm was on the menu today.

"Oh, that's quite all right," he insisted, plunging his hands into his pants pockets. Clearly, he was the smarter of the two.

"What brings you to my door?"

Ordinarily, I'd hound them for a reference, but I was intrigued. I was the player on a stage in which the script had been written, and I was curious to know what my lines were supposed to be.

Let me guess, I thought, supplying the dialogue. *We're here looking for our son.*

"Our son is missing," the woman spoke cheerily, shrugging her purse from her shoulder and rummaging through it before producing the picture. Rings on her fingers reflected light into my face. A buzzing sound emanated from her purse and I stared until a fly wriggled over the lip of her zipper like an onyx bead before flying off.

I half expected a different picture, but she offered me the exact same one hanging on my fridge: happy, gap-toothed "Clay."

"Keep it," I suggested. "I've got one just like it."

"Oh," she said, her lips pursing. She stained them red, a 1940s starlet red, but it clashed with her skin tone so what should have been alluring looked like a blood smear instead. "We miss our son and would give anything to have him back, Mr. Adamson. Can you help us?"

The wires in my jaw made an audible, metallic *snick* as I smiled—Gods, the effort!—and Mr. Rogers flinched. I was dead, but I still had my teeth, punctuating my grin with an uneven, serrated edge.

"Anything at all, Mrs. Rogers?"

"Name your price, we'll be happy to pay it."

"Can you get blood out of everyday household items?"

★

Mr. and Mrs. Rogers Redux, as I came to think of them, blinked in the same fashion as the ones who came before them. When they spoke, they were as wooden actors reciting lines from a poorly written play. I could have grilled them with a series of questions, something along the lines of, "How many more Rogers are there, exactly?" or the more direct, "Why are you people fucking with me?" but if there's anything you learn dealing with shady people is they only answer direct questions with so many mangled lies you're better off with no answer at all.

Judging by the set of Mrs. Rogers's mouth, my reaction had not been expected; they were unprepared to deal with a monster like me.

I repeated my demand.

"That's what I said. If you want me to help you, you're going to have to live with me and clean my house."

They were in no position to refuse. If they were systematically being sent here, logic followed that they were under orders and they could not refuse. They'd say yes, and when they did, they'd be under my watch and care. If my goal was to gain my son back and Mr. and Mrs. Rogers would not willingly help me, by keeping them close I could draw the mysterious masked shooter closer. Close enough to trap.

"Oh, I'm not sure . . ."

I sidestepped to the windowsill, where I picked up a bottle of ammonia spray and turned, depositing it into Mr. Rogers's hands.

"Thanks! You start today."

Mr. Rogers looked at the bottle as though it were an object he had never laid eyes on, and after a moment, he turned to the window, picked up a discarded rag, and wiped down the glass without a word of protest.

Mrs. Rogers looked at me, strangling refusals. She wanted to say no, but whatever her orders were, they left no room for rebellion. She swallowed it and waited for me.

"Any good with a power washer?"

★

If they were unsettling in conversation, they were more so in action. They moved like puppets or automatons. Even I had more life in my bones. I did paperwork at a desk—taxes—but it afforded me a better opportunity to watch them as they went about the business of setting my house to rights, dusting old knickknacks that once belonged to Jessica, unsettling years' worth in accumulating layers of skin cells, hair, and cigarette smoke as they went. I got the impression that in the world where they lived, house work was not a priority—or perhaps they did not live in houses but survived in underground caverns akin to Morlocks.

They did a well enough job, though common objects mystified them, particularly in the kitchen. They opened closets and looked at my suits as though they were tourists at a zoo, pondering a new species exhibit. I showed Mr. Rogers how to make a bed. He touched the sheets with a sense of confusion that left me wondering if he had ever slept in a bed at all.

When they were done, I sensed them moving about me, like children trying to get a parent's attention. *Daddy, are we done yet?* Light flickered over the television screen. Lana Turner slinked across the frame, curls and all, in black-and-white glory.

"If you got nothing else to do, I need you to stay here. I have extra rooms. It's not like I use them."

"Mr. Adamson," the woman began, protesting. "We just need you to look for our son—"

"Then you have to stay here."

Her breath huffed out of her in exasperation, a rare display of emotion. I did not turn around, but listened, curious. I couldn't force them to stay, but I wondered how badly they needed me. How far I could push them and how much I could make them dance before they gave up.

"But I . . ." her words hung in the air as she struggled to find the right excuse, the right reason, before she faded into silence. Was it that hard to tell me to go fuck myself?

"Make yourself comfortable. You like old movies, eh? Either of you?"

After a moment, while Mrs. Rogers was busy swallowing her dialogue, Mr. Rogers settled into the chair next to me and watched Lana Turner with quiet admiration.

"Yeah, I know," I spoke into the silence. "She's a babe."

★

I began the evening ritual of locking down the house. From one door to another I drifted, checking the locks and slanting my weightless shadow across windows. A faded ghost in my moth-eaten suit, ever thinning into two-dimensional space.

"What now?" Mr. Rogers asked in his quiet, strangled voice. I got the impression that either he had taken a vow of silence at his day job or chose not to speak at all. His voice sounded disused.

"That's right," I mused. "You need to sleep."

One of those human necessities I had all but forgotten. I already had the television schedule for the night plotted out like a sailor's navigational course and my dreams determined by an idiot box.

I found the linen closet, not sure what I would discover when I opened the door. I hadn't opened it in years. A puff of dust exhaled from within, and I pulled out several old blankets and thrust them into Mr. Roger's hands. He and his wife followed me like they were checking into a seedy motel, frightened and wary, taking the linens I offered.

"This way."

I led them down the hall. Was it me, or did my steps become heavier as I went, a shuffling in my gait?

I reached the end, until there was nowhere else for me to go, to escape to. The door was as cold, as immovable as a mausoleum door.

After my wife and son had died, I had resumed my residence at the house we had bought together. I'm not sure if I can call what I did grieving—I was dead, all the way through to my rotten heart, with a rotten soul to match. I refused to touch the room that had been our master bedroom, where Jessica had first found me, boiling inside my own skin on that night. It was also the room where we had laid together with our fingers interlaced, the bed we shared on our wedding night, a collection of a thousand moments strung together with kisses, hungry yearnings. The ordinary fable of doomed, ordinary love.

I had not slept there since.

A team of scientists and military personnel had scrubbed the place from top to bottom; Jamie had seen to it that when I returned I need not be confronted by the brutal reminder of that bloody evening. But in a pale, afternoon light in winter, one can make out the faded blood stains embedded in the carpet nubs, the drywall. No amount of bleach and elbow grease could erase the past, and it persisted still, like cheap perfume in a strip club.

Clay's room was no different. Barely evolved past a nursery, a smaller bed had been set up for when he had outgrown his crib, still adorned with the trappings of early childhood: the trendy cartoon of the moment, a cat and a mouse capering across the walls and onto the sheets and the bedding as well. The coverlet turned down, waiting for a boy to slumber who never arrived.

A coldness penetrated the atmosphere here, pushing through the walls and into my skin.

"I'm sure you can make do," I snapped, and left them hovering in the hallway, exchanging glances from one room to another and then between themselves.

Zzzzt. Zzzzzzzt.

A fly whipped past my face and settled against the curling wallpaper in the hallway. I stopped and stared at it. My house never had flies, but lately I encountered them with greater frequency. In the land of the living, this is a minor nuisance. To a dead guy like myself, it's a fucking apocalypse. I didn't like to think about what an infestation of maggots would do to me.

It helicoptered in a semi-circle, transparent wings vibrating as it tasted the dusty wall.

"Eat me," I muttered and crushed it. Sheetrock gave beneath my fist. The blackened, squashed body fell to the floor and I stared before returning to Lana Turner. She was waiting for me as I settled into the chair.

I checked the Glock and tucked the weapon back into the holster. I closed my eyes and leaned back.

I couldn't sleep. But the shooter didn't need to know that.

So I rested my eyes and pretended like I had enough of a soul left to dream.

★

The mind is a curious weapon.

Dead or alive, I was still human, with all the psychological characteristics; I could not dream, but the desire remained. At ease, and without amusement, my consciousness filled the emptiness. We may be social creatures, but the proof of our lone-wolf nature is our persistence of imagination. My closed eyelids provided a blank canvas, against which images filed past as though thrown against a projection screen, a silent movie with snippets of my old life, and a new, nightmare one interchanged.

I thought of Clay, of Jessica. But these thoughts were old, worn out hats. The pain of them was familiar, safe; a pity party where I was the honored guest. Instead, I turned away from them and the shimmering picture frame of Lana Turner. She became Niko in black and white. My thoughts were as developed as an adolescent's. Her lithe figure danced before me, beckoning, inviting, and I wondered if she really liked me or if she flirted with every corpse that came under her care. Hmmmm, Niko. What I would do to her if I were alive.

Maybe you should be thinking about your son, I remonstrated myself.

Except he was dead. *Supposed* to be dead. But now, I had Twit 1 and Twit 2 showing up at my door, insisting he was somewhere out there and that only I could find him. Lafferty had referred them in the first place; maybe I should have gone straight to him for the rest of the story.

And then, there was the creepy tarot card to consider.

"Fuck it," I muttered, and shifted like a man dreaming.

★

Nothing happened.

I had not been sure what to expect; but with the Rogers in lockdown, I need only wait to draw in my adversary. I checked on them as though they were errant children, opening my old bedroom door. Huddled shapes in the early morning light, they slept innocently, drawing long, deep, untroubled breaths. I envied them their shared humanity, their capacity to dream.

I left a note for them explaining I'd shoot them if they left the house and not to let anyone in. As an afterthought, I found an old package of cookies and left it on the counter for them, like a parent might for a child. I sniffed one, just to see if the old memories of a chocolate cookie, the taste and smell, might be aroused, brought into life. If I might hunger for such an obscure piece of my old life.

No reaction. No salivary glands churned into action, nothing at all.

★

I wasn't hurt enough to justify the visit, but I wanted to see her.

I slipped the lock at the funeral home and entered the darkness. I sorted through the events as I slinked through and found the back room where Niko conducted her work. A corpse was there, waiting for her. He was naked and covered with a sheet, anticipating her attentions. And she would touch him, in all the ways I wished—

That's ridiculous, I cut into the fantasy abruptly. In my condition, sex was out of the question. But I remembered all the times when it had not been, and though I no longer functioned in that way, my most essential sex organ—my brain—was far from dead.

Then why are we here? I asked myself.

I used the excuse that I needed a safe place to think. It was getting difficult to do that at the house with so many dead bodies piling up at an alarming rate. In the darkness, surrounded by the metal gurneys casting predator shapes in the moonlight from the windows, and the heady aroma of formaldehyde, I felt at home. My mind was free to wander.

The hour passed and I dosed myself when the time came, crunching on my gravel pills with a dry mouth. It was like eating tarmac.

The door clicked open and fluorescent light shuddered on. From where I sat, in an uncomfortable metal chair behind the farthest gurney, she did not see me at first. She was dewy from the early morning rain that had been falling when I first entered. Droplets shimmered in her hair, and I admired her from afar. Some might not have felt as I did and might have seen only a gothic freak; they would have no appreciation for her attention to detail, her desire to paint herself with tattoos like a canvas. She had fashioned herself a work of art, and it would take a talented man to look beneath that and see the other wild shapes hidden behind the flash and the presentation.

I enjoyed the moment undetected. She took off her raincoat and hung it on a hook; she busied herself with gathering tools from drawers, washing her hands in the sink, turning on a radio. Morning music filled the air, reports of the weather, and then a tune with Kurt Cobain's wailing voice. He sang about a heart-shaped box.

Her eyes found me as she drew close to attend to the body.

"How long have you been watching me?" she asked.

"Not long," I said, standing up. A wide brimmed hat cast a long shadow over my destroyed face. She couldn't see the damage— she already knew I was ugly, but there was no need to emphasize it without something to mitigate my appearance.

Coming here had been a mistake. I had a job to do, and Niko wasn't a part of it. I'd come here to fulfill an old man's whim and nothing else. She stood there like a frightened child with a plate of scalpels in her hand. I owed her more respect than this. I realized I hadn't come here for any good reason.

One should consider the lives they change and influence just for the crime of showing up; I could think of no good I could bring her by being here, other than to shake up her predictable world and wreak havoc on the ordinary.

"I'll be on my way," I grunted, but she reached out, setting the tray down and drawing me back with a touch on my arm, pulling my sleeve toward her.

"Stay. There's blood on your collar. And you seem . . . distracted."

Was I? To be under her scrutiny was more frightening than being shot at. I relented and allowed her to push me onto the empty chair beside the gurney.

I gestured to the gurney supporting the shrouded body beside me. "I don't expect to be sitting on one of those anytime soon."

She drew back the sheet from the corpse she was working on. He was an old man, his face deeply lined, large bags beneath his eyes. A whirl of white hair capped the skin of his ashen skull. He looked sterile and waxen. She strapped on a set of latex gloves.

"I don't recall you explaining why that hasn't happened to you yet," she said, opening jars of strange, foul-smelling liquids. They gave off a flavor like mint if you set it on fire first.

"Tell me what you think," I answered. "Tell me what you see."

She took a large swab that looked like an oversized Q-tip and dipped it into a jar before facing the corpse on the table. Her gaze assessed me in the poor light, hat shadowing my features. She frowned. With a quick motion, she swabbed the corpse around the nostrils, the eyes, and into the mouth and along the gums. His lips peeled back with a wet, slurping noise.

"You're not like I am. I think you were once. I'd say you were dead, but you walk and you talk, you act like anyone."

"When I'm not falling apart."

"There's that, as well."

"What do you think happened to me?"

"I wonder if a witch cast a spell on you. Like a fairytale. Did she?"

I laughed softly. "Perhaps that's what did happen. But the witch is a man, and he is my brother. His name is Jamie."

"Hmmm," she murmured and moved about, running a snaking tube into the corpse's arm, one end disappearing into his flesh and the other leading to a cylinder resembling a massive syringe. She flicked a switch and the cylinder began to pump, pushing fluid into the old man's dead body.

"That makes things complicated."

"He was misled by his good intentions, I fear. In his arrogance, he failed to realize the spell would last so long. Or cost so much."

"I would want to know how to break the spell, then," she said.

She stripped her hands of the latex gloves and disposed them. Her black dress hugged her curves in a bombshell sort of way but made her more fearsome than seductive and it was hard to say why—the same way timeless stone idols inspire awe. They hold the blood of countless sacrifices deep in their pores, their ancient cracks and crags.

"It cannot be broken."

When she returned to me she drew up the plastic sheeting over the gurney beside me. The length unraveled and made a sound, impersonal, rippling plastic like chattering teeth.

Playfully, she turned a corner over. The edge fell onto my arm. My good hand remained still, sensing the plastic against the new flesh, and I looked at her, curious, surprised. She gathered the sheet in long, whispering sheaths between her fingers like a girl gathering flowers and slid them off the edge of the gurney above me, where they fell into my lap just below. She perched herself beside me on the arm of the chair so I was forced to withdraw my hand and make room for her, lean legs brushing against my own.

My mouth was dry; but then, death always makes it so, and my tongue fumbled for a response, for a protest.

"Maybe you should get up," I suggested.

"Can the spell break with a kiss?"

She drew the plastic around my shoulders like a cloak until I swam in the sheet they used for the dead men. Her fingers splayed over the polyurethane, feeling my sunken chest beneath the funeral wrapping. I had the sensation of a butterfly pinned inside a frame. It was both delightful and terrifying.

"Never," I spoke with regret. "A kiss can . . . spread the spell, if you will."

Her fingers were small, the nails painted black with glitter. She took the edge of the sheet and tightened her grip until I was cocooned in plastic. Her touch no more than a bare whisper, but when you've spent years in a pitch black house with only Lana Turner for company, every small contact is explosive. My skin crawled with anticipation.

"Then I guess we'll have to figure out something else, won't we?"

It occurred to me then that I was in the hands of a siren, a temptress; she was a classic femme fatale from a pulp fiction movie, and here I was, falling into her clutches, setting up the surprise third act of a predictable story, when she would draw her gun on me and explain why she did it, how fragile she was, and *wouldn't I just love her and forget about how bad she'd been?* I groaned, a long lock of her hair brushed against the questionable skin of my neck. God, I really hoped she would be bad. I thought of reasons to refuse her, to push her away.

Then, she lifted the plastic over my head, crowding me, enclosing me in sterile, hospital smells. If she were a femme fatale, perhaps this was a clever way to kill me by asphyxiation, not realizing I was impervious to such attacks. But she was not a femme fatale.

She leaned and pressed her chest insistently through the plastic, into my suit, and into the skin beneath. Sensations long forgotten upwelled through me. Nipples so hard they could cut through the fabric of her dress. Her hand rested against my neck and her fingers threatened to melt through the plastic and she pressed in to kiss me. Her mouth closed over mine with only the thin synthetic barrier between us.

The sensation of being so close to her and simultaneously withheld made my hands clench into fists to funnel my building frustration. Her heart beat out time like an oil-slick cylinder in a hot engine.

"Saran wrap, next time," I breathed, and with either hand at her waist, pulled her into me for another, stealing away her lips without being able to truly connect. I groaned, my hips a collection of broken bones grinding against her, like teenagers out late on a school night—embarrassing, adolescent, thrilling. I tasted formaldehyde.

"Stay the night," she whispered. "We've got coffins."

I laughed, delighted. Of course! There would always be a place for one more at a funeral home.

Beyond her, in the background, the corpse sat up.

The old man jerked into a sitting position, bending at the waist and knees, his mouth open and a long, wailing groan escaping his lips. No sooner did I detect the shadow of movement when I reached for the firearm. She cried out.

"No! Vitus, it's the—"

Helpless to stop, I shot off a round. A hole appeared in the plastic and the bullet punched through the head of the old man. His skull exploded from the back and painted the wall with an impressionist expression of brains and bone. Gasping, I ripped the plastic away from my face with my free hand.

"—gas," she finished feebly, her mouth turned down into a frown. Her raven hair tousled and messy and medieval. A sorcerer casting love spells on me. At least, right up until I pissed her off by shooting her work.

"Sometimes they do that," she said, moving the plastic away. The rest of it slithered from my lap. For a moment, I thought I had an erection, that a part of me had sat up along with the old man, but no; wishful thinking. I was still as dead as the corpse. And not much left of me to get excited with. "Gas or the ligaments can bring it on."

"Sorry," I whispered, holstering the gun. "Can I—"

"No. No, Vitus, you should go. I have a mess to clean up, and a bullet hole to explain."

"I could—"

"You can't. Go."

I cursed myself silently for screwing up.

"Well, at least *he* didn't notice."

She paused to stare at me, and I waved a hand at her, heading in the direction of the exit.

"I'm going. I'm going."

And I was gone.

✴

As I passed through the foyer, still dizzied by my encounter with Niko, I paused before the suit of armor once more. If the suit of armor was meant to inspire me with thoughts of chivalry and noble deeds, I could detect none. This was the suit of armor for a knight who saved damsels—yet, it looked like the coat of armor you chose to wear if you were in the business of killing them, a nightmare world where dragons ruled and set fire to the miserable earth.

I admired the dirty, stained sheen of metal beneath the cold, sterile lights. I could not shake the sensation that the dark visor slit followed me as I left.

★

Time to pay Geoff Lafferty a visit.

Officer Lafferty used to be a police officer. In a small, suburban area like the one we lived in, there isn't a huge crime element that exists in a city, so rather than walking a beat, he had his own cruiser for catching speeders and tourists. Like everyone, he hated paperwork, knew most of the townspeople, and gave speeches to kids in class about how drugs kill.

He was hooked on prescription pills at the time. In retrospect, he realized there's little difference between popping pills your doctor profits from and pills your pusher does, but at the time it seemed like a good idea. He'd had a kidney stone, and when they gave him something for the pain, he completed the course of pills. And then decided he'd like to complete another. And another.

A slim, shorter man, he lost weight as the habit started to dig in, take hold. He was functioning, but from time to time he'd nod off in the cruiser and wake up just in time to return at the end of his shift. One nod out too many, and he was T-boned at an intersection where he fell asleep inside the cruiser while a kid plowed into the side. The car spun and hit a traffic light. The force of the spin snapped his spine, causing a lumbar injury that left him paralyzed from the waist down.

In that split second, he was both paralyzed and cured of his addiction; back injuries such as his deprive the user of the sensations that make opiates worth taking in the first place. Sober and handicapped, the police station gave him the only job they had for officers in his position: desk jockey. In his case, evidence room manager.

The first set of Rogers had name-dropped Lafferty, so it stood to reason he may know something I didn't. Lafferty knew me from the old days—we'd graduated high school in the same class, and he and Jamie used to pal around. Geoff had been instructed to refer people if he thought they could use my specific services, and he'd been reliable—until now.

I parked the Thunderbird outside the station, pulling my hat as far down over my face as I could manage, and approached. The police knew me, knew I was a friend of Lafferty's. According to Geoff, I had reached a legendary status—they knew the military base wasn't far away, and I was involved in strange goings on there. A few beers and a Bourne trilogy later, it was unanimously decided I was a government spook and officers were telling their children if they didn't stop the goddamn racket they were gonna send Vitus after them. Thus, a legend grows.

An officer by the door glanced at me and then attempted to take a second look without being rude. He was young and fresh off a factory line. I brushed his shoulder enough to move him an inch with my bared teeth pulled back from my rotten lips, breathing out a growl so he could smell the stench of death. My eyes were ghost-lights transfixing him like roadkill, his shock punctuated by his unhinged jaw.

"Mind your fucking business," I said, and slipped past him and inside the door.

The pale officer looked away and continued to hold up the wall by the door, shrinking into it in a failed effort to disappear.

I didn't expect trouble here. I've been to states where random strangers wave and say hi, but here in Jersey, being nice is an invitation to a personal fuck-over. Someone's always out to get you and nastiness becomes an ingrained way of life. Gang members wear three-piece suits and 1000-watt smiles. Dear Granny pimps out her children to strangers to support her coke habit. If there's a way to make a profit off human pain and suffering, someone in Jersey has perfected it. Usually while huffing toluene. And if profit can't be squeezed from you, they kill you and strip you for parts.

I took a flight of steps down into the basement of the headquarters.

This is where they housed the evidence. A crime is committed, and anything left behind that could be used as evidence for the prosecution is bagged and inventoried and sent off to the basement, where Geoff Lafferty comes in. In a wheelchair behind a desk, he takes in all the strange items left behind at robberies, murder scenes, rapes, and drug busts.

When he's not running evidence, he's finishing mountains of paperwork other people don't want to do. Every once in a while, someone passes through and misses him, expecting someone several feet taller than the man seated in the wheelchair below. Whether it's a woman who lost someone close to her or a man who needs information, Geoff Lafferty is there to supply a name: *You want something done the police won't do, talk to Vitus Adamson.* My own personal carnival barker.

"Lafferty," I greeted him, leaning against the counter. He wheeled over to the counter with a weary look in his bloodshot eyes. The walls around him are plastered with push pins and wanted fliers for missing children by the truckload who disappear and are never heard from again.

"Vitus, here to provide evidence that you're full of shit?"

"You don't have a bag big enough, Lafferty."

"Is that what passes for wit these days?"

"'Shit.' Not 'wit.' Get your ears checked, old man."

He chortled, smiling briefly; Geoff was not the type of guy who smiled much, his mouth a thin line to match a flat, emotionless face; if you were a fool, you fell for it, believing his poker face was the real one. He gave nothing away behind his eyes, measuring you from the background. Occasionally, I got to see the man behind the wall of silence. In return, he got to see me from time to time, as well.

"I had someone show up on my doorstep," I began.

Geoff shuffled papers into proper order as I spoke, but I knew he was listening. As though to make up for all the hours of his drugged-out haze, his sobriety was supercharged—nothing escaped his notice now.

"How's this my problem?"

"They're dead. But they're also liars."

"Trust, but verify," Lafferty sighed, quoting Reagan. "Haven't referred anyone in a long while. You need to refresh my memory."

"They called themselves Rogers. As in Mr. and Mrs."

"Seriously?"

"Does it look like I'm making it up?"

"No. But they must have been, because I never met a Mr. and Mrs. Rogers."

"You know the name of the last person you referred?"

He stopped shuffling his usual mountain of papers and opened a drawer. He reached beneath, pulled out a slip of paper, and passed it across the counter.

I took it from him and opened it up. There were several names, but one in particular grabbed my attention.

"Madame Astra? Either a hooker or a fortune teller."

"She came out of processing dressed like the trade, you know?"

"Where do I fit in?"

"She was pissed. Bitching about the cops being involved in her business, not doing anything, same old song. I asked her what her business was, she said they were harassing her, for no reason." Lafferty shrugged. "I'm sure there was a reason."

"Doesn't sound like reason enough to refer me. What made you give her my golden ticket?"

"I thought you could use the company."

"So, you referred her because you thought I could use a good lay, is what you're telling me?"

He grinned. "Might change that sourpuss expression of yours. Or maybe it's sour pus?"

"You're a fucker, Lafferty."

He laughed. "I guess she didn't show up?"

"Not unless she was calling herself Mrs. Rogers."

"You'd have known it. She was different. Strange."

"Thanks for the tip, Geoff. Maybe you need to find some company of your own, eh?"

He grinned. "I did. I went and married her."

I waved him off, thrusting the paper into my pocket and leaving.

★

Later, I returned to the house.

Any fool with a gun can call himself a hunter; patience is indispensable. With my eyes half-lidded, I settled into the familiar sounds of a sleeping house—the breathing of my houseguests as they slumbered in my sheets, the hum of the empty refrigerator, the wind against the vinyl siding, time and slippage working against my humble home over the course of decades.

I waited. If you've ever been posted in one spot for too long, most people feel their limbs go numb when the circulation slows. I was dead, all of me was already numb, and when I got up, there would be no part of me left to come back to life. My brand new gun hand twitched in the darkness and then lay still.

Hours passed in this fashion, one long silence stretched out across minutes and seconds. The television cast images against the wall, a silent film playing out an urgent drama, volume down low. Mitchum smoked in something noir-inspired. Tree branches scraped along the house, and still I waited. I tried not to think about Clay, about the case. I tried not to think about anything at all, missing a time when I could have dreamt.

Crickets stopped and started from time to time and aroused me to alertness, only to pick up their rhythm again and lull me back to waiting. The black-and-white reel swapped places with the modern and the opening credits of *Jacob's Ladder* unfolded with Tim Robbins as tormented Jacob Singer. Flashing lights sent me drifting back into an uncanny queasiness, with the small hairs on the inside of my ears singing and rasping and coming up empty. I lost myself in a television land of scenery and discordant images. Time staggered out of true until I thought I was staring at my own image through the screen and jolted up out of the darkness, thinking I was trapped inside the movie in a nightmare from which I could not wake—and then realized the television was off. The convex glass reflected my face and I could not remember turning it off. I sat with my hand on the remote and the other on my gun and stared at the black screen.

Minutes dragged out in this fashion.

And then I heard it.

A long, strangled squeal of wood and metal being coaxed apart. I opened my eyes, adjusting to the darkness. How clever was my shooter? Was he trying to gain entry through the door, or the window? I watched, still. My heart lay dead against my cold Glock.

The sound originated from the front of the house. The squealing hit a final note and diminuendoed into taut silence.

I laid my new hand across the weapon and withdrew slowly. Synthetic, hard plastic rasping against fabric. My quartz-stone eyes panned the room and I rose from the chair. One step at a time across the floor as I backed against the far wall.

If I were alive, I could describe to you the glitter of sweat and the rank scent of my own adrenaline pushing up through my veins and my teeth reduced to gravel in my mouth. Lips gone to coarse grit sandpaper. The only genuine article I had left was fear.

"Show me your face," I whispered, as though I could separate the darkness from my target with will alone. Past the window, I eased my way there to peer through the outside hedges, searching for him.

My brother and I used to read stories of hunters stalking panthers in continents halfway around the world where men and women had the sense to fear the night. This brought things long buried through the dense material of my consciousness and reminded me of one such story. In it, two men passed a cigarette between each other where they were stationed in the wilderness until his fellow held out his cigarette and no one took it. An ember burning in the nothingness to illuminate the empty space where the wild cat had snatched his comrade away without a sign or a sound. Smoke churning the void he occupied seconds before.

I was returned to this sense of childhood dread; one hand outstretched and waiting for someone to take the smoke from me and waiting, waiting, waiting for the moment of revelation to dawn. A yawning emptiness whose static condition made me aware that anything could be elapsing beyond my sight, leaving to the imagination any number of horrors equipped to steal my courage piecemeal.

And then the screaming began.

First the shatter, then the screams. Sound exploded from the opposite side of the house. I cursed as I turned on my heels and ran, sliding against the wooden planks for the bedroom door. Shots erupted behind the walls. Spackle and drywall exploded apart in puffs of gypsum dust as bullets exited out the other side. The knob jittered around my shaking grip.

The fools had locked the door.

I stood back and shot out the lock to jerk open the splintered door. My feet sloshed through blood and I knew an echo of ancient memory: adrenaline and blood close against the skin. The room lay out before me was torn apart. Bedding and mattress soaked in Mr. and Mrs. Rogers' blood. Their bodies fallen over one another like discarded toys; feathers floated in the air, contents of their pillows scattered with their brains.

He stood there.

The shooter stood above Mr. Rogers's body, shells expulsing from his weapon and bullet holes ventilating the wall. The sound of the door electrified him into locomotion. Glittering eyes through his ski mask slit. He sucked in a breath as he brought me into focus and swung his gun toward me with precise and level care.

I'm dead, not slow.

I met his gun with my own; fractional seconds and limited space gave me no room to shoot but thrust the barrel of my gun to strike his weapon out of the way. Flesh mashed against my grip and crushed the knuckle of his trigger finger. He grunted surprise and pain as I stepped into the circle of his body until he and I were chest to chest like lovers illustrated in a poisonous *Kama Sutra*. If he wanted to shoot me now, we were too close; he would have to risk shooting himself or move his hand at an odd, awkward angle that would take up too much of his reaction time.

I could feel the rapid beating of his heart through my cold chest drum up in tandem with the taste of his scent in the air, quickening pre-deceased senses and driving hunger pangs through the center of my belly. Saliva collected in a puddle around my tongue. I tasted my latent hunger and wanted more. Wanted to get in close and unhinge my jaws and snake-swallow him and satisfy this chronic hunger. And, then satiated, end my season in Hell.

I struck him with the butt of the gun on his shoulder instead and broke the spell of my ravening. His grunt gave way to a hefty gasp.

Zzzzzt.

A fly buzzed past my ear in the fray. Distracted, I jerked away and out of its path. The intruder pressed his advantage. He introduced his fist to my face. It was a quick meeting. My cheekbone snapped with a rotted crunch against his knuckles and my head whipped back. The room filled with our labored breaths panting out a seething aggression, mingling his sweat with my carrion smell.

The man launched into a run to escape through the blown-apart window he had used to gain entrance. I snatched his hooded sweatshirt into a fist with one flailing hand, drawing him back. He turned, striking wildly at me. Bits of me cascaded to the floor, shaken loose by each punch that found home.

"You're in danger. Get out of here, Vitus," the man hissed.

A final wrench and he broke free and left me clawing the air after him. He reached the window and shook the floor with the force of his exit as he vaulted through the jagged opening and landed in the broken glass outside. Bloody at the hands where he had chosen to grip the glass and escape rather than slow down and risk being caught.

I lifted my gun until the iron sight covered his retreating figure and drew it steady. The man stopped halfway across the lawn as though he sensed the bead marking his back. He turned with his shrouded face and the slit of eyes, like deep slashes of midnight, vacant darkness, stared back at me. I was reminded of the empty suit of armor at the funeral home.

My finger stayed put along the barrel at neutral.

He was dangerous. He killed four people and shot me.

Panting, he held his own weapon to the side. He had a clear shot, yet he refused to lift his gun and take it.

Then, he tucked it out of sight in the back of his pants and walked away.

"Fuck," I muttered, and put away the gun.

PART 2

LORD OF THE FLESH EATERS

Madam Astra.

She had an office situated in the quiet part of town, where people liked to park their cars and window shop as they walked. I did the same, feeding quarters to an old parking meter and stepping out into the misting rain.

She had a listing in the phone book and a small advertisement that ran in the weekly circular. On the surface, she appeared to be a legitimate business woman, but anyone advertising tarot fortunes, astrology, and palm reading is suspect in my understanding of the world. I attribute very little of misfortune and, by proxy, the future, to the fates when the human components are all too easy and obvious culprits. So much of our lives are moved by bad meals and decisions made on two hours' sleep and a half a bottle of vodka that I found the idea of the stars plotting our course laughable. Just as likely, she was a con artist stealing from her clients in the dubious business of hopes and dreams.

As I walked, I continued thinking about my midnight altercation with the shooter and the two rotting bodies at the house. I'd folded up the unfortunate Mr. and Mrs. Rogers, stuffing them into contractor bags for the time being. I'd gotten rid of asbestos shingles that way; but the room was a bloody mess of brains and body fluids. The most regrettable thing about that circumstance was the mess their deaths had made of my marriage bed.

The man had not wanted to hurt me. Had refused to shoot me, acknowledged my clear shot, and turned his back to me. What did it mean? And his cryptic warning. What possible alliance did this man hope to forge with me? Did he know where Owen was?

I touched the photo of Owen Rogers folded in my pocket. I made great effort to think as little of him as possible, not only because the thought of my son pained me, but because I needed to martial all my energy for this case.

I was hired to find Owen Rogers and I believed that at the end of this trail I would find Clay Adamson instead. It was too hard to think about what would happen if I failed, what my life would be if I was wrong, if this was just another stepping stone in a clever trick designed to draw me in.

There's Niko.

Indeed, she had found her way into my life. Gorgeous, young, vibrant, and giving herself away to a corpse. How did I know she wasn't on the take? I didn't. She could be involved, for all I knew.

I stood on the street smoking a cigarette. The rain ran into my eyes and I pulled my hat further down, shadowing my brow while my thoughts agitated back and forth.

Niko had been working at Pleasant Hills when they brought my family in—what remained of them.

Dark days. I took a moment to remember them, forgetting the uneven texture of the cracked sidewalk beneath my feet, forgetting the biting cold of the damp wind. I shivered now like I had shivered then. Side by side with Jamie, subdued in a straightjacket. I remembered he had worn a blue suit. In the early days, it was all trial and error. They had no idea what dosage was necessary to keep me upright and functioning, so every day was a violent whipsaw of emotions, disintegrating into a zombie at a moment's notice.

He had not wanted to take me to the funeral home, but I insisted. He had me on a tether like a rabid animal, and I hated him for it, for reducing me to this *thing*. I had begged him over and over again to end it. I did not want to go on like a half-animal, knowing I ate my son and wife. I wanted to see Dad, but Dad wouldn't come, and I seethed with hatred for the old gray fox and everything that happened in Sarajevo between us, between my mother.

But I did go on—Jamie made me go on. They packed me into a Ford with tinted windows and armed guards to go to the funeral parlor. I sat in the back while a guard with an AR kept me on a short leash, Jamie at the wheel and his seven-year-old son dressed in his church clothes, a blue suit. I remembered thinking his tousled hair reminded me of Clay, and the knowledge that my son was dead hit me again with force, consistently surprising me with its ferocity. We had passed by a string of soldiers awaiting our arrival, and Jamie's boy, Amos, sat up straighter in his seat, cocking his hand like a pistol at the armed men and shooting them down with huffing noises through his mouth in imitation of a gun blast: *bang!* It had drawn a long, sad smile from me.

From there to a waiting room in a long coat meant to hide my straightjacket, and a soldier on hand in case I needed to be put down. Jamie spoke to the funeral director, and in the background, with roses in her hand, a girl with Bettie Page good looks, bombshell style. Curling black hair. Niko.

I remembered staring at her hands. Her fingers small and I thought, *Those fingers put my family back together.* I could not stop staring. She spoke to Jamie. Their voices rose and fell from fathoms away; I was underwater, deep inside myself.

She passed me, and as she passed, she turned.

The soldier stepped forward with a hand on his rifle, and what was he gonna do? Spray the lot of us with bullets? Jamie intervened, caught her by the shoulder with an insistent hand, whipping her back and away from me when I realized again that it was me they were securing her from.

In the instant before the guards could whisk her out of my life, she reached out with a rose, white petals like pearl-skin, and pushed it into the fabric fold of my arm; her fingertips brushed me. Her wide, moon-shaped face wore a look of curiosity, confusion, shared grief. Jamie let me keep the rose. I held it that night, white rose in a fist, until congealed blood oozed from thorn punctures like gas station oil, thick and black.

I never forgot her. She had forgotten me.

She can't be on the take. There's no way. That's an intricate con, to be working at a funeral home when you happen to kill your wife and child, just to screw you over a couple years later. Best con I ever seen.

"That's because it's not one," I muttered, annoyed, and cast the burning butt into the street before I crushed it with my heel. When I stepped away, torn remains of yet another missing child poster littered the pavement. The picture of this new unfortunate boy was disintegrated until it looked like a caricature of a zombie itself, decaying in the rain before my very eyes. Didn't anyone use milk cartons anymore?

Let's see this Madam Astra. Let's see how good she really is.

And with that, I headed to the shop with the glowing hand in the center window, advertising FORTUNES, FUTURE, AND FATE! Madam Astra tells all!

I opened the door, coming in from the misting rain. I made soggy footprints on the carpet as I stepped in. I left my hat and coat on as I took in the dim interior. Lazy smoke swirls of incense filled the air, the way I imagined a bonfire filled with hippies might smell after dousing themselves in patchouli and weed.

Darkness and colored light, red and pink lamps with ornate shades of fringe. A confusion of bright velvet and silk garments strung throughout the interior gave it the appearance of a gypsy caravan. A glass case against the wall showcased tarot cards and amulets, crystals; some for sale, some for use in the reading. A plaque on the wall advertised the different services, fortunes reading like an order off a fast-food menu. *I'd like a double whammy super sized, with a large order of fatalism.* A person could choose several methods of divination, from astrology chart, to tarot cards, to palm reading, or all three for a discounted price.

I perused my options. Palm reading was out of the question, unless she wanted to use my newer hand, which was only slightly less decomposed than my old one. My old one had yellow bone showing through rents in the flesh, obscured by my black gloves, a necessity in undead wardrobe.

Tarot cards and astrology chart. Jessica had always read our horoscopes aloud, tracking them in the daily paper. I didn't have faith in the stars; what good was astrology for a dead guy like me? Stars and fates were for the living.

Tarot cards were the most appealing option, but still sounded like a rip off at twenty dollars for a short-term reading, as opposed to forty dollars for a life read. *To tell you what, exactly? How terrible and empty this human experience is, and then you die? Or whatever passes for death,* I considered. I reached for the bell and tapped it, sending noise throughout the shop.

In the back, a curtain swept aside and a figure emerged from the shadows; slight, a willow frame in a swirl of skirt and theatrical fabric. Long blond hair that swept to her waist. I imagined she was what a fairy would look like if that kinda thing were real; but beneath the charming patina of polished made-for-TV smile, beneath the small, pointed features, an unsettling version of fey nature lingered—not in a Hollywood cute kind of conventional fairy, but rather, the original version. The ones with their underground palaces, the ones ready to strip the meat from your bones with their teeth and sample the marrow. A mischief as capable of leading you in front of the path of a sixteen-wheel Mack Truck as a secret paradise in a shire or a mountain.

In short, she was everything I was not.

Whereas Niko was darkly intriguing, with a somber air that hinted at mystery, Madam Astra was a high school cheerleader in gypsy garb. She'd traded in pom-poms for tarot cards, and her blue eyes were oddly empty, like a puppet's. Button nose, perky breasts. Her bright, bubbly blondness only served to highlight my monstrosity; my sunken eyes, my rotted face falling apart in strips and seams, the skin cracked like hard packed mud where I used to smile.

I had the pleasure of noticing that, as she drew closer, her walk slowed, considering me for the first time, truly seeing the awful face beneath the shadow of my hat. My rotted lips peeled back to bare crooked teeth as I watched her approach. I know what the wolf felt when Red Riding Hood came to his door, the hunger in his bottomless belly, his bottomless heart.

Most people who stole close to me, close enough to see and smell the decay and the carrion, the meat rotting off my bones, chalked it up to unusual skin diseases, cancer, even leprosy. Amazing what we'll overlook in favor of what we prefer to see. Few used the word *zombie*, though it lingered on the tip of their tongues, too unbelievable a notion to voice. She stared longer than she should have before finding the center of my opaque, decayed eyes.

"Can I help you?" she asked. Her voice was steady, and she disguised her distress well.

"I'm interested in the future," I began.

"Unusual. Most of my clientele in this town are women, you know. The majority of men I receive as customers are those looking for their wives."

"I'm looking for someone," I said. A knot formed in my throat. I swallowed it back into my esophagus.

"Oh?"

I pulled out the picture of Owen Rogers, laying it flat on her counter and pushing it over to her. I studied her face as she leaned over it, blond hair brushing her red velvet sleeves.

"I'm looking for my son," I said. "His name is Clay Adamson."

Zzzzt.

I responded to the noise instinctively, gaze flicking to the glass countertop like a snake. A fly—brilliant emerald green thorax punctuated with black wings—buzzed lazily by her fingertips, sampling the counter with a tube-like proboscis. Nausea roiled in my belly.

I hated flies.

Attempting to ignore it, I concentrated on Madam Astra once more. The sound rang in my ears like a humming electrical line, making conscious thought difficult.

"I've seen him," she said.

Confirmation. A knife thrust into my belly. I choked on my heart, which was steadily climbing through my throat and out my mouth. If this was what hope felt like, I longed for my days of despair.

"He goes to my church," she continued. "But his name isn't Clay; you must be mistaken. He's Owen Rogers, and his parents are a lovely couple."

Interesting. I could feel heat creeping through my collar and up my neck, a building rage. I was tired of playing these interrogation games, pretending to slowly circle my prey; I was tired of being cautious. Weapons and instruments of torture took the place of my heart. I wanted it to beat again, trade my vena cava for a firearm and blow out bullets with each pulse.

With a long sigh, I reached up and took my hat off. I was a monster. It was about time I acted like one. Thin light cast over my barren skull, bleached bone showing through the top where the flesh peeled away around wisps of straw-like hair. Her face grew slack as her lips parted and her saliva dried up, turning her tongue to bone.

I left the hat on the counter and turned back to lock the door with a quick flick of my hand. Her eyes were as wide as dinner plates when I faced her.

"Now, let's have us a real conversation," I growled. "You have my son, and you know Mr. and Mrs. Rogers are dead, so why don't we cut the shit and get down to business?"

I pulled out the Glock and let it hang by my side, my arm loose and relaxed, a precursor to a storm. I was ready. The hour was growing late, and I was due for my medication soon. I could taste her meat on the air, the blood pulsing through her veins and capillaries. Enough time without my medication, and she would be sweet. Ripe with all the hectic juices fear could provide.

Her face held the same stunned, confused, innocent-me expression for a long moment as I stared at her. Then her features smoothed out and one small hand picked up the photograph, holding it up so I was confronted with the face of my son.

"You and your son have been chosen, Vitus Adamson. It is an honor to stand in the presence of our Lord."

And to my astonishment, she genuflected, as devout as a nun during a Sunday mass in her red velvet skirt and downcast eyes.

★

Beep-beep.

I cursed, stepping away from the woman. She bowed so low before me the tips of her blond hair brushed the carpeted floor, and I reached into my pocket without looking, popping off the cap and shoving two pills into my mouth. Anything to stave off this wild and unrepentant hunger. They always tasted so bitter, each time.

"You're keeping the kid in a cage, that it? You got him shacked up in a house somewhere, like an animal, because you think he's a god?"

She lifted her head. Her pupils narrowed to black pinheads with her eyes fevered and bright. Her cheeks flushed with new blood.

"We are honored to have him. But you are mistaken, Vitus. We must cage him for his own safety. What of your pills?"

I blinked and looked down at the orange prescription bottle in my hand.

"Are those any less a cage? Are they not designed to protect you, as well as those around you? We can no more set Owen free than you can roam loose without your medication. He does not understand the Lord inside himself any more than you understand the Lord inside you."

"What Lord?" I asked.

Her voice floated on a deep, husky undertone and, if I were to close my eyes, I knew I could easily imagine a sex phone operator. She could have been describing her underpants with a voice designed to seduce and lull me. Selling me propaganda off the tip of her tongue with a smile behind her glassy eyes. Her mascara turned up at the edges to accentuate their shape, but her gaze was disconnected and out of sync. A smear of—was that dirt by her temple, wending into her scalp? *Grave dirt,* I thought without reason, and attempted to clamp down on my meandering thoughts. Why was I so distracted? What was it about her that was setting me on such an edge of nervous anxiety?

"Lord of the Flesh Eaters, the King of Dark Matter. The Master of Monsters."

She bowed once more before me. I could see the lacy edge of a bra showing through the plunge of her shirt and the view invited and implied desire; deep in the gutter between her breasts and ribs, I caught a flash of something black (mold? Was that mold deep in her core? No, it must be more lace, why in the world would I think mold?) and then she rose.

I held up a hand between us as though I could ward her off, but she insisted on taking a step forward. She posed me no real physical harm—she was too small and fragile for that. It was her religious fervor I found frightening and even more the jitters rammed up my limbs and through my nerves the closer I got to her.

"We have read your scripture, your dark gospel; we know the pain of your existence. You have been called upon to do terrible things."

I laughed. "That's an understatement."

"You see, Vitus? We know your hate, your rage. How long have you been living now, like this? No purpose, no direction? The pills aren't keeping you upright—it's your seething hatred. It's your bitter anger. And you carry it alone."

I said nothing, blinking and stupefied. The truth was, I'd never heard my life summarized in such a way, through another's eyes. It caught me off guard and cut loose a howling voice on the inside of me. So I listened to her, spellbound by the rhythm of her voice.

"And so he will build a life of sweet things, a thin wall he erects against the darkness. One by one, he will eat his security, his love, his happiness to fill the void that can never be filled. So it is written, praise the Lord of Flesh Eaters! Master of Monsters! He can only be sustained by flesh and blood."

She brought her hands together until her fingers formed a steeple.

"You worship this condition, is that it?" I gestured to myself, tapping the edge of my frayed lapel. "I'm a corpse. *Pre-deceased.*"

"That's not who you really are. You think you're a monster? Who told you such a lie? Jamie? You'll believe him, the one who arranged for you to be like this in the first place? What proof do you have that you are such a monster?"

I stared at her.

"I ate my wife."

"Did you? Or did Jamie have her killed so he could keep you to himself? Why do you think Owen's been in hiding all this time? We couldn't let Jamie find him."

I was prepared to dismiss her words as ravings, as though she were only a Kool-Aid cup from madness, but her last words emptied my mouth of protest. How much did she know about me? Enough to know about Virus X, about the experiments, and about Jamie.

Enough to have my son in captivity?

"They showed you scraps of your wife. How did you know it was her?"

"They found me with them," I protested. An odd tremor built from my legs into my spine and punctured the decomposing muscles of my arm as though the dead nerve endings came to life and sent racing flames through my veins. "They found me with her! I had her blood in my mouth, I tasted her perfume . . ."

"Is that what you remember, or what they told you?"

My breath caught; I had no memory of the event, only Jamie's version, how he had found me in a room strewn with body parts and blood.

Jamie would never have killed Jessica. He would have done everything to save her. He was the best man at my wedding, for Christ's sake . . .

But oh, lying was very much Jamie's style. Him and the old gray fox.

A most uncomfortable sensation formed in the center of my guts, where my stomach churned with the bile and venom and the bitter pills holding my existence intact with a thin chemical veil—doubt. Doubt was opening a crack inside me that would widen into an abyss.

She inclined her head so the light from the window caught her hair like a halo; thin wisps of incense smoke filled the air until the room spun and chased the tail of the horizon. Only the gun in my hand was real, burning an outline into my palm.

Kill her, I thought grimly. I could stop this vivisection of the past and break her hold over me and all it would require was her life. *Kill her.*

"In all the time, with all that you've been through, did Jamie ever say he saved you because he loved you?"

I should have stopped breathing. I gave up air in the well of my lungs I didn't know I had left. Scattered tarot cards beneath the glass counter and constellations charted out until their shapes resembled grinding teeth and then she was pressing a hand over my chest. Fabric crinkled and rasped as she pressed my white button-down shirt with her palm. My chest an iceberg, her fingers icicles.

I couldn't remember the last time *anyone* ever said they loved me.

"We need you, Vitus. Come with us, and you will know your son again. You can have the life they took from you."

"Nothing can change this," I whispered. "You're lying."

"No, Vitus. But we will wait for you, because we love you for what you really are."

She stepped away, withdrawing her frozen hand from my cold chest. My gun hand twitched. I wanted to put a bullet between her eyes, but all I could hear was the question, over and over again: *Did Jamie ever say he saved you because he loved you?*

Not once.

Never.

★

I slammed the door hard enough to crack the glass as I left and trudged out into the mist. I clutched the gun in one hand, heedless of the pedestrians. Some gave me wary stares and others were too stupid and distracted by their techno-gadgets to notice. I holstered resentfully.

Before the car, I hesitated. Where was I going, what was my plan? What kind of life was I returning to? With my hand clutching the door handle, I saw the panorama view of my life unfolding forever in one endless loop. Just one case after the other, of foolish people doing dangerous things, dirty things. Watching people tear themselves apart, husbands and wives without trust or faith, children abducted and ruined, employers and employees spying on each other—I was looking at an eternity of watching people tear at themselves as though they were . . . zombies.

I slammed a fist against the car hood. The metal popped as I clenched my broken, wasted fingers inside the glove. I felt nothing, I felt everything.

The bitch had my son. And she wasn't giving him up—not without gaining me as her own personal chess piece. I couldn't trust anything she had to say, and no doubt she knew about the Rogers—emissaries designed to draw me in? The conspiracy widened. I took in a short breath that thrilled my muscles with a sensation of panic. Had this all been an elaborate ploy with one intention—to entrap me?

How did she know so much about Jamie, about Virus X?

I feared to ask—the answers may be terrible to behold.

Get a grip. Start from the beginning. Unravel the mystery. You have an objective: you want your son. All the rest is bullshit. How do you get your son back?

"Force or persuasion," I muttered.

I cast away the feeling of the moment and refocused. Logic and strategy would lead my way out of the mire. Use of force was questionable; she was as vacant as a churchgoer who charms snakes and writhes on the ground in a pantomime of demonic possession. I could threaten her with death, but in the eyes of a religious fanatic, that was a reward. She'd jump at the chance to be a martyr for a cause, so physical threats were out of the question.

Come with us, and you will know your son again.

She wanted my participation in their church in exchange for my son.

"It's a fucking Roman Polanski film," I hissed and shoved a cigarette in between my lips just to keep my mouth occupied. I got into the car and started the engine.

I guess that leaves persuasion.

I groaned and pealed out of the lot.

★

Rain came down in heavy drifts by the time I pulled into my driveway, making it difficult to see and navigate. From the porch, with keys in hand, I paused warily before the entrance.

My front door stood ajar into a slice of darkness. I hovered with one hand over the weapon as a gambler might his talismans. Prick-eared and alert. I heard nothing and detected no movement from within. I tapped open the door with fingers spread and entered the house.

A shadow on my left.

I choked the figure back against the wall. My arm locked over his throat and I pinned him. An umbrella clattered beneath a kicking foot and a picture frame see-sawed in a ninety-degree angle before dropping to the floor and exploding glass across our scuffling feet. I yanked the gun free. All shadows and smoke, he squirmed beneath my grip.

"Vitus!"

Shit. I released the shadow and stepped away. The gun fell to my side like a heavy pendulum.

"What are you doing here, Niko?"

I moved aside a curtain to let in the feeble rain-light. She stood illuminated in a slicker, black hair curled and moist with the rain; her lips an inviting apple red.

"I had to talk to you."

"So you broke into my house?"

"Like you broke into my work and forced me to fix your jaw at gunpoint? You don't have a phone, and I had no other way to reach you. And anyway, I was going to wait for you outside. You left the door open."

I sighed and lit a cigarette, breathing in the hot fumes of tar and tobacco. Her eyes glistened in the half-light as she watched the ember trace an orange outline in the air. I'd locked the door before I left; perhaps one of Madam Astra's minions had paid my house a visit in my absence. I'd have them doing my landscaping next, at this rate.

"Why didn't you tell me?"

"Tell you what, exactly?" I asked, suspicious.

"I remember you now."

An uncomfortable silence bloomed between us. I looked away to the window. In the yard, trees bent and twisted and cut dark paths against the neglected yard. While she spoke, I listened to the interior of the house and scanned the world around me for movement, watchful. Hyper-vigilance dogged me even in the quiet.

While I leaned by the window, keeping constant vigil over my surroundings, Niko unfolded her story. Earlier in the day, the fumes from the formaldehyde began to bother her. Dizzy, she took a walk out among the graves where she passed my wife and child and the headstone above my empty grave. The flowers I left behind were still fresh and blooming, and latent memory in the background of her thoughts pulsed through her splitting headache until the feeling passed; clarity replaced pain.

She found me then, in the long lost corridors of her mind, like a pressed flower buried in the gutter of a book. The white roses I left propped against the gravestone set off a cascade of recollections.

"I remembered you," she whispered.

I did not look at her. I exhaled smoke and tasted my own blood sandwiched on either side of my decomposing tongue. I wished all that was left of me was a memory; if I could dream, I would dream of living six feet underground in a six-sided box. I would not be here, looking out a dirty window and pretending to look at everything but her, play-acting a monster with a mind as dead as my heart.

She waited for me to speak, and I know I disappointed her. This was the moment I was supposed to give her the tender heart of me, to show her I was a human, that I had once lived and loved. Maybe even procure tears for her amusement. My tear ducts were as dry and broken as abandoned tunnel ways from a dead civilization. I had nothing left to give her that I had not eaten or cannibalized in the end.

Beep-beep.

The siren song of Atroxipine broke the silence. I remained still until the digital beep faded and then took out the bottle, uncapped it, and knocked a dosage into my mouth. Pills rattled against the back of my throat. My broken teeth ground them into dust against my molars. Metal clicked inside my jaw.

"Goddamn you, Vitus. You think you're the only one who's lost someone?" she snapped.

Furious, I rounded on her.

"You don't know anything about me. If you're smart, you'd leave."

"You're the one who keeps coming back!" she returned and took a step forward, matching my advance. Her courage took me aback. What had I expected? A meek girl, all fear and trembling? How foolish I had been. I calculated curves and softness—behind her feminine mystique was barbed wire. Hold her close and I'd come away with rust and punctures for my trouble.

"You think I really don't understand, do you?"

"You don't," I stated. I blew smoke out between us, a lazy ring. I tested her patience, and she knew it, but what I really wanted was to drive her away. If being rude and obnoxious did the trick, so be it.

"I lied to you, Vitus."

I lifted an eyebrow. Beforehand, I believed the only thing she really had going for her was a pretty face and a nuclear figure that could melt nails. This new admission of duplicity excited my interest, awoke me to all the secrets bound within her. I took a breath.

Confession time. Here it is. She's involved somehow.

She'd been a villain all along.

"I didn't tell you the truth about Hawaii."

Her words flowed fast upon the other and dismantled my suspicion and paranoia in one breath, though I did not show it. I kept myself locked within my mask as though I did not feel; but for each word she spoke, I felt everything, married with the shame that I had ever doubted her.

She told me of Hawaii. Born in the moist, tropical air. Loving parents and the waving palm fronds cradled her in youth; rills of Pacific water washing up on shore. Her pale skin, her raven black hair, all genetic gifts from a native Hawaiian mother and a father who had been stationed on a military base. This young soldier wandered off the main road one day, following a dirt trail to a communal house in the middle of palm trees, sugar cane, and celestial waters.

"It was a Lazar House, Vitus."

I pinched the end of my cigarette with two fingers, listening to the sound of my flesh sizzle against the extinguished tip.

"You're talking about the leper colony, aren't you?"

They called them Lazar Houses, a long time ago in the dark ages. Even with a medical system struggling with reform in our present day, the pestilence of a millennium ago made our present-day concerns look palatial by comparison. Hard to imagine a world where leprosy was so virulent, every town in the English-speaking world had a Lazar House, lepers living together and begging for charity from strangers. Advanced stages have been known to numb limbs and open the way to gangrene through bacterial infection. Limbs rotting away. Flesh dissolving into the primal mud from which an ancient, vengeful God is rumored to have formed us. And in their time, to be a leper was to be punished by God. Hell visited you on Earth instead of troubling you to go there yourself.

No one would ever mistake me for a leper—our conditions were radically different, but equally stigmatized and displayed on our faces. Still. What was it like for her to look at my face? Did I remind her of the ones she'd left behind?

"My mother used to hold me," she said. "Long hands. Graceful. Like a bird. As time passed, that became more difficult, because she lost her fingers to secondary infection, one by one, until all that remained were the nubs of her palms. She'd hold them together in prayer. She would sit by my bed and stroke my hair with a stump instead of a hand as though she could feel it still. And somewhere along the way my father left; hard to say if it was those hauntingly reduced hands of hers, whose bones inspired terror in the neighborhood children, likewise terror in him. When they had first met, she was whole, lithe, beautiful. But she fractured over time, like a flawed diamond, relentlessly tapped until she shattered."

The words dried up. My cold, cold heart felt colder still. It didn't take a special kind of moron to realize I was a decayed surrogate father figure. She took a step closer to me. I held my ground, but the mood, the moment, was steeped in volatile emotions. I dared not breathe.

"Do you know, the rotting, the gangrene, isn't the worst of it? No one will touch them, Vitus. People fear to lay their hands, like so," she whispered, moving in closer.

I backed up against the end table, cornered in the darkness.

We both held our breath, her palm open and approaching my face. Her touch met my skin. My cheek, rough textured as rope, as concrete, weathered with damage.

"I know what it is to be touch-starved, Vitus."

I swallowed, metal clicking in my jaw, and did not respond with a look or a word. Her hand fell away. She faded into the background, dissolving into the darkness.

"It's a terrible affliction to know the pain of those whom no one else will touch. She wanted me to stay, but she wanted her daughter to have a better life. She couldn't have both. So she sent me away. And I left. And do you know what I found when I got here?"

"What?" I asked.

"I find a coward! A low-life, dead-beat junkie!"

I flinched. Somewhere inside my dark chest, my dead heart moved in eerie pantomime of a heartbeat.

"It's not like that—" I protested.

"What was it like, then? Time and again, you thrust yourself into my life, unwelcome, unasked for, and you didn't think telling

me was important? You didn't think you owed me the story of
what happened? I can forgive whatever happened to you—I can
let the past remain buried in the past. But you couldn't even look
me in the eyes and tell me—"

Before she could eject her final, bitter words, I was moving
across the expanse, knocking over the end table, sending a vase
of moldy water and dead flowers splashing onto the floorboards
where the smell of decay persisted. I held her by the neck,
pushing her back, undead eyes blazing with a jack-o-lantern
glow, animated with a force beyond death. I smelled the heady
aromas that constituted her, the perfume—beneath the perfume,
her sweat and her tissues throbbing in erotic harmony, calling
me in to take a piece, sample the flesh, taste it—

"Look at my eyes," I hissed.

She jerked backward, but I was unrelenting, and I hated myself
for it. It must be done.

"Look into these eyes and tell me what version of the truth
you'd like. You think it gives me pleasure to spend time with the
woman who pieced together the remains of my wife? I look at
your hands and I think of her."

I released her with a jerk, my breath coming in quick pants.
She fell backward, but her eyes were unfrightened, her expression
lemon-sour.

"You think I enjoy inhabiting this rotting, decomposing body?
That I could ever spend a second with you and not remember the
man I'd once been? Wish I was him again, just long enough to
be whatever you need me to be? Your kiss is like a knife stab. It's
just a reminder of how dead I am on the inside. I'm a corpse. I
don't have the self-respect, the *soul* of a leper."

The conversation was over. She was smart enough to know it;
she turned on her heel and took out a picture frame as she left.
It smashed onto the floor. Glass shattered in the frame over the
faces of old friends from Alpha company, guns in hand, posing
for me behind the camera. Tough guys about to be dead.

I'd meant to throw that out anyway.

She opened the door, and then stopped to look at me one last time.

"A guy was waiting here for you on the porch. He wanted me to give you a message: stop looking for Owen."

And with that, she slammed the door shut and left, the sound reverberating through the darkness.

★

What can I say?

I'd had enough of this place.

My shoes crunched over glass as I watched her through the window, descending the steps to her car parked out on the road. A black shape caught my eye: the vulture. He watched her in likewise, detached fashion, beady eyes following her from his place on the far end of the porch until her car pulled out; leaving the vulture with a sad and regretful air.

Or maybe I had him confused with me.

Whatever the case, I didn't sweep up the glass or clean up the mess. I continued to stand by the window and consider my options.

Stop looking for Owen.

Who had it been? I turned away from the molten lava of my self-loathing long enough to collect my thoughts anew. At the back of the room, I engaged the computer and brought the security feed up on the screen.

Within moments, I had a visual. Security footage saved up to the last forty-eight hours, just long enough to incriminate you if you killed a hooker at your house or if you let someone in to hand out religious tracts and you wanted to get a better look at his face.

The bastard was clever, and it was my shooter, I was sure of it. He'd taken a cowboy hat, shadowing most of his face from the overhead view, and I cursed. I could tell it was him by his carriage, his steady walk, which ate distance with a persistent efficiency as he drew close and waited for me to show up.

Instead, he found Niko first. I watched as she ascended the stairs and he stepped out of the darkness, announcing himself without any indication of who, or what, he was. What interest he had in my welfare was hard to understand. One thing for sure, no one helps no one in New Jersey without something in it for them, and that includes your dear old Granny.

Stop looking for Owen.

Which, in its own way, was an admission that there was a Clay to look for in the first place.

★

I packed nothing for the journey. I thought about calling someone, as though I were a man with one day left to live. What would I leave behind for the people who had known me? I had nothing of real value, just a house full of bad memories and a well-stocked liquor cabinet.

I began to write a note with one of Clay's old half-chewed pencils, but halfway through, it felt too much like a farewell speech. Too much like love. I picked it up and ignited the end with my cigarette tip, watched the smoke swirl over the surface and catch the flame before dropping it into the wastebasket, where it sputtered hungrily.

I regarded the vulture on the porch one last time as I locked the front door with a jingle of keys.

It's a stupid idea. The vulture blinked lazily and his head bobbed in the wind before he returned to the business of ignoring me.

"Yeah," I agreed. "I know."

I went anyway.

If that bird stuck around long enough, I'd have to give him a name.

★

Outside the fortune shop, a man in a sweater vest with his hair neatly combed stood by the front door. As I drew closer, the similarities to the Mr. Rogers of firefights past became all too evident, as though sweater vests were the new jogging suits of hive-mind mentality.

"Rogers?" I asked as I passed.

His eyes narrowed as he watched me, unmoving before the glass door.

"Yes, do I know you?"

I ran a hand over the brim of my hat to block my eyes and draw his attention away from my face.

"Do you guys come off an assembly line or something?"

Apparently, humor does not run in the Rogers family, because he looked at me as though I spoke a complex language he only half understood.

"Never mind," I muttered. "You work for the lady inside?"

He did not answer, but licked his lips nervously, as though I weren't supposed to know that.

"That must be a nice setup, huh? She brainwashes you guys. Cheaper than paying bodyguards, I guess."

Rogers did not answer, so I brushed past him. It made me wonder how many of them there were, and I thought of the journal, Owen's words of guardians and watchers. The Rogers? Likely, I considered, watching him pace the cracked sidewalk outside before I pushed the door open and entered with the chime of the bell.

Astra stood at the counter. Nothing had changed, and I was struck by the sensation that she had remained in that exact spot where I'd last seen her, never moving—if it had taken ten years to make up my mind and return, she would be there, still in her long skirts, incense clinging to her flesh in a thick ring.

"So soon," she whispered.

Her lips formed a red, pulsing, elongated heart; every word dipped in blood.

"Why wait?" I asked her. I did not mention there was no one left in the world who would notice I was missing. She didn't have to know how pathetic my life was.

The shop was the same as when I had left it, with the same gypsy caravan decor, the same empty, musty interior. I wondered if she ever had many customers or if it was just a front, from the crystals to the cards to the hippie-inspired garb. Her makeup looked slathered on so thick it formed a separate mask from her face. An undersmell persisted; old gym socks or fermenting yogurt.

She smiled through her red heart mouth as though we were lovers with a string of trysts behind us to cement our relationship. I still wore my old ill-fitting suit, moth eaten at the sleeves, stained with my decomposing juices of years past. I shook out a cigarette and lit up. Tobacco competed with the smell of patchouli. I was pleased with the result.

"Tell me how this works, Madam Astra. You have my son at an undisclosed location, and you want me to enlist in your mind-fuck army?"

Her smile hesitated, but did not fail. Not yet. She wanted to keep her mask in place just long enough to lead me into her hive. Venomous queen bee. I remembered 1996, Hale-Bopp, all the crazies in the jogging suits who were found dead on a floor with their testicles cut off in amateur fashion. Helluva way to die. I hoped whatever Madam Astra had in mind was a little more creative, because while I may be a "zombie" in layman's terms, cutting off my junk was just going to piss me off.

Most of it had fallen off already anyway, but it's the principle that matters.

"Vitus, you have a way with words."

"That's what the strippers tell me."

"Well, you'll come with me, of course. And I will lead you to the congregation, who will show you the ropes, so to speak. We have a wonderful, communal place, and once you've become acclimated to everything, you'll have the chance to meet Owen. We are celebrating your arrival with a special feast and ceremony."

I laughed, a dark chuckle of white smoke issuing from my yellow, tombstone teeth.

"Do I look like a chump to you?"

"Pardon me, Mr. Adamson?"

"Don't give me the stupid, doe-eyed look. Some ritualistic 'ceremony' you need my help with? You're a tawdry villain from a B-movie, lady. You'll lead me to some compound where three generations of inbred fools quote scripture, or better yet, say 'thee' and 'thou' and await the holy apocalypse, and then I'll find myself the focus of your human sacrifice."

She blinked. Her expression was slack and vacant, and I sighed with exasperation. Didn't she watch any movies, read any pulp novels? Maybe they didn't keep those sorts of things in the "compound."

"Far from it, Vitus. No one is sacrificed. You are the guest of honor, and you are the one for whom our holy Lord will come forth for. No blood need be spilt, no sacrifice but what you're willing to give."

"Or take from me."

"No! No sacrifice, no death! *Transformation.*"

Now, she had my attention.

"Into what?"

Her lips curled; one second she played the supermodel with her carefully molded face and in the next, a coquette. She wore a mask for each word and tailored them for my benefit, driving her duplicity deeper. Ever-shifting and unstable. The smell of foul yogurt and rancid gym socks was stronger here.

"You know a little something about transformation, don't you, Vitus? What they've done to you. Wouldn't you like to have the chance to become something more? I'm offering something greater than your son. I'm offering the chance to be born anew, in the image of our Dark Father."

"To be born, I must die."

"That's the beauty, Vitus. You're already dead."

She had a point.

★

"Lead the way," I said.

Her Trojan Horse smile articulated as though cogs and gears were at work behind it. She turned it on and off according to her mood, but the vacant look in her eyes remained. She was a hundred pounds sopping wet, but I didn't like her. I felt intimidated without reason and threatened without cause. Something in her was colder than I was, frozen temperatures packed into a hot body.

"Come with me, Vitus. We are honored to have you."

"Yeah, yeah. Show me my son, we'll talk more."

"As you will," she conceded, frozen smile; she came around the counter and led me toward the back, sweeping aside a fabric curtain heavy with the smells of incense. I followed her into the interior of the shop, senses alert, ready for anything.

The whole business reeked of a trap, but I decided after Niko had left that my first objective was to find my son. After that, I would worry about the mess, how many people I needed to kill to get out of it, and ask the questions later. I could mend bridges I burned and make up for being a bastard when I was back on the upswing of things.

Nothing else mattered but Clay. He'd only been two on July 25, 1999, when the world fell apart, but 1999 was long ago and far away. It occurred to me that Clay would not want to come with me. If he was attached to this cult and brainwashed, I'd have to carry him out by force. And abducting a kid is a lot more complicated than getting a five-finger discount on a candy bar at a convenience store. Kids asked questions. Kids who weren't kids anymore were adults and they'd fight back. Who was to say he'd even remember me?

I was going to leave a trail of burned bridges behind me at this rate. Sloppy work, and I didn't like sloppy—sloppy got you killed.

You're dead already, Vitus. What's the worst that could happen?

Zzzzzt.

A fly alighted on the lapel of my suit coat. I paused in the dim light, as Madam Astra led the way toward the back, and glanced down at the fly. He had no inclination to move, enjoying the brittle fabric and the cold, rotten meat of my body beneath.

I crushed it with my fist, grimacing, and smeared insect parts across the cloth. Unsettled, I forged on.

We traversed a stock room filled with boxes on shaky industrial metal shelves, shelves leaning against the back wall, and a black door with scored and peeling paint. She waded through the dusty interior, the hem of her skirt dragging over the floor littered with scraps of discarded paper and dust bunnies. Faded and yellowed invoices. I stepped over what looked like old blood stains on the concrete and they aroused questions I couldn't answer. A stray earring. (And was that a piece of earlobe attached to the metal charm on the end? No, surely not.) I shuffled after her faster with every sense and each dim eye hunting for evidence of the snare closing in around me. I could all but feel the loop of wire set across the game trail, waiting only for me to stick my neck through it.

She opened another door and I followed her through and into a narrow pathway of descending steps. Total darkness broken by bare bulbs set in the ceiling. They glowed like distant stars in a gasping void. Down we went. Damp and musty air. I kept my hands loose and ready to pull the gun. Would a series of brainwashed goons swapped out from a cheap horror movie appear at the bottom and apprehend me? No one appeared, and I craved such familiar and identifiable enemies to comfort me and give me a framework for this trepidation and fear drumming up from my very marrow.

At the bottom, my feet touched down on concrete. She'd been here before, I could tell by the confidence in her gait. Well-versed and certain of her terrain even in the darkness. She made a hard right with a sweep of her gypsy skirt so the fabric twisted like minnows darting through a flow of water. My footsteps echoed her tread. Another door yawned ahead, illuminated by a yellow light.

"Welcome, Vitus," she said and opened the door and stepped aside to beckon me in. "They've been waiting for you."

I stooped to duck through. Permanent midnight engulfed me and I turned to look for her, but she was gone. The door swung emptily behind me. I could leave if I wanted, retreat back up the steps. I dared not call out her name, and in the shadows beyond the entryway; I heard sounds beyond—shuffling steps, whispering clothes, steady breathing.

I attempted to penetrate the darkness with a touch. My fingers met with fabric, smooth velvet. The sound of my steps echoed the substance of wood, and while I attempted to understand what new level of maze I'd been forced into, the darkness broke like the shell of an egg.

Overwhelming light flooded and blinded me. I held my arm up and shielded my face. Heat enveloped me. A collective gasp of a thousand held breaths broke the silence. A whirring of velvet curtains parted before me. I pulled my arm away from my face and I saw my shoes firmly planted on a wooden stage that dropped off into nothingness several feet beyond.

My dead eyes adjusted and I let the brim of my hat do the work for me as I looked down.

I stood before a large room with a hundred people in long red robes standing before the stage, watching me. Their faces immersed in shadow beneath the peak of their hoods and I wondered if I had not been kidnapped by a series of Harry Potter wizard wannabes who wished to induct me into a bizarro Hogwarts school.

"Honor your Lord!"

The voice projected from the back of the room in symphony with the hum of unseen speakers. In unison, the congregation fell to its knees, a rustling of red cloaks and hoods. A sea of red poppies falling in concert. I moved for my gun, but did not draw, remained frozen with my fingers over the shape of it, unable to articulate the fear that peeled my lips back from my teeth—a grown, undead monster terrified by a gathering of innocent children.

I had never felt such an excruciating focus brought to bear upon me; I knew what insects knew, to be poised beneath a magnifying glass under a shaft of hot and burning light. A hundred sets of eyes studied me as their red figures genuflected.

They pulled their hoods back from their faces, emerging like worms from cocoons, their bright, coffee eyes—their soft, corn silk hair.

"Clay," I whispered.

Clay was there. And Clay was also next to the first Clay I laid eyes on, and next to him another Clay, and another, and another.

A room full of a hundred Clays.

A hundred sons that should be dead, but weren't; sons I killed in my blood-soaked memories, over and over again.

My fingers clenched over my gun; I did not have enough bullets. I had sixteen shots; not sixteen hundred. But is that what I had come here to do, kill my son?

My *sons*.

"Who are you?" I whispered. I asked the question as though they were one entity conspiring against me, and they would answer with one collective voice. But they never had the chance.

"I kept my promise, Vitus."

Madam Astra emerged from the archway toward the back. The stage lights limited my vision and I held a hand up to focus and lock in on her. The heat sweltered beneath the lights. She waded into the ocean of red. My lips were dry and cracked as they parted to release breath. And all this time, I thought there was nothing so terrible as myself.

"Now you keep yours."

★

What does a man do when confronted with a hundred children from Christmas Past?

A better man—a living, breathing man—might have fallen to his knees and cried. I stood in a sea of children, reflected ghosts of my son. But they were not only my son from the moment he had died, that chubby toddler still learning how to walk a straight line and practice his vocabulary for his proud father—no. Each one was Clay, from his blond hair to his brown eyes, but they were Clay from every age. A ten-year-old Clay, a six-year-old Clay, a fifteen-year-old Clay. A living timeline.

Clones, I thought frantically, my eyes jumping from figure to figure in a desperate attempt to connect them, to make sense of the trick that had been played on me. Their faces took on science fiction proportions as I imagined a laboratory filled with scientists—scientists specifically lacking in moral fiber, like my brother Jamie—filling petri dishes with dividing cells soon to be my hundred sons.

But they were not clones. In this dark and musty basement, with the millions Astra made from fortune telling? Unlikely.

The fevered moment of panic passed from me. These were not my sons. They could not be. Logic took over and ticked off a thousand reasons, deconstructing the desires of my heart. They were strange children gathered with the purpose of pulling me into an intricate trap whose shape I was still determining. Nothing more—no son here.

And then the first of them reached up with a hand and clasped my gloved fingers in his own. I felt the warmth of his young skin against my dead, cold flesh. His touch punctured a bullet wound, shot straight up from my wrist to the tip of my spine, rattling every bone.

I looked down, and he looked up at me, a ten-year-old Clay, with large doe eyes. His face a cherub's, unlined and so unlike my own, free of the corruption of age and bitterness.

"Will you come with us, Daddy?"

I sucked in a breath.

"I'm not your Daddy."

"Who will save us?" the child wailed. He latched onto my gloved hand with his other one, pulling and tugging at me. His face collapsed in on itself as tears leaked from the corners of his eyes, his mouth pulled down as dry, heaving sobs escaped his lips.

Disconcerted, I kneeled down to his height, bones creaking against the concrete. Brown eyes watched and studied me from every corner as I set a hand against a curl of his blond hair, and he stopped his howling.

"Listen," I whispered, "I'm not your Daddy, but I'll save you, okay?"

He pouted, making fists against his hips. "Only Daddy can save us. So you have to be our Daddy."

"Fuckin' Christ kid—"

"You said a bad word," he whispered, his eyes wide and round.

I never said I was a good father. Only that I was one.

"You drive a hard bargain. I'll be your Daddy, and I'll try to watch my mouth."

The child watched me, searching for a trick, a lie behind my opalescent white eyes. When he was satisfied with my sincerity, or show of it, at least, he turned and the crowd of Clays absorbed him, blending back into their crimson robes and their similar faces.

Sure, kid. I'll be your Daddy. Right up until I figure out what the fuck is going on. And then, like every true relative, you'll learn to hate me.

I smiled down at the congregation, and a slightly older boy, perhaps thirteen, parted through the crowd. Astra stood at the back, combing a child's hair back from his forehead, rubbing a smudge out of a red robe in motherly fashion.

The boy approached me, his eyes as wide as all the others. They stared at me the way I imagined natives had greeted the conquistadors.

"Madam Astra says I should show you your quarters, now."

"Lead on," I said, and gestured that he should lead the way.

★

In the underground dampness, the altar room led out into a hallway, branching off into separate rooms. I glanced through the doorways as I passed and noted the bathrooms, the guest rooms with small cots set up beside end tables and vases with red and white flowers, and picture frames.

A paused before a door while the child continued forward, unaware I stopped to peer through the threshold. What caught my eye and stopped me dead in my tracks was the picture frame in every room. I took a step forward to confirm what my eyes perceived.

It was my picture. Not just any picture—Jessica and me on our wedding day. If my heart wasn't already stopped, this was enough to ensure it never started again.

Jessica and I stood side by side. A white rose nestled in the lapel of my wedding suit; her hair twisted up and curled in blond cascades, the same hair she would pass on to our son. I would keep the darkness for myself and thank God every day I had not passed it down.

In the picture, I was human, alive, dewy skin that breathed and glowed like any human's. The contrast startled me. A reverse portrait of Dorian Gray. I had no more pictures of myself, and to be confronted with one here threw off my balance and sent my internal compass spinning.

"Clever," I whispered. "We'll see how clever you are when you're picking lead out of your skull."

"Sir?"

The child's voice broke on the word and he winced, waiting for me to turn and acknowledge him.

"I'm coming," I said, turning away from the photograph to follow once more. A perfect square of hurtful memories.

I took advantage of Astra's absence; all the rooms appeared empty and there was no one in the hall to interrupt us.

"What's your name, kid?"

"Owen Rogers."

"I mean, your real name."

"Owen Rogers is my real name."

I sighed. He stood before the door of my room. A simple cot with white sheets, a vase with roses, and the terrible picture of my wedding day repeated here, as it was in every room. A reminder of everything I had lost.

I entered and picked up the frame before setting it face down on the end table.

"Where were you born?" I asked him.

"Here."

"And you don't remember your parents from before?"

The boy regarded me with a blank expression. My questions did not strike him as unusual and he answered in hushed notes as though he did not understand what I was getting at. His conversation sounded coached.

"What parents? You're our father. And Madam Astra is our mother."

"Do you like Madam Astra?"

I crossed my arms over my chest and leaned against the wall beside the door, not quite blocking his exit, but making it clear I was in the way. He did not move and remained in his eager to please manner. A puppy programmed by a trainer with endless dog treats. Anyone will salivate when they've been given a steak enough times.

"I love Madam Astra. She's my mother."

"So by that logic, you love me as well?"

"Of course! We've been waiting so long for you. Madam Astra has been unhappy all these years, preparing for your arrival."

"Has she."

My words were not phrased as a question. I could stand here and shoot the shit with this kid all day, asking him question after question, but his answers were getting me no closer to what I needed to know. Madam Astra was a clever brainwasher—she'd secured these children's most basic needs. They wanted for nothing, not for food, security, shelter, and most of all, unconditional love. By providing that, instead of the normal cult tactic of withholding it, she'd bought their loyalty lock, stock, and barrel. If I wanted to break that, I needed to offer something new that Astra could not. Something a boy in his teenage years might want.

I confirmed once more that we were alone with a furtive glance down the hall and reached into the suit jacket, withdrawing the Glock.

"Ever seen a gun before, Owen?"

"No, sir."

His eyes became larger, if that were possible, round as saucers. His brow wrinkled in severe concentration as he studied the lines of metal in my palm, the sleek black surface of the most perfect killing machine. For his benefit, I dropped the magazine out onto my palm and opened the chamber to empty it of the round inside. I deftly caught it in the air as it ejected and deposited both bullet and magazine into my pocket.

I held the empty gun out to the boy.

"It's safe now, so I'll let you hold it, if you want."

Gingerly, he reached for it, small fingers on the butt as he lifted it into the air, as though it were a snake that might reach back and bite at any moment.

"Don't put your finger on the trigger. Yeah, you've got it, keep them along the barrel. That's right. How does that feel, sonny?"

"It's cool," he spoke, his voice a near whisper. He held it in both hands, aiming at an imaginary target in the dark corner of the room, making a shooting noise with his mouth in imitation of a gun blast.

Now. Spring it on him now.

"What kind of games would you play with a thing like that?"

"Um, I don't know." He stared at the barrel. "I like arrows better."

I laughed. "That's probably for the best, because weapons aren't toys. But ain't no harm in pretending, eh?"

"No-oo." He shot it into the wall again with his imaginary sounds.

"What do you picture shooting?"

"Dragons! But I'm pretending they're arrows."

"Did you ever get to play with guns before?"

"No, Mommy wouldn't let them in the—"

He stopped, a horrified expression filling his features as his cheeks flooded red. His lips formed a thin line as he turned the muzzle on me, maintaining his shooter's stance. With the black hole of the barrel before me, I didn't appreciate his gun enthusiasm.

"You tricked me!" he accused.

I smiled, rotted lips cracking and dropping bits of flesh as they expanded.

"Madam Astra doesn't need to know. It can just be our little secret, eh? So what's your Mommy's name?"

"I'm not supposed to talk about them. She'll be angry."

"She'll be angrier if I tell her that you slipped up, buddy."

"You wouldn't do that!"

I smiled again and let the silence draw out between us. Sweat beaded on his upper lip and his forehead as he stewed in thoughts of the consequences of his actions. I saw no signs of physical abuse, no visible bruises, but who knew if Astra had mastered the art of hitting without leaving a mark.

"Why should I care what happens to a boy who does nothing but lie all day?" I pointed out, and his facade cracked like a shattered diamond, broken apart by its own flawed nature. His happy boy mask came away, revealing a hollowed, haunted child underneath his eager-to-please demeanor.

And he began to turn the gun on himself.

The chamber was empty, I had seen to that myself. I tore it from his small fingers with vicious locomotion and he reeled backward against the wall, eyes frightened and broken.

"Don't tell her!" he begged, collapsing into sobs. Look alike Clay cried between his soft, pink fingers, covering his hot face in layers of shame. "Please don't tell her! She says if we aren't good, you'll go away!"

Quickly, I turned and closed the door behind us. Even alone, our privacy could be an illusion, and I wanted as many layers as I could manage between us and Astra. I returned to the boy, pulling up a wooden chair and seating myself before him so we were on level with each other.

"What does she do to you if you talk? Does she hit you?"

I was going to rip each of her toenails out and make her dance Swan Lake if she so much as laid a hand on these boys. I reached out and hesitated an instant before letting my hand fall on the boy's shoulder. He didn't move away or flinch at the contact but gathered strength from the fatherly touch. As though it were something he missed.

"No, it's just that . . ."

"What? What is it?"

"I told you already," he whispered. "If we're bad, you'll go away."

"That's why you are crying? Because you're afraid I'll go away?"

He swallowed a great gulping breath, before continuing on, his tear-wet hands falling away from his face as he looked me in the eye.

"We've been waiting for you for so long."

★

Beep-beep.

Time for candy.

I turned away from the boy, reaching inside my jacket for the bottle of pills and knocked two of them back. While I dry swallowed my dose, the boy's words ran back and forth in my mind. I knew when I had entered that nothing I would find would bring me peace, but I had expected something more overtly sinister. Instead, I was in a labyrinth where every answer plunged me into dead ends. Logical deduction came to a standstill; rational conclusion sent me into a further tailspin. What would the cost be to me, to these children, if I could not decipher this twisted game?

"I should get back," the boy broke in, motioning for the door. I stepped before him, blocking the way.

"So soon? I've only just begun to get to know you, sonny," I said, pulling out a pack of cigarettes. I lit one up, bitter smoke filling the atmosphere between us. He stood there, watching me, with something like worship and fear.

"Smoking's bad," the boy said.

"No shit," I answered, and the boy gasped in further offense. The door vibrated behind me, the brass knob turning, and then accompanied by a steady rap of knuckles against wood.

Annoyed to be interrupted, I stepped out of the way. The boy lost no time, happy to be out of my clutches; the door swung open and Madam Astra stood there, delicate features in a thin face, nipples straining against the thin fabric of her gypsy garb as the boy scurried past her in his crimson cloak. A deep funk entered the room with her and I thought to myself I should follow the stink and see where it led.

"We don't provide very lavish quarters, I'm afraid, Mr. Adamson."

"Why have you told these kids I'm their father?"

She blinked, a confused look like a dazed rabbit. "These are all your children."

"I had one child born to me, and I have yet to see him."

"Vitus," she whispered, pleading. "Do not upset us so. Do you know how long they have been waiting for your return? Only all of their lives. And you will crush their hearts, hurt their feelings so, by denying that you are their father? Are you so cruel, Vitus?"

I had expected outrage, an argument, maybe even a knock-down-drag-out with a broken vase and spilled flowers as a follow-up to the last meeting I had with Niko. Hair pulling would have been preferable. In all my travels and violent cases, pleas of mercy were only accompanied by gunfire. This tender plea was out of my realm of expertise.

First Niko, now Astra. Since when did I have a female fan club? And when had Astra declared herself president?

I groaned.

"My patience for this game is wearing thin," I warned her.

"You should meet them. All of them. They're upstairs waiting for you, where the feast is being prepared. Please, reserve your judgment; you are free to come and go as you please. Make yourself comfortable and join us upstairs. The children love you so, Vitus, and they want to see you."

With that, she vanished down the corridor with her blond hair swinging after her like a curtain.

★

I wandered back over to the picture frame, lifted it up. I had broken the glass when I slammed it down on its face. Stray shards tinkled against the end table surface. My young face. A face untouched by rot and mold, a face tanned by warm summer suns, not cold and blue-tinged and marked with striations where the flesh had pulled apart.

And her. My Jessica.

I sighed and ran a thumb over her face briefly. My thumb paused there, and then trembled.

I cast a glance back over my shoulder, down the hallway where Astra had disappeared.

Her long, blond hair. My Jessica had long, blond hair.

Suspicion took hold. Hooked tentacles dragging through my gray matter. I balked at first. But each passing second only served to increase the sensation of fear and I had to consider the possibility. A trembling built inside my chest where a beating heart should be and threatened to send me to my knees.

Not possible.

But I believed my son had lived, didn't I? Why not my wife as well?

Well, for one, she would have to be infected. And Madam Astra did not look like zombie material, which put her out of the running.

Yet, it would explain why she knows so much—knows about Jamie. About our son.

And that smell. That curious scale of green at her hairline . . .

I did not wear my wedding ring anymore. Obvious reasons— when the flesh of your fingers rots off on a regular basis, it's hard to keep a good fit. That, and the marriage had been over since I killed her—why hold on to the memory with that thin, gold band of pain? I pulled out my wallet and opened the billfold. Nestled beside a few crumpled bills was my wedding band. I kept it on me always, even if I did not wear it.

Let's put the theory to the test then, I thought, pulling out the ring and cupping it in my hand.

★

Upstairs, the main altar I had arrived at had been turned into a feast room, tables and chairs lined up against a concrete floor, great swaths of fabric draping the tables like misshapen animals. I stood at the door, watching the children bringing in flowers from their rooms. They were the most polite, cooperative children I had ever seen, and their eyes were far from the empty, vacant stares of brainwashed cult members—they were excited and brimming with youthful energy. I was to blame for the excitement; they were making great efforts to pretend I wasn't there, watching me from the sidelines. They couldn't help snatching glances in my direction, with the same atmosphere of fear-worship I had already been subjected to.

The child I spoke with earlier in my room set plates and linens on the table for him and the other children and I studied him, as though I might have a second chance to crack the facade he wore and delve beneath the surface. To my frustration, he maintained his joyful presence and hid the darker monster beneath. As I watched him with cold detachment, a fly landed on his cheek.

I pulled a face of disgust.

The boy stood still. He sensed the fly's presence and deferred to it, remaining frozen with a stack of plates in his hand, silverware gathered in the other. My eyes narrowed as I observed him, and he waited until the fly was done sampling his skin. The insect flitted off into the darkness, satisfied, and with a long sigh, the boy resumed his duties.

What the fuck was that all about?

Nothing good. I had a sharp longing for Niko—to be able to see her, to talk to her, but that was all over with now. She wanted nothing to do with me. I couldn't say I blamed her.

Through it all, Astra moved between the children, dictating and giving orders. Nothing sinister there—from time to time, she tousled their hair or squeezed their shoulders with all the warmth of a natural mother. Except now, I could not help but compare her to Jessica, looking for similarities. When she helped a child set a platter, was that the way my Jessica had done so? Impossible to tell. Asking questions got me nowhere.

Then maybe you should play the part. They've set up a grand stage, and you're supposed to be the loving father to the children, husband to her wife; they expect your defiance. Throw them off balance by acquiescing and see what shakes out.

I nodded to myself and took a moment to breathe deep. I disliked such a charade. These were not my children. That strange, fey woman could not possibly be my wife. Pretending that they were offended me at my core. And why? Haven't you guessed?

"Because I can never go back," I whispered, tracking her with my eyes. "Those days are over. There is no more pleasure, no more happiness. I can never, ever, get them back."

I would still be as dead tomorrow as I was today. No amount of pretense could bring me back to life, coax my cells to divide anew, my DNA to reawaken like hungover crashers at a drunken party and carry on with their lives.

What if she were my wife, alive after all these years?

Who said I even wanted her back?

The pain of losing her was sharp; no less knowing that I had killed her. The dead man I was now knew no other existence than that heart-rending pain. Without it, I was nothing. The man I had been stood in awful counterpoint to the man I became: honest, naïve, integrity, courageous, a non-smoker. I had stood for something pure, something greater. I was a twisted shadow of my former self, and now that I had tasted the blood of my family, consumed them down to their marrow, I knew no other way to be. The darkness was my home now. I chose my evil of my own free will.

Straightening my suit jacket, I waded through the children—my children—to Astra.

★

She turned as I breached the distance between us. I hesitated, and then pushed forward, fighting against my basic instincts. Everything inside me rebelled; but time and circumstance and bitter memories are persuasive factors. With great effort, I choked the sentiment into my words.

"Jessica," I said.

Astra remained still, frozen. Continuing the charade, I reached out with a gloved hand and caressed her cheek, moving a strand of her hair away from her face. This was the sort of motion I would have made when I was alive, a tender gesture. I often did so when I came back from service, coming up the porch in my fatigues. She'd run outside with a shriek, throw her arms around me. So small, she still had the power to squeeze until I gasped to catch my breath.

"Vitus," she said.

She did not deny it!

I wanted to turn my open hand into a slap, ring her across the face and demand the truth. Jessica was dead. Why was she pretending? What could she hope to gain by this insult, by throwing the death of my wife in my face?

To keep you under her thumb, to throw you off balance.

My fingers twitched uncontrollably. From this distance I could almost taste her blood, the meaty texture of her flesh. I contained myself, swallowing back my rage and letting my hand fall to grip her comfortably around the waist. I moved in close to whisper in her ear.

I could kill you here. I could eat you just like I did my wife.

"Are we ready, honey?" came out instead.

She smiled, a sway in her hips like an excited schoolgirl. Her lashes dipped over her cool eyes, bedroom eyes.

"I thought you'd never ask," she whispered in return and, taking me by the hand, led me to the head of the grand table, where plates and silverware and wine glasses set out before us. I bit back a groan as she ground my decomposing finger bones against each other in her grip, leading me to a seat with her place setting beside it.

While she turned her back to usher a child into a chair beside us, I dipped the wedding ring into her drink. A gold ring descended in a swallow of wine and settled on the bottom of the glass.

You think she's a faker. How did she know about Jamie, then?

"No," I muttered.

"What?" she was back beside me, watching me with hungry eyes. Difficult to define the emotions I saw there—more than worship, I was a god whose light she borrowed for an instant. A cruel word from me could extinguish it forever. Her level of devotion was frightening.

"Nothing," I said, and waved her off.

Far from throwing her off her game, I was the one who was unbalanced.

Get control of yourself, man!

But I did not have control. Silence fell in the altar room, now transformed into a dining hall, and she gestured with the raising of her graceful arms. Together, they sat as one, moving in eerie concert. Children of so many ages, in my experience, are noisy and excitable, but they were on their best behavior, speaking in soft tones amongst each other, often looking toward where myself and Astra—Jessica—remained seated.

The plates were empty. I glanced down the line of children with their blond heads poking through their crimson capes, a hundred twins. I meant to ask about the food—what was on the menu tonight? But the words were mangled, shriveled, would not suffer my clumsy tongue.

Something else came out instead.

"I never got a chance to tell you," I said aloud.

"Yes, dear?"

Just like that, a lilt in her voice, a turn of her head. Astra watched me with Jessica's cobalt eyes.

Did I eat her eyes?

God, did I?

"I never got a chance to say I was sorry," I blurted.

"That's all in the past now," she returned smoothly.

"I don't remember that night."

"Calm yourself, Vitus, you're—goodness, you're trembling. Are you well?"

"No, no, I think I need . . ."

I stood, nearly upsetting the chair, the tablecloth, the glass beside it. The gold ring at the bottom of her wine glass winked at me, like a yellow eye in a draught of pus. I reached convulsively for the pills inside my suit pocket, my fingers pulling out the prescription bottle.

My wristwatch should have noted the time for my last dose, but the lights were burning overhead in the cracked ceiling, brighter than they should have been. I looked at the watch.

The digital face was empty. The surface was a dead mirror, reflecting my rotted face back into my white eyes. If I had life functions, I imagined I would have experienced a cold sweat, hairs standing on the back of my neck. Instead, there was a wire of panic winding around my belly, then up my spine.

I missed my dose.

It's not too late, I thought, and began to struggle with the childproof bottle. My fingers grew thick and clumsy in their gloves, clawing and sliding. My coordination slipping, a sign of my slow digression into monstrosity.

"That's not what you need," she spoke gently, and lifted the bottle out of my fingers, the way she used to take a rattle out of Clay's hands. The pills shook inside with musical noise, amplified a hundred-fold.

"I need that," I protested. "Don't make me—"

"—hurt you?" she filled in, her voice deep, husky. "Like you did to me before?"

Her last words felled me and sliced me at the nerve. I fell back into the chair, staring into her eyes. Locked to each other as pythons constricting into a single, crushing knot.

She handed the bottle to a child. Another Clay disappeared with it, fading into the crowd of red Clays where he had come from.

My throat and my chest tightened, choked with iron bands. Every dead, rotting cell in my body pulsed with decay, a decay far deeper than that of a corpse. All my guilt, my shame, my devastation was bound inside my undead body and the tide threatened to drown me. The tide was coming. The tide was death, ultimate undeath; a great mouth that ate and gnashed and devoured everything before me, a hollow opening from the inside out.

If I did not have my dose soon . . .

"Jessica," I whispered. I opened my mouth to beg her to bring back the pills, but it occurred to me that this was the reason I was here—what I had done to my beautiful wife must be repaid in full. No judge or jury had ever exacted retribution or justice for my crime. Instead, Jamie had plucked me from disaster and saved my unlife with no consideration for the lives I took or the price that must be paid for the abomination I had become.

I had begged him to kill me and he had refused. To live as a monster was unconscionable, but as a monster that had killed its own wife, every moment elevated into agony.

I deserved this; I deserved to be a monster.

She lifted the glass to her red lips, refracting a semicircle of light as she swallowed the wine. The ring tapped against her teeth and, startled, she looked at it once more, plunging a delicate pinky finger into the bottom and bringing out the wedding ring.

"Oh, Vitus," she sighed, lovingly.

My sick heart thrilled at the sound of her voice.

She turned and gripped my hand in hers and peeled back a layer of black glove from my fingers. She slipped the ring over my wedding finger, pushing metal against flayed flesh that parted beneath the pressure and lacerated bone at the faintest urging.

I did not object or shy away, but let her, as though we were newlyweds before the altar.

Abruptly, she let go of my hand and rose before the dining room to command the attention of all the children. Their eyes tracked her like a thousand fireflies in their curious Clay faces, the most well-behaved, brainwashed children a father could have.

"The time has come, my sons! Your father needs you now! His evil brother has starved him so! Years we have gone without our Lord, been deprived of his holy presence, and we are not the only ones to suffer, no! Your father has spent these ten years in search of nourishment, and what did they give him in return? Nothing! Snatched the food from his mouth, delayed the moment of feast! Let it begin now! We take back all that has been taken from us!"

A great cry rose, a ringing clatter as countless small hands gripped silverware and banged forks and knives against glasses and plates in enthusiastic applause. Stupefied, the sound filled me with a miasma of emotions impossible to define. Jessica gripped me by the shoulder and raised me to my feet. Before, their scrutiny had been a dissection, but here was an entirely new sensation that had me gasping for air and struggling not to drown in the feeling.

Admiration. Pride. Overwhelming love.

They loved me. They were my children and they loved me.

Few seductions prove so powerful. Booze couldn't replace it, sex couldn't allay it, there wasn't a drug or experience in the world that came close. Unconditional acceptance. Undying love. All my life, torn from happiness and tossed among the waves of misfortune, brought home at last. The maelstrom spat me out after a thousand years on the fringe of a downward spiral and this is where I landed.

Just as I was about to open my mouth to speak—without any understanding of what I was about to say—the eldest Clay beside me picked up his knife, jerked up his shirt, and cut into the flesh of his abdomen.

★

Blood spurted across the white table cloth.

With my mouth open, I stared like a village idiot, tongue like raw meat hanging down between my teeth. The smell of the coppery blood, metallic and salty and earthy and delightful, hit the air like a mist. I could taste his youth, his lipids still circulating through his blood, cells dividing in a frenzy of enthusiastic youth. Like a non-smoker holding a first cigarette until I was dizzied and swayed by the taste of his blood on the air.

God, I needed those pills.

"Make him stop, Jessica!" I cried.

Speaking hurt my head, riving it into halves, a too-ripe pumpkin run riot with decay. Brain-seeds spilling out from the leaking tissues.

"It's happening all over again," I groaned and stumbled, Jessica's strong grip still upon my shoulder and her fingers dug in through the fabric of my suit to pull me back and steady me.

"You must feed," she hissed. "It never would have happened if they had only given you what you truly needed!"

"I need my pills!"

My breath wafted as sweet as exhaust fumes from a past-era diesel truck. My fists clenched convulsively to satisfy a desire to tear and rip and claw my way through the world. *Bring me flesh, I'll bring Hell.*

"And look," she persisted in arguing with me, "they've turned you into a spineless junkie. This is not the man I married."

"He's dead!" I roared.

"Here, Daddy," a quiet voice spoke beside me.

The older boy who had cut himself moments before held his plate out to me. On the surface of the glass, gristle of fat and meat, no more than a fingertip in length. His pale face stared upwards, awaiting my approval. My lips peeled back from my teeth in horrified disgust.

I wanted it. My stomach churned in anticipation.

With effort, I turned away but fared no better in the other direction; down the dining table, row after row of children were lifting their knives and cutting pieces of themselves, butchers flaying meat off their own bodies. Their blood hit the air like a breaking storm when the barometric pressure dropped, stitched through lightning and thunder.

"An offering, Vitus. For you."

And God, I was starving.

"No," I whispered.

"Deny your own children!" Jessica accused.

I took her accusation with a flinch, forgetting entirely about the Glock nestled in my holster. Who would I have shot and for what crime? It was as dead as the rest of me, forgotten in the failing sectors of my brain. My mind was a tall building whose lights were slowly being shut down, each floor closed off with crime scene tape and shut away behind locked doors. One by one, each room plunged into darkness.

My temperature ratcheted into stratospheric levels. Heat crept into my dead and torn cheeks, fevered with the ravaging virus.

Soon, there would be nothing left of me to stop the inevitable, and Jessica knew it. The tilt of her head, the fall of her blond hair, put me in mind of my porch vulture, watching me to see what I would do, if I would cave in or refuse. The air was thick with their shared scent of blood and skin and hot, breathing bodies. They crowded in upon me until my back was up against the stage. It bit into my spine. Their images parsed through my senses as jumpy and frenetic frames.

"Eat, Vitus. Your family awaits you."

Abruptly, the

last

sentient

part of   me

met with

darkness.

★

Zzzzt.
Zzzzt.

★

And then, I awoke.

My head throbbed, my skull reduced to fragments of a broken bowl encased in a thin layer of rotten flesh. The ceiling of my cell in Madam Astra's—Jessica's—quarters, loomed above me. I attempted to sit up and wrench myself into an upright position and failed. I was pinioned against the uncomfortable cot, a metal band across my neck, more lashings constricted around my wrists and ankles.

If I were alive, I might have liked this, I noted with gallows amusement, attempting to arch my back and get a better view of my surroundings.

A rustling. A shadow moved beside me.

The dark figure drew closer. A cameo illuminated only by feeble light from a bulb in the wall socket. A ski mask shrouded his features, but I knew him from his lambent eyes and his lean and starved gait: the shooter.

"You," I hissed.

He raised a finger to his lips, his eyes darting to the door and back again. He held a gun in his grip. A silencer protruded from the end. Footsteps shuffled at the closed door behind him and sent shadows through the threshold before they passed on with their business. In this underground lair, it begged the question of how he'd found me at all.

I pondered this new turn of events, attempting to remember something, anything, from the moments before, leading up to this one.

All that was left in my fractured memory were broken images of the dining hall. Faces like shuffled cards. I ran a dead tongue over the surface of my teeth. I tasted blood, hints of flesh stuck between the serrated molars. These remains were the only proof

I needed of what had elapsed from my last conscious memory, of the children closing in on me in the dining hall, with Jessica by my side, to now.

I cursed myself, like a drunk recovering from one bender too many. Jessica had taken my pills away. What had happened that I was awake now? I doubted she was feeling benevolent and decided to dose me before trussing me up like a Christmas turkey. To whom did I owe my brief spell of lucidity?

As if in answer, the shooter opened his gloved palm. On the flat surface, he produced a bottle, my pills rattling inside of it. I recognized the bottle—my emergency stash. I kept it in a hidden compartment in my vintage television housing at home, along with a porn magazine I'd never thrown out and didn't even like.

"What'd you do with the magazine?" I whispered.

His eyes narrowed in consternation, and if I were in a better mood I would have laughed. I had already decided he wasn't here to kill me. If that had been his intention he would have done it already. He glanced back at the door and I struggled in my bindings.

"Get me out of here," I demanded.

He did not answer. Instead, he set the gun aside on the end table beside the picture of me and Jessica in the shattered frame. After a moment of reflection, he studied his shoes, heaved a sigh, and with one hand, lifted away the ski mask. It slid away from a mop of blond hair, pale features.

I was looking at a double of myself.

I gaped openly, until he cleared his throat and shifted, uncomfortable with the scrutiny.

"Clay?" I whispered.

He looked sad, then, his lips twisted. He struggled with the answer, and the minute the words escaped his lips, I knew it was a lie.

"Yes."

He's lying!

You thought that about Jessica, too.

I considered that thought, handling it like a lit stick of dynamite. After a moment, it was easier to blow out the fuse.

His identity, real or imagined, was not important yet. Getting out of this hellhole and away from my angry wife and a hundred bloody, zombie-food munchkins was.

"You fed me the pills?"

"You weren't much good without them. You wouldn't open your mouth at first, but when I held my fingers out you tried to snap at them, so I just chucked the pills at you until I got two in."

"Oh," I said, wishing I had not known. "Help me out of here."

"I can't," he whispered. "They closed off the main entrance with concrete blocks. Cemented it in."

"How are they supposed to leave, then?"

He looked at me, so like myself at that age—about to marry, join the army, and ruin my life in general. Before Kosovo. The resemblance was both ghostly and eerie. Maybe he *was* Clay.

I shoved that thought aside.

"Don't you get it? They're not planning on leaving. This is it. Swan song."

Rage flared suddenly and my temper was blown to shreds with my patience. My wrists chafed uncomfortably against the metal cuffs.

"So what's the plan, recite poetry and light farts? You should have left me like I was."

"I didn't know any other way to wake you—"

"That's the idea, stupid! Leave me dead, leave me animal, leave me a monster! The idea is to never wake up. *Never.*"

I averted my gaze, looking off into the ceiling. White space interspliced with shadows cut across the surface. An awkward, hurt silence filled the space between us, and he cleared his throat before speaking again.

"I just wanted to tell you I love you, Dad," he spoke gently, and picking up his gun, yanked his ski mask back over his face.

In that moment, I was certain that he was not Clay—he never had been, never would be. All this chasing a longlost ghost to discover my wife had been the one who survived, not my son. My "son" was the decoy to seduce me to her door, the one thing Jessica knew I'd never stop searching for. The truth was obvious now that I was confronted by an imposter—if Clay were alive,

Jessica would not need a hundred copies of him to surround her, because she would have been satisfied with the original.

I thought of the missing child posters scattered across town. On signposts and convenience stores. I passed them when I bought my cigarettes and crushed them beneath my feet when they fell to the tarmac. Which of them was the young man standing before me now?

Clay was dead.

The grief cut me afresh, and I turned to the man who believed I was his father.

"You were the first one, weren't you?"

He stopped in mid-stride, a black figure in the center of the room, tall. He looked strong, the sort of son that would make a father proud—somebody else's father, to be sure. I wondered how long his natural parents spent searching for him, or if he had been a convenient orphan Jessica had picked up along the way, the first one to begin the terrible spiral into madness.

"Yes," he answered. He turned back to face me and finally seated himself beside the mattress, cold brown eyes watching me with quiet wonder. He had waited all of his life for this moment; I hoped it was everything he imagined, like a cheap melodrama designed to exploit the vulnerable, the young, the inexperienced who didn't yet know life adhered to no script and offered only cold indifference for each measure of your love and bitter experience. *Good,* I thought, *let one of us get something he wants.*

"She brought the others after. At first, it wasn't a big deal. But after awhile, there were so many . . . she sent me away before it got that far. She said I was not her son anymore. I was too old."

"The cage?" I whispered, and my fist clenched involuntarily. "Everything in that journal, that diary . . . was that real, what I found? Did you write that?"

"It's real, the cage," he answered, and looked away. "But whatever you found, it doesn't belong to me, but it's real, Vitus. Who knows what unfortunate child wrote it, and what miserable end he met with."

He might not be my Clay, my real son; but the memory of the journal, the adolescent tears staining the ink on the yellowed pages, invoked a protective rage. She had used it against me, and I had followed the lure all the way back to the source, the barbs of her hook set deep in my throat.

No, he wasn't my son.

But for a while, I pleaded with myself, *let me pretend*.

"And what then?" I asked.

"Everything changed. Events might have been different, if I had stayed a boy."

"But you grew up," I filled in.

"She sent me away once I began to ask questions. I was not like the others, I was curious, I was—"

"You were smarter. She couldn't maneuver you as easily."

"Then, I left. Escaped. I . . . killed one of them," and he spoke with pained regret. By rights, he should have been a boy worried about girls (or boys, for all I knew) and picking out a career path after high school. Instead, his young face bore the marks of trauma in training—something wizened lurked behind his eyes. "He was in my way."

I had never had the chance to see Clay at this age, to know him as an adult, and never would. Faced with my boy's doppelgänger, I was at a loss. I could console him with what limited emotional resources I had. That's what a father would have done, and I found I wanted to be fill that role, even if only in these dark hours.

"You did what you had to do," I offered, and hoped it would be enough.

Cold comfort. He remained still, then shrugged, refusing to look me in the eyes.

"My questioning was bad enough. That, maybe Mother could have lived with. The beginning of the end was the night I found her without her face."

While he spoke, he lifted the gun and began to unload the weapon just to pull out the magazine and the chambered round. Fingers that should have been doing something more mundane, like texting or working an after-school job, serviced a killing machine instead. We don't all get that kind of idyllic life and I knew it well. That he weathered a different kind filled me with pride that I had no right to feel on his behalf.

I said nothing and waited for him to fill the silence, as I knew he would.

"It was a warm night and I was thirsty. They locked me in, but I'd already mastered lock-picking by the time I was ten. I remember creeping out into the hallway and the bedroom door was open just a crack. And beyond her mattress, the room opened up into a bathroom, and I could see her, standing at a mirror. She was my mother, the only mother I had ever known—and she didn't have a face.

"She was studying her reflection. What for, I don't know, it was horrible to behold. I could see all the things beneath her skin, roping veins and red, wet tissue, the shape of her teeth in her jaw and the hole that was her nose. Beside her, there was this deflated . . . mask, I suppose. Her face a sheath of skin, like a shedding snake."

I hitched in a breath.

"Dead," I said between clenched teeth.

Astra evaded definition and capture because I couldn't summon the logic to understand how she could be my wife and still be alive. If I had bitten her, I had infected her. Reason stood that she would be every bit a zombie that I was, minus the pills.

It was falling into place now. The smell that followed her in a thick miasma. The hint of mold in the shadows of her dress.

"Yes," he agreed. "Something about it . . . even her real eyes were milky gray, like yours. She hides them. Sometimes with contacts. Can you imagine my fear, my overwhelming terror, to wake up and realize my mother was dead, and she wore masks? That I had never seen her true face?"

He shook his head and began to reload the magazine.

"After that, things weren't the same. I thought she hadn't seen me, but she acted different. Maybe she sensed me, smelled me, but she knew I'd been there. She didn't want me interacting with the other kids and giving her away. So she sent me away. Years went by, I got away, started living where I could—on the streets, in empty houses, anywhere I could make a space and sleep at night. I kept contact with some of them. We'd swap notes and leave messages for each other in empty mailboxes and under the porches of foreclosed houses. Do you know how many McMansions are just sitting empty out there in abandoned developments? And then, a few months ago, one of them let me know that they were preparing for the Lord. I knew they had found you."

He pushed the magazine back into the gun with his eyes trained on the door. When he was satisfied with his loaded weapon and could detect no movement beyond the wall, he turned back to me.

"They used the Rogers to lure me in," I concluded.

He nodded. "Once she took the children, she'd locate the parents. They were broken, disconsolate in their grief. It made them vulnerable to suggestion. She managed to take them on once they were broken by the loss of their children. People are so vulnerable at that moment. They work for her now. They are loyal, and most of them are the ones she stole the children from. They've never seen the compound. They just do her dirty work, believing when they die they will be saved and reunited with their lost children. Little do they know that just beneath their feet their missing children are housed in a compound and taught to believe Astra is their mother. Mrs. Pied Piper herself."

"So you shot the ones she sent for me."

He nodded again.

All this time, he'd been trying to stave off the inevitable. His efforts had been to protect me, not to put me down. I cursed myself quietly.

"Kid?"

"Yeah?"

"You're a helluva shot."

He smiled but could not meet my eyes while he did it. The contained expression on his face was telling, revealing a man who received the barest minimum of support and love from the world. I wondered if I should be the one to tell him it only gets worse from here.

"Get out of here, Owen," I said.

His expression changed swiftly, immediately concerned.

"I'm going to take you out of here—"

"You said it yourself, they blocked off the entrance. If we try to leave together, we get caught together. I'm dead already,

Owen. You're still alive. You've got a chance. Hide. Search for a way out. When you find it, take it, and don't look back."

"No," he said. "I'm in it with you. I'm not leaving."

My face hardened. I brought up my next words from the harder spaces inside myself.

"You're a sorry excuse for a son. Wouldn't matter if you died anyway, huh? Clearly, the college life isn't in your future. Pissed that away." I forced a sneer to match the words, a sneer I did not feel. He flinched before me, creeping back an inch, as though I were filled with a heat that would burn him.

"You're lying," he snapped. "I can tell. You want to drive me away."

His eyes turned hard as he reached out and gripped my hand. Warm fingers on my own, and for a moment I thought he was going to hold hands with me like a frightened child. A nice gesture, but not really helpful. Instead, he pulled out a marker from his pocket and bit the cap off with his mouth.

He wrote across the side of my index finger and when the marker sunk into the spongy membrane to poke at the bone beneath, he cursed and continued on with dedicated patience until he had big, clear letters: DADDY.

"What's that for?"

He put away the marker.

"For you to remember when you forget everything else."

He rattled the pills in his hand.

"God, not again," I whispered.

"There's no other way. Listen, the dose will run out before morning, by the time they come in to take you away. This word on your hand, look at it."

I made a mental note to ask him when he started moonlighting as my personal pharmacist. This kid knew more about me and my habits than I was comfortable with. Did he gain all that through surveillance? Internet searches? It left another bad taste in my mouth among the many, but there was no time for it now. *Later,* I told myself. For now, I attempted to do as he asked, bending against the restraints to examine his handiwork. Black marker on my dead, rotten skin.

"Something about the disease . . . kills the consciousness, destroys the frontal lobe. I'm not a doctor, I can't stop it, but it's basic psychology. Hypnotic suggestion. Use the word to trigger the subconscious."

"How about we screw that and just use a real trigger, eh?"

"I'm serious," he insisted. "Triggering the subconscious won't change the drive of your base instincts, okay? But it could modify your behavior. Give you . . . second thoughts, in a manner of speaking. Focus you. You'll still be a monster, but you'll be a *motivated* monster instead. Got it?"

"How do you know that'll work?"

"I don't. I just read a lot of books."

None of this explained why Jessica still retained her higher brain functions without medication or the use of special trigger words. I said as much, and Owen considered it a moment.

"I don't know why she doesn't act like you when you're off the meds. I've never seen her take a pill, but I think . . . I think . . ."

He paused and looked at me strangely.

"The reason I think the trigger word will work for you is because she uses a trigger, too."

"Something that focuses her? So much she can actually reason?" I asked.

I was incredulous. I couldn't penetrate the memories of my time as a shuffle-shuffle moan-moan, how the hell was she conscious and conniving to boot?

"I think if you find her trigger, she'll regress. She'll go back to being a monstrosity."

"You realize what you're asking me to do, don't you?" I whispered. "You're asking me to destroy my wife all over again. Who said I would do it?"

He smiled, an odd quirk of his lips.

"Because I know the secret."

"What secret is that?"

"You don't love her. And maybe never did."

And with that, he picked up the gun, resumed the mask, and eased out of the room like a wisp of smoke.

★

Irony, it turns out, tastes worse than my medication.

In the wake of Owen's absence I was left to ponder his parting words. I clenched a fist in my restraints, the long snaking marker DADDY curling along the line of my finger. The word that would focus me, allow me to hold on to a shred of consciousness. The idea had merit; the brain was a muscle, after all. But I was still yet a weakling—how could I pull myself from the murk of pre-deceased, low brain function? How could I rise above a reptilian limbic system that demanded flesh, and more flesh? I doubted myself, doubted I was capable of such a feat. This particular brain muscle was weak.

Owen had made that brutally clear in his parting words: *You don't love her. And maybe never did.*

I laughed softly into the stuffy basement air. A weak man who made a weak marriage. He was right. I hadn't loved her. At eighteen, I thought I found love in the back of a Toyota with a blond young thing named Jessica. And for awhile, that was all of love I knew. We played passion games in dark rooms at house parties, one hand up her dress and molding the shape of her hip, the other pulling her closer to me, closer to me. Like I could eat her. A shadow of our future.

Then, two years after, I was in Bosnia. *Kosovo.*

I groaned. How long until the dose wore off? Did I have hours, or only minutes? The disintegration of my waking mind was no longer an event to be feared. Now, I wished to retreat into a darkened world where no new memories were made, no old ones to haunt, and nothing to live through or to live for. Give me obliteration, give me an undead life. Instead, I went reeling back into the past.

I had got the call in Mississippi, during boot camp. Jessica was pregnant; white knuckled fingers on the phone. I was the same age as the shooter in the ski mask that I pretended was my long-dead son. I hadn't spoken to Jessica in months. The warm thighs of a Southern woman hot from the delta had been keeping me company during long, humid nights. I showed her what I knew and she wasn't impressed.

In that distant past I examined myself as I had been. Not quite a man, no longer a boy. Sweat and mosquitoes, I was suddenly a father, a role I had never pictured for myself. The old gray fox had been my only template for a father, and fear-sweat filled me as I heard the empty notes of Jessica's voice—shock, surprise, wonderment. I shot rounds off at the range but I was terrified of a fetus smaller than a bullet.

I told her I would give her an answer. But I never really did; I came back to her house when boot camp was over and she took me in, announced our engagement to her family. I had none left to announce anything to. The old gray fox was unreachable and refused to take our calls. My mother in exile. Jamie told me not to do anything stupid. My fate was decided by my fear, fearing to abandon, fearing to act. In a moment of hesitation, I became a father and a husband.

No, I did not love her.

A particular fondness, loyalty, devotion—perhaps love was nestled somewhere between those concepts and had carved out a space beside my cold and deadened heart. Ancient history.

★

Things were heating up in Kosovo, and rumors of ground troops were followed by Clinton's refusal to send them. But we all knew it was a matter of time. The more Slobadon refused to yield, the more NATO bombed, which brought us closer to the brink. Ground troops would be inevitable if the Serbs did not capitulate soon. Bondsteel Camp wasn't even on the map yet.

I met with Jamie in Kosovo, which was an unplanned event. We talked about the air strikes, NATO, the whole mess. He said they'd called him down with the initial troops on our "peacekeeping" mission to look at the mass graves. Information was dodgy. Every side had a different version, and rumor was something had happened in the farmland. People gone missing. He was there to help excavate. That was the first drink.

By the second drink, he explained they were working on something really revolutionary, the sort of thing that could change the way wars were waged. No more death, no more suffering.

By the third drink, he was slurring his words and I thought I heard him wrong.

Where are the mass graves? I asked.

What mass graves?

The ones we're fighting this fucking war over, dumbass.

He chuckled into his drink, and then ordered a fourth.

About that, he began slowly. *I'm gonna bring them back to life. How'd you like that?*

We never talked about that conversation in Kosovo again. I took him back to the barracks and helped him into bed while alcohol seeped from his pores and fermented in his sweat.

The next morning, he requested I join him as part of an armed escort with a handful of troops to the mass grave excavation. This wasn't what I had signed on for, and we stood by while a bulldozer raised the earth and broke apart its crust, shoving black dirt this way and that in heaps and mounds.

There was nothing there.

Jamie became agitated as the minutes passed and bulldozer's metal jaws continued to come away with nothing but dirt; no bones, no meat, no corpses.

A soldier beside me cracked a joke: Maybe they walked out, eh?

But Jamie wasn't laughing. He had a hard, desperate look in his eyes. I shared a smoke with another soldier and he asked me what the fuck that guy's problem was. I shrugged and said nothing, but wondered what had my brother under so much pressure that he bit his lip and paced the outer edge of the hole like a prisoner before a set of bars. Something about that empty hole in the ground, his barely concealed rage, filled me with an apprehension the Balkan chill could not disperse. They'd find bodies much later; but for now, I could have sworn my brother *wanted* a massacre to supply him with corpses. Needed the corpses. I didn't ask why.

The next morning, he told me they had something they were working on that would make our careers in the military, if I wanted to be a part of it. I hesitated, distrustful, cautious. While

I pondered my choices, Jamie talked about his project—Virus X—with me from the back of a convoy for cover, and in heated discussion I failed to notice the vehicle moving and swaying. Conveying us to the helicopter pad.

He had been depending on the mass graves to further his scientific goals and use what he found as fodder for his experiments. Without them, he must turn to the scant reserves of volunteers, he explained, looking at me hopefully. He was impatient; mass graves would be discovered mere months later. That didn't rule out the possibility that the corpses from the abandoned site hadn't walked out on their own after all. Anything is possible.

It's a chance to change the world, Vitus. No more death. No one has to die. We could reverse every dumb-fuck thing our father ever did, you know that? Give the old man something to make the rest of his hair turn white.

In two years of hoping for advancement and receiving none, I took Jamie at his word. And in that moment of hesitation, my future was written. I was pre-deceased; I just didn't know it yet.

★

All those things—long ago, far away.

Another man walked in my shoes. I never really got to know him, the boy that I was. At twenty years of age, he died ignobly as part of a military sanctioned, pharmaceutical experiment. In his place, I was born—a darkling encased in rotting meat, a walking, talking corpse, still picking pieces of his wife and son from his teeth. A convenient tragedy packing heat. I was a pathetic human and I made for an even more pathetic monster.

I flexed my hand again. The length of the word DADDY waved and I re-examined the word. Being Jessica's husband had been an empty experience and a duty I had sought to fulfill out of a sense of obligation—as had my decision to join the military. My father had been a soldier and so I believed I should be one.

Fatherhood had been different; I had watched Clay like a scientist unsure of the organism that had just outgrown the Petri dish. Even at the age of two, Clay had his own ideas about where he wanted to go, who he wanted to be. He didn't want my help, or Jessica's. He hated naps and enjoyed running from us.

Until I stopped his running forever.

And that left a hole in my heart I could not name.

What does it mean to be a father? I asked myself, looking at the word. I tried to imbue it with a sense of responsibility, but all my responsibilities had been failures. No, DADDY wasn't my word; it was Owen's word. Owen, who believed he was my Clay, and that we were reunited at last.

Instead, Owen had probably been snatched from an arcade while his parents left him there to shop at a neighboring store; or maybe Jessica had spotted him outside a school playground and the likeness had struck a chord in her that could not be silenced. How many children went missing every day? Enough so that a young boy, the first boy Jessica chose, would be lost in the mire of paperwork and AMBER Alerts.

He was the first domino to fall. Once Jessica had snatched and indoctrinated Owen, it was only a matter of time before dissatisfaction set in, and she began to take others to fill his place. And whose fault was this but my own? In the long chain of unintended consequences, I was the living embodiment of chaos and everyone around me had been swallowed in the widening gyre.

What had it meant to Owen, who must have buried the memories of his parents deep, so deep he could no longer remember? Instead, he was willing to accept me as his father with no questions asked. He gave his trust without hesitation; he gave his love without reservation and condition. His gift was profound in its depth, its size; I could not measure up to the pedestal he wanted to raise me to. And did I not owe him more, if I was the catalyst for all this misery?

I looked at the word again.

You wanted to pretend Owen was your son. Maybe the secret to this word, DADDY, is that you finally accept it—accept the role Owen aches to fill. Accept this new son in place of the old. You owe him that much.

It's sick! I lamented, stifling a wail. I refused it still. And inside, an ache crept steadily up my spine like a writhing snake and all the way up to the base of my skull where the ache expanded to ocean-size proportions.

Not much time left to me now. These could be my last moments of consciousness before I was lost forever. I stared at the word fiercely. I thought of Owen and what it cost him to turn away the memory of his old parents in favor of a new one. Maybe his parents had never truly loved him anyway. Why else would he abandon their memory so eagerly, be so complicit with Jessica?

And he spent his life waiting for me. Waiting for my arrival.

Owen's father wouldn't lay here, bellyaching over the past. Time to pay back the love given. You know how precious that gift is. It's too late for Clay—nothing can change the mistakes of the past. But there is still time for Owen. He's giving you an opportunity to die with a final shred of dignity—knowing you did something for someone other than yourself—something for your son.

Zzzzt. Zzzzt.

A fly buzzed energetically against the concrete wall. I watched it with hatred rising through the fibers of my broken cells and leavening through my deadening brain matter. I wanted to eat the fly and consume the world and shove it into my jaws and keep going. My salivary glands worked overtime, wetting my lips with anticipation. The hour of turning was upon me.

Curdled eyes rolled in my sockets. My belly churned. The time was now.

"Hang on," I whispered, I begged myself. Consciousness scrambled for purchase along the edges of my darkening mind. Did the light dim yet? "*Hang on.*"

What was the word again? I found it hard to remember. There was a boy, a boy I had known. Just here. I was. Where. Hunger. Find the boy. Keep the boy. Safe.

Keep. Him. Safe.

Keep. Him. Safe.

Keep.

Safe.

★

There is no past. There is no future.

"How did we sleep today, dear husband?"

The Dead Man looks up.

A woman crowned with long blond hair occupies the space before him. His nose crinkles like a wolf's until the dead skin parts beneath the pressure. He smells her female smell, a mixture of incense and patchouli, but they provide a barrier for her real smell, the smell of rotting flesh, of long-dead corpse flesh.

She is like him.

His moonstone eyes meet hers from the bed where his hands clench and spasm in the iron fetters around his wrists. He wants to taste her and swallow her.

She sees the feral look in his eye, the hungry look, and smiles knowingly, like an experienced woman about to lead a virgin into a bedroom.

"I'm going to let you up, Vitus. I'm sorry I have to keep you on the leash, but hopefully that will be temporary until we have you trained."

The Dead Man watches her small, fine-boned fingers work a metal strap over his neck. A hard, steel edge rubs against the deteriorating flesh of his throat as he spasms against it.

A sensation erupts from within the Dead Man as though two people looking out from behind his eyes and reflected inside one another into infinity but then it's lost in the yammering background of his thoughts. Mirrors propped against one another.

Trigger word, Vitus. You got the word?

The Dead Man flinches but the Dead Man is me and I am him, and abruptly the conscious thought bursts like a bubble on the wind and whatever understanding he almost reached is gone.

He is only a Dead Man watching a Dead Woman unlock his wrists from their iron prisons.

He makes a grab for her and then hesitates with his head tilted in uncertainty. Her flesh is spongy as old cheese underneath the meringue swirl of her dress, and he retracts his hand as he realizes she is no longer a viable food source. Her rot is hidden beneath the clever application of spices and incense, and up close with his monster senses he recognizes her for the dead corpse she is.

He frowns as he sits up, clenching and spasming fingers at his side, waiting for her next command.

A long link chain leads from the collar around his neck to her small fist, where she clutches it as though he might fight against her at any moment. He cannot remember if he ever has.

DADDY.

The word written in black across the edge of his hand fills him with a torrent of trace memories and sent his thoughts cascading back with images and scents and trace impressions of a flimsy past that will not hold still; a man in a ski mask, blond hair, candid brown eyes. A father and a son.

Me?

The concept of *me* fractures and fragments and the Dead Man cannot seem to connect them.

Vitus! You're the father! You are me! Do you have the word?

He does not have the word.

The nattering voice clamoring at the edge of his thoughts makes his teeth clench until metal clicks inside his jaw. The sound echoes nostalgia and a woman's black hair with a burst of exuberance and then, the Dead Woman tugs him along. Across the room he shambles with broken and uncoordinated movements. He moves like a marionette with only half the strings cut.

Out into a hallway. Little boys are stationed outside their rooms in flowing red capes like soldiers or superheroes. The Dead Man smells the scent of their blood, and recent wounds upon their bodies still weep blood beneath their bandages. White blood cells on top of the red like cream on milk. He makes a sound deep in his throat like a German Shepherd. Low, snarling growl.

She tugs at the chain with force. The collar chokes off his windpipe, but he resists and tests his raw power, little more than sheer will behind collapsed and decayed muscle. Closer, closer, close enough to bite into the beckoning flesh and feed with abandon, without reservation.

"Now, now," she cautions and leads him down the hall.

Boys watch him with wide eyes and try not to stare but snatch glances at him as he follows the Dead Woman at her heels. He snaps at one young boy who shrieks, and she sends the Dead Man reeling backward with a yank so hard he gulps at the damp air like a fish. He does not need to breathe, but the discomfort addles him as he struggles upright against the leash.

"See, dears? He's harmless, I'd never let him hurt you. We just have to get him fed, don't we, Vitus? And I've got a special meal for you."

The boys rush past, wild snatches of crimson fabric down the hall. Their feet tap out eerie, discordant time against the concrete.

Pied Piper. The Pied Piper of Hamlin, he thinks, but the thought disconnects into a free floating balloon above his head until it bursts and evaporates. He remembers a blond-headed boy that a man named Vitus used to read fairytales to. One of them was the Pied Piper of Hamelin.

I used to read the Pied Piper *to Clay.*

The moment of clarity is brief and the Dead Man looks down to stare at the DADDY word written in the skin of his hand again.

"Wwh. Wh."

Blond hair swirls as the Dead Woman pauses to look at him, her brow furrowing. The Dead Man struggles to make the words but his lips trip like a pair of clumsy feet.

"Who. Ooooo. Whooo. Who is."

A splitting headache rips into the side of his frontal lobe, the tender, spongy brain matter controlling logic, reason, and good manners. The pain is excruciating and delivers pulses of earth-shattering agony through his forehead and down to his splintered nose, his rotted lips, and his lacerated cheeks. He struggles with the sentence.

"Is. Vight. Us."

Who is Vitus?

The Dead Woman smiles and does not answer. Instead, she pulls him forth so hard that he falls onto his face and breaks the thin cartilage piecing his nose together against the concrete. Gore falls out and all that remains is a triangle of dark emptiness, accentuating his skeletal appearance. He wipes a long smear of broken bone matter and blood over the front of his suit and barely has time to do so before he is dragged forward once more, struggling to keep his feet as she draws him closer to the altar room door. A hunk of metal presses up against his chest, concealed within his suit.

Gun. Old gray fox likes 1911s and you swore you'd never carry a 1911 just to piss him off. Gun. Firearm. The Glock. Your baby, the Glock. Don't forget.

And like a cassette tape ribbon unraveling in a wind, the thought is gone, an errant radio transmission lost in space.

"I was going to provide you your usual meal, but you are our guest of honor. And you always did have such passionate appetites, Vitus. Ah."

She sighs, gone misty with past memories, and what she needs now is a little Vaseline smeared around the memory lens like a two-bit soap opera. Dream sequence. The tinkle of a harp. She blinks and her manner changes, forgetting the rosy-colored past and catapulting into the stark future.

"Well, no more waiting, then. Here you go, Vitus."

She opens the door and closes it behind her, reaches for his collar and unsnaps the chain, setting him free.

★

The Dead Man's senses were far from dead.

Zzzzt. Zzzzt.

An errant fly drew a lazy circle about the room before settling on a white plate piled high with strips of bloody flesh like raw bacon. A room of concrete, with a table and chair at its center. Walls dripped with slow lines of dark sweat while a bare bulb swung back and forth on a chain. Stains proliferated and embedded the pocked surface of the floor.

From the far shadow in the corner, a man stepped forth.

The Dead Man's eyes adjusted to the dim light. The man in the shadow raised a cigarette to his thin lips and produced a lighter. He lit up with lazy satisfaction, pausing to look at the Dead Man with a penetrating gaze beneath the brim of his hat.

The Dead Woman seated herself before the table with the plate of festering flesh. She helped herself as though the strips of human flesh were delicacies, oysters on the half-shell that she gobbled one by one with hungry, slurping noises. She licked from her lips as though she were experiencing an orgasm with eyes half-lidded and her breath hitching fast.

She took no notice of the man in the corner.

The Dead Man growled. People were food sources, nothing more; it was not a cognitive thought reaction, but something he pursued on instinct alone; primordial forces drove the Dead Man when all other functions ceased.

But the man in the corner was different.

He moved with fluid grace, smoking at his leisure; rings of blue smoke circled his head in a tenebrous corona and a slice of his mouth made visible in the shaky light. While the Dead Woman dined, oblivious to the distress of her zombie pet, the man in the corner spoke directly to the Dead Man and she did not seem to notice at all.

"Vitus."

The Dead Man stared, dim witted, slow—unable to connect the name to the collection of rotting tissue that defined him bodily.

"Don't you recognize me?"

The words were meaningless, and the Dead Man met them with silence, cocking his head like a dog attempting to discern his master's voice.

"Do you have the word, Vitus?"

He did not have the word.

"Noo. Ooooo." The Dead Man blew rotten breath between his sore lips like a locomotive, overtaken by a panic he could not explain. A new sensation in his limited faculties. His clumsy skeleton shook and shivered until every joint ground painfully and collapsed in on its decaying supports.

The man left the corner and approached the Dead Man with the confidence of a grown man who has left the uncertainty of youth behind and embraced the prowess that only experience can temper. Assured. More than self-confidence. Kinesthetic ease. Ashes fell from the tip of his cigarette and the Dead Man cowered before him as his face lifted into the light.

The Dead Man's brain split into two halves—each one a radiating migraine, exploding with stars and light. He clutched at his head with trembling fingers, tearing at the dead skin like old cheese as though he could extract the pain with his splintered, yellowed fingernails. The man filled him with fear but the pain crippled and annihilated what was left. He could not cower but hold his position, frozen before the man's approach.

"You're me, Vitus," the man said. "I'm the you that served my tour in the army and came back to raise a son. I'm the you that could have been, the you without Virus X, the you without Jamie."

The words were like pennies dropped into a well. They made a tinny rattle, but the Dead Man could barely hear it through the axe strokes boring repeatedly into his skull. He clapped his hands over his ears, determined to stop the ache from there.

The man took off his fedora and braved a step forward into the Dead Man's sphere of influence—clear brown eyes to his spoiled ones. He set the hat on the Dead Man's forehead. His skin split beneath the pressure, like overfilled denim tearing at the seam.

Once he'd placed the hat, he brushed off the Dead Man's suit with a paternalistic air, inspecting him like a prize animal. He straightened out the lapel with a sad gesture of familiarity.

A handsome man; hair cropped close against his scalp, his eyes clear, lucid, a man well-satisfied and at peace with himself. He studied the Dead Man with an apology written in his mud-brown eyes; a regret that pierced him deep and called up lost moments, broken promises. A life that could have been.

"I was there, watching you when it happened. I'm sorry I couldn't stop it. I was just a background watcher. I'm the guy in your dreams, your Id that demands and hungers and wants and feels. You're like an older software version of me, y'know? Back when we were lizards, with scales instead of skin. Right?"

The Dead Man said nothing, and the other man took it as encouragement to continue.

"You don't remember what happened to your son or your wife. You always could have asked me, if you really wanted to know; but then, you never *really* wanted to know, did you, Vitus?"

He was silent a moment, collecting his thoughts.

"I know thinking is difficult for you right now. And that meat over on that plate must be really distracting. A clever trick, that headache, right? That's the sensation of your frontal lobe trying to process forward thinking thought, choices between good and bad, recognizing consequences, and a lot of other boring shit. A bitch, huh? Don't worry. Some people aren't even zombies and they can't manage it.

"Do you want to know what happened that night, Vitus?"

The Dead Man stared, and dark eyes met moonstone ones. The man sighed, as though speaking to a small child, and forged on, relentless. The Dead Man trembled to hear his voice, feel the pain shiver through his ear and into his soft, gray matter.

"You should know," he said gently, and reached out to touch the Dead Man's shoulder. "Sometimes, I'm there in the background when you remember a fragment of the past, in that time just before sleep, or when you're awake but not quite there, yes? Make no mistake about it—we can never go back to the way things were before.

"Hell, Vitus. You made Hell in your home. You killed your son outright. Deep down, you know Owen isn't Clay. You knew it from the beginning—but still you tracked him down, doggedly, loyal to the end. For what loyalty is worth.

"And your wife, the one you married because you were too dickless to do the right thing and set her free? If you had, she'd still be alive right now. Our fate turns on the many things we lack the courage to do, as well as the mistakes we commit to.

"Well, you didn't quite kill her. That would have been a mercy, compared to the hell she lives in now. In case you haven't noticed, she's not quite all there. She believes a dark force animates her, an evil god, and we are all manifestations of that Dark Lord—you in particular, Lord of the Flesh Eaters. Here she is, still trying to be the perfect wife, feed you, love you, gain your approval in a final, desperate attempt to heal the wounds of the past—wounds scarred over many times with thick and unreliable tissue. She is not the woman you married. She is a devil of your own making. And deep down, she's not truly evil. She believes she's helping you. With just enough nourishment. With just enough love, you could be made whole again. But we both know that's not possible.

"Do you know what you did, to her, Vitus, the thing you block out that you cannot remember? You tried to kiss her. One last act of love. But you turned while you were kissing her. Ate her face off. While you were busy cannibalizing Clay, she escaped, and all this while, she's been focused, intent with one purpose—to find you, bring you back, and resume the life you both had before. That is all that animates her, drives her, makes her conscious. Without that, she is as animal as you are, dead inside are you are at this very moment. And the ghost of your dead child between you both. How goes the saying? Ah, dear old father would have known: *Amor vincit omnia*—love conquers all. And destroys all, in the same measure.

"It would be so much easier if she was just a two-dimensional villain, wouldn't it? Something you could kill without regret. But inside, she doesn't really understand why death came to her door in the form of the man she loved, the man she worshipped, the man she put up on a pedestal, just to watch him crawl down to eat everything in his path. Still, even after all these years, she doesn't understand. Remember Jackie Kennedy, pulling the brains and bits of skull from back of the car, desperately trying to put something back together that is beyond saving? That's your wife. Still putting the pieces back together.

"Yet, they don't fit, they cannot enmesh and unite once more. They fail, they darken, they decay. And still she persists, waiting for your love, your approval. You cannot let this cruel existence continue.

"It's time for me to go, Vitus. But before I do that, do this last thing before we part."

The man set his hand against the Dead Man's heart, but there was no heart—only a hunk of metal and dense plastic called a firearm, and the man smiled at the touch.

The Dead Man smiled with him—in imitation or genuine pleasure, impossible to know.

"Unmask the bitch and end her suffering."

★

The fog lifted—and I stood there a long moment.

They were gone, the Dead Man I was, the stranger I had once been, a new monster restored in its place. The splitting pain dividing my head faded to a steady, dull throb and I swayed, dizzy and disoriented.

Jessica remained at the table. She left a portion of the plate in reserve for me, for when I was ready to dine with her— very un-zombie behavior. With her blond hair like a halo in the trembling light, I memorized her as she was at this very moment. I did not like what I saw, an emotionally crippled monster wearing the flesh of a woman, destroyed from the inside out. Her lips were red with blood, her teeth with bits of boy-flesh between them.

Is that what people saw when they looked at me?

Is that what Niko saw?

There was still time to make things right, for her and myself.

I approached and with each step made my measurements and calculations and strategies—no longer the shuffling of a pre-deceased corpse. The collar around my neck chafed against the skin and heightened the sensation of claustrophobia. The walls sweated in damp lines.

I put a hand on the back of her chair, the sort of thing I used to do when we had both been alive. My wedding ring winked in the feeble light, a circle of reflection. DADDY scrawled across the hand—Owen's desperate plea to bring me back to life.

I deflated a long sigh into her ear. Jessica turned in the seat to stare up at me.

"My love," I whispered.

Up close, I made out a seam by her scalp, extending down along the base of her jaw. Spots and lesions of rot made visible, imperfections she cleverly hid with the assistance of scarves and clothing. Until now. Her flesh bared in all its hurt and waiting for my ministrations.

Zzzzt. Zzzzt.

The errant fly would be dealt with later. I had a wife to tend to, a woman I promised I would be faithful to, for richer and poorer, in sickness and health.

'Til death do us part.

And the time had come to part.

★

I leaned down to kiss her. The past merged with the present, the long-buried memory surfacing and overlaid across time like transparent paper. The moment of turning, divided between monster and human and crossing the line of consciousness. I did it again. Lucid and aware to taste the rot of my saliva as I opened my mouth and kissed her. With our lips interlaced, I bit down hard and pulled away with force, feeling her flesh give between my teeth and taking her entire face away with me.

I made it quick; moved with the velocity of a snake strike. She did not expect it and went reeling back into the table, sending the cutlery, the dishes, and the furniture upside down in a clatter that filled and echoed throughout the room. I stood with the flap of skin that was her face in my hands, leathery, as though my wife just asked me to hold her purse.

Zzzzt. Zzzzt.

I turned it over in my hand. Against the side of glistening red decay that fit against her inner face, things crawled and squirmed over the surface. My eyes stared but could not process what I saw; could not make sense of the white worms writhing and stitching through her tissues.

Maggots.

She was riddled through with maggots. Flies giving birth in her veins.

I dropped the mask of skin. It fell to the floor like an empty pancake. Maggots erupted from the surface and scattered. A shrieking commenced and filled the room like a siren.

Zzzzt. Zzzzt.

The sound of buzzing grew persistent and rose in volume. Her mask hid the festering gobbits of larvae all this time and grew in the damp heat of the underground lair. Now they hatched by the thousands as she writhed and screamed, sending torrents of flies from her open mouth, crawling along her tongue, from deep within her belly.

Later, I told myself. I would deal with the flies later.

Take care of her, Vitus, my Id breathed from within.

She ran for the door. I drew my weapon and squeezed the trigger, once, twice, three times. The first shot went wild and punched into the door frame inches above her head. I heard a sizzle as the second bullet caught a tangle of her hair in midair. The stench was lost amid the other rank and vile smells preceding it. The third caught her in the back of the throat where it exited and exploded through the door. Gore and maggot guts followed and sprayed the wall around it.

The buzzing increased in intensity. The final shot impacted too low and missed all the important bits—not high enough to take her head off and incapacitate her. She ran, shrieking through the hole in her throat as she yanked the door open and pounded through. Swirls of skirt flowed behind her in one eclipsing shadow.

Too late, I cursed, and slapped the back of my neck. My hand came away black with fly guts. My lips peeled away from my teeth and I hissed my disgust. They were everywhere. Filling the room and pacing the walls with their pin-prick feet, with their emerald and sapphire bodies, tasting, sampling, mindlessly eating everything they touched. Some crawled into my collar and another grazed my ear. They alighted, settled, and flew off like snowflakes in a blizzard.

While I stood there, repulsed and horrified, slapping at the horde of flies come to eat of my flesh, my wife closed the door and threw the lock.

My brief moment of lucidity faded; the headache returned with greater force and my overwhelming fear in the face of these dirty insects sent my consciousness reeling back inside myself, throwing forward the monster part of me, better equipped to deal with the horror and disgust of the flies.

Not now, I thought, groaning.

I dared not open my mouth for fear they would dart in and insert themselves along the lining of my gums and plant their children in the spaces between my teeth. I stared at the word written across my hand—DADDY. I thought of Owen, who was already taking the place of Clay inside my head, until their two identities were indistinguishable from each other, one and the same, and then where was I flies *zzzt zzzt* I am *zzzt* so hungry

dark

zzzzzzzzt

zzzzt

zt

z

PART 3

KNIGHT RISING

*S*uck. *Thump.*
Suck. Thump.

Like a heartbeat. I have not heard that sound since I was alive, the steady thump of four chambers in a beating heart coursing with blood. The sound comforts, recalls me to a time when I was a fetus in the cave of my mother's womb; fingers curled in imitation of the weapon I would fire when I grew up.

Suck. Thump.

The sound does not originate from inside me. There is no legitimate heart in the dark, empty cavity of my chest. Images blur and thoughts grow sluggish. These are sensations I felt when I was alive, when I was stupid and young and drunk and woke up every other day nauseous and hungover.

I did not feel young. I felt mummy-ancient.

I moved my fingers and tapped a porcelain beat against a metal gurney. I lay on a table. The ceiling above me came into focus, industrial tiles arranged in rows and columns. I blinked, but the action failed to complete. My vision fuzzy. I focused but the dark and rotted spots in my eyeballs had destroyed parts of what

I once could see. I blinked again and failed. My eyelids must be pinned open, because despite my best efforts they would not descend and soothe the dryness.

I opened my mouth to call out; the wire in my jaw clicked, amplified to movie-theater sound. My thoughts sped up and thawed and gained coherency. I was not in the basement anymore. Dust puffed from my mouth in an effort to speak. All that issued forth was a pained groan. My fingers tapped again and the persistent sound in the background became louder. *Suck. Thump. Suck. Thump.* I turned my head. Plastic rippled beneath me and there it was—the pump Niko used to embalm corpses.

That's odd, I thought. *There's no one else here.*

The room was empty. Gurneys lined up in rows and prepared for new intakes, but there were no corpses. Except for me.

I heaved a sigh with relief. Of all the places I expected to wake up in, the Pleasant Hills Funeral Home had not been one of them.

Niko, I thought with a twinge of regret. Her resentment would be a benediction, a face I correlated with feminine warmth, someone who could look me in the eye without fear.

I opened my mouth to call her name. *Niko.* A dry wind husked from my mouth, a garbled set of words. My teeth clicked together when I spoke. Numbed, I could not feel my lips move. I struggled to lift my hand to my mouth.

Bone against bone.

My fingertips tapped against my face like china plates thrown against each other. I startled, shaking, and pulled my hand away to hold it in front of my destroyed eyes.

Nothing but bones. Bones with little shreds of pink meat at the ends, here and there. Dangling ligaments and tendons snaking between the bones. The last remaining tissue holding my hands and fingers together. In places, soft tissues went missing entirely. Someone took mortuary wire and snapped together bone-to-bone in their place instead.

I wiggled my fingers. I could identify each carpal bone, the tiny bones of the metacarpals, the knuckle joints and the longer ones, threaded and connected to the wrist.

But no flesh. No fingernails. No hair filaments, no rotted skin to hold it together.

I gasped and made ready to howl, and nothing came out.

Suck. Thump. Suck. Thump.

My hand was nothing but a skeleton.

What about the rest of me?

My glance followed the line of my wrist down the length of my arm. An arm is defined by more than its motion; it has flesh, muscle, tissue. Red blood pumping beneath the surface of the skin.

All I had were bones. Long bones connected at the joints. Hint of sinew like dental floss. Thin shreds of meat by the bone surface.

I raised my skeleton hands to my face. I could not feel my face with bones for fingers but only hear their syncopated tapping against the planes of my skull, where there was no skin to pad their contact. I searched for eyelids, but there were none, only what soft jelly remained of my destroyed eyes that I could touch, but could not feel.

I screamed and screamed and screamed.

Suck. Thump. Suck. Thump.

★

I passed out.

Like a hysterical woman from a Victorian picture-show, I swooned where I was on the table, a long skeleton, a collection of bones. When I first turned into a pre-deceased monster, I must have been arrogant to believe that death was the worst that could happen, the worst that could ever be.

I was wrong. Even a zombie still has something left to lose.

★

I came to again. How quickly I mastered the art of sleeping without being able to close lidless eyes. Images present themselves, but the mind shuts down and refuses to compute. Second by second, consciousness broke the surface until I was aware, awake inside the skeleton of my body. Voices drifted from the room next door, a door of frosted glass separating the mortuary from the room outside. Words floated in with the draft.

"Don't go. Not yet."

Niko's voice, pleading.

"They're all children down there. Children alone with a pre-deceased monster."

"They could be dead already, Owen."

"You know why I have to go back. It's got to be contained."

A grim silence followed the lull of their conversation.

"You need his help. If you leave before he's up on his own, it'll tear him apart. I don't think he's got the strength for it. If he wakes up and finds out you're gone . . ."

"What? What will happen? I'll be back. I got him out; I'll get back in and out again without him, easier without him, actually. I'm made for this. I've been doing it my whole life."

I was filled with a rush of pride; my boy.

"I can't leave the children there to rot. I'm going after them."

"Owen! Don't!"

I frowned, or felt that I did, if I had a face left to frown with. A long, uncomfortable silence spanned time and the moment of feeling pride for my boy eclipsed by a darker set of emotions—feelings of jealousy, envy. Did she . . . *like* Owen?

Their voices picked up again and hushed; in that moment, I could imagine a number of romantic interludes passing between them, whispered adorations of love, admiration, perhaps even stolen kisses.

Oh, you fool. You didn't really think you had anything to offer her, compared to what Owen had? A living body, an intact soul. I didn't even have a rotting body left to me anymore. How long had I been unconscious on the gurney while they had time to get to know each other, while she had time to appreciate the handsomeness of his features—just like mine when I had been his age. She would get the best of me, and what better way than through my would-be son?

Not that he actually was my son, after all.

That's nice, I thought. *One second, he's the son you never had; the moment you think he's moving in on Niko, all of sudden, he's not your son. It would be better for everyone if you stayed dead with flimsy internal narcissism like that.*

I groaned and summoned the energy from my guts. I still had a few of them nestled in my rib cage. Tapping bony fingers along the metal gurney, I grasped the rails in my skeletal hands to force myself to a sitting position.

I caught my reflection in a mirror by the wall. Horrified, I took in the face of the monster I had become. Eyeballs nestled in the bone sockets of my face. Missing nose. Only a gaping, triangular hole marking the center; the awful, permanent wolf's grin of every serrated tooth revealed behind long lines of sinew remaining along the cheekbones; other than that, most of the tissue erased from the skull. I looked like a discarded skeleton from a laboratory study.

How can anyone love a pile of bones?

I shuddered. Bone from bone to bone clattered upon one another. Through the white slats of rib I could see parts of myself as through a curtain. My blackened lungs were still in place and wound with dark snarls of red tissue and veins inside the center of me. Niko had pushed a tube into me to send embalming fluid through the center of what little remained.

I saw my heart. A tough, sinewy muscle, it beat artificially with the rhythm of the embalming pump. I considered the irony of Niko making my heart beat again as I swung my legs over the gurney and out over the cement floor. Fluid gathered and swirled down a drain by the gurney wheels. Beside the slotted drain, several maggots lay still and dead, soft white grubs rendered into curled commas.

She killed them with the embalming fluid. Clever girl, I considered. She must have hooked me up to the machines as soon as Owen brought me here. It was not hard to piece together how events dovetailed and coalesced. Maggots don't keep eating when there's nothing left to eat, do they? No doubt Owen had followed me ever since the Rogers showed up at my door, so he knew I came here. The flies pumped out with the rest of the dead blood inside me, but what had been the point, really? What was left of me worth saving?

I heard the knob turn, the door open.

Reflexively, I shielded myself, holding my arms up above my head. But they were not arms, not anymore. Two bones shielding a skull. My eyeballs peered out over them, looking at her. Niko. Black hair piled up on her head. Her face was paler than I remembered, her eyes were red, as though she had been awake for many hours. She wore a cobalt blue dress that accentuated her goddess figure as though she'd stepped off an Egyptian stele. She looked lovely.

I looked like a horror film reject.

Ashamed, I turned away from her. Bones clicked, joints popped, alarmingly loud without flesh to muffle the sound. I struggled to leave the gurney and pull out the embalming tube from my middle with a violent jerk of my skeletal fingers. The tube was difficult and fought back until she stepped across the floor and hurried to help me.

"No!" I hissed, jerking away from her.

She ignored me, turning off the pump and reaching for the tube I already clutched. Our fingers brushed, her small hand, fleshy and ripe like peach skin; my own hard bones, whose touch I imagined as cold as bullets, white as snow.

I was inhuman; how could she stand it, to look at me like she did, with her intact eyes? I saw a skeleton reflected back at me from her pupils. Nothing about the skull resembled me anymore. There was nothing left of the man I had been.

"You should put me in a box and bury me."

"Maybe," she returned, "but not yet, and a little thanks for all this work I do on your behalf for free would be nice every once in awhile."

The embalming tube slithered between us, spewing fluid to the floor. My bone thighs dangled from the gurney, connected to an bone ankle, to bone foot carpals and little bone toes.

"We'll have to hook you back up to the machine tonight to get your dose to you. Owen has been crushing up pills and we added it to the fluid, hoping it would work."

"Are you satisfied with the result?" I asked her bitterly.

Under better circumstances, I could have made an effort at kindness; this newest atrocity left me with no civility, no remaining sense of empathy. Privately, I wished they had not resurrected me. Better to have left me a ravening monster without the self-awareness to understand what Jessica had done to me with her maggots. Lord of the Flesh Eaters, indeed. What purpose did it serve to bring me back to life, a new monster, as nothing but a skeleton? I was a Halloween nightmare.

"The result sucks," she responded, her words matching mine, tone for tone.

I bowed my skull. I deserved as much. My last words to her had not been so kind.

"Vitus."

The door opened. Owen entered, garbed in black—in stalking gear—once more. Niko ignored us, cleaning scalpels at the sink. She did it to give us a semblance of privacy, and I waited as Owen came forward into the room. Watching him approach, I was struck by the contrast between us, the vitality that informed his steps, the smoothness of his skin, the rippling muscle beneath his clothes. He exuded a life force that had been extinguished from me long ago, and looking at him was like studying a mirror image of myself: *that is what I looked like once.*

I looked away, gathering myself.

"I wondered where you were," I said.

He stopped before the gurney with several feet between us. He was polite to a fault, understanding without being told that I desired my privacy and my distance.

"I came for you as fast as I could. The whole place erupted into panic once Jessica made it out of the room they were holding you in. I didn't quite understand what was happening, the children were . . . they lost their purpose once Jessica lost her reason. It was as though she snapped; there was nothing left holding her coherent thoughts together. She ran from corridor to corridor, and I saw her. There was nothing left of her face, just this—"

"You found me," I cut him off.

I dreaded the thought of hearing him describe what I had already seen. She was still my wife, even if she were dead, or crazy, or damned to Hell for eternity. No language spoken could match the power of standing witness before her corrupted, maggot-eaten form.

"I tracked you down. I would have been there sooner, but I was clearing the way through an old ventilation shaft. I could not get through the door where they had blocked it off, and I fear they are all still there."

"How long have I been here?"

"Two days. I had to . . . wrap you in a blanket. I feared to lose the parts of you that were falling off."

I raised a skeleton hand before my eyes and flexed the finger bones. Wires interlaced the smaller ones, and it occurred to me that it had been painstaking work to connect my bones in such a way, like shattering a puppet and then sewing it back together. Hours and hours of labor on par with that of a master craftsman, just to give me back the most basic of articulation.

I glanced at Niko. Had she even had time to sleep? Or had she spent the last forty-eight hours working on me? My shame expanded.

"I'm going back, Vitus," he announced.

"Oh?" I turned my attention from my hand. Niko had finished washing the surgical instruments some time ago. She occupied a dark corner in silence as she watched us.

"I can't leave them. I can't leave the children there with that . . . thing."

"What makes you think I would let you go back into that place with that *thing* that is my wife?"

Niko said nothing; no gasp of surprise or shock. No doubt Owen had relayed everything to her while I had been passed out in the intake room. That, too, evoked a sense of shame, Niko having to hear from a stranger that I had not, in fact, succeeded in killing my wife, but only maimed her. And what did she think of Owen? Had he presented himself as my son? *Oh God*, I groaned, *what did she think of me now?*

Owen sighed. His expression held a poker face, but he was an inexperienced player; he struggled to contain himself. Of course, a skeleton does not have half the complications involving duplicity a living person with a face and human expressions does.

"You can't stop me, and you can't do it yourself."

He pointed out my obvious helplessness, an incapacitation I refused to accept.

"So you're the great martyr, hm? What happens when a fly lays claim to your flesh? Have you thought about that?"

"Your flesh was rotten, it made for an opportunistic—"

"Infestation? Perhaps. You do realize there are a thousand varieties of flies, and there are those that feast on live flesh as well as dead? Sure, mine was the most convenient. But you've got no way of knowing you'll be able to find your way out once you make it back in. Plenty of time for anything to happen."

His features hardened, perhaps even irritated by my calm explanation of what awaited him in the dirty, damp basement with the hundred damned children of the Flesh Eaters.

"I assure you, Owen, when you are dead, you will have many hours to ponder all the fear a maggot may hold; until then, I forbid you to go."

His face suffused with red from the collar of his neck to the roots of his blond hair. It made me wonder if that was how I had looked when I was angry, when I was told things I did not like to hear.

"You know I'm going anyway."

I leapt off the gurney. I should have reconsidered. My skeleton feet connected with the concrete and rattled me all the way up my spine. I groaned with the pressure it sent through what little remained of my body and took two steps to stand before Owen.

The red blooms in his cheeks faded, turned into ice; his eyes widened and he stepped back, his lips parting.

He was afraid of me.

"For what purpose did you bring me back here, Owen?"

"Purpose? I'm your son—"

"Like hell you are, and you know it. Try me again, with an answer that makes sense."

Niko's glance flicked with interest between the both of us, and I hoped a day might come when I could explain it all to her. For now, explanations would have to wait.

"I couldn't leave you there!"

I stared at him, but he held steady.

"You would have been better off leaving me for dead or killing me yourself. If you walk out that door, you'd better be prepared for what I'm going to do to come after you. Everyone so fucking eager to save me and then discard me when it turns out I'm not here to be your personal yes-man. You don't like what I have to say, kill me. I'm serious. I keep asking for it, and everyone keeps not doing it, and I'm not sure how much more self-destruction I can pull out of my ass to prove it to you, because I don't even have one of those anymore!"

He swallowed. A thick, muddy sound in his throat as his Adam's apple bobbed in fear.

"Kill me."

I invaded his space, snapped the gun out of his holster, and returned it to him, pressed it into his hand. My skeleton fingertips reduced to squares of alabaster against his palm. He startled with the sensation, which sent his skin crawling as goose bumps ran up and down his arms and every little hair lifted off the flesh.

His hands trembled. But he would not pull the trigger.

At last he pulled away with a violent jerk, his breath hitching in fast.

"You can't even pull the trigger with a monster standing in front of you," I whispered, "and you think you can handle what's waiting for you in the basement?"

I didn't try to stop him—what could I possibly do? I was a collection of bones. He slammed the door shut behind him as he left, leaving Niko and me in silence.

"He's not your son, then?" she asked.

"No," I sighed. "My real son would have killed me. No, he did exactly what Jamie did. Everyone and their fucking misguided conscience."

I turned, a skeletal foot tapping against the floor, and studied her face closely. I hoped to catch something, any kind of reaction at all to Jamie's name, wondering how many family secrets she shared now; at any point she could have asked what I was talking about, but she remained silent.

★

Fluorescent lights flickered and I looked upward, listening to the bones in the back of my head creak and balance my skull on the occiput.

"Turn out the light," I begged her.

She watched me, her eyes as large as tea saucers, and flicked the switch off, plunging us into dimness. Feeble light poured in between the blinds and cast half-shadows around us like prison bars. The darkness relieved me and set me at ease. I was more naked than naked—no clothes, no flesh.

I wanted to continue my old habits, those physical things we do without a second thought. The way you might lean against a wall and prop up a leg with your heel against it or cross your feet in a casual stance. All these things required new strategies. I was light and unburdened without the flesh, but the cost left me desensitized and hollowed.

"I didn't expect to see you again. At least not like this," I began.

We had the room to ourselves. Owen was gone whether I liked it or not. He was young, too young. Was he prepared for what he would find in that basement? There might be children—but would there be anything left of them? And when he got there, would he have the strength to do the hard thing, the right thing? Kill the children he once knew as brothers?

I did not think he had such a darkness in him; I had cultivated evil in my life, I had a talent for killing what I loved. He was still learning those brutal lessons and I feared he would fail that education.

Niko spoke, breaking the thought.

"I had not intended to. I have . . . seen my share of walking corpses. I feared to be the sort of woman who looks for my past in other men, hopelessly seeking a love that can never be returned. Do not feel too badly that you see your son in him. We are always looking for those we've lost in other people."

We were still in the darkness, her back to me as she faced the sink. All of her chores appeared to be done, she had no excuse to turn away from me. I longed to bridge the distance and comfort her, but I had only brittle bones, carrion to offer.

Owen could offer her so much more. Owen was alive, warm, flesh.

"And what about him?" I asked.

"Him? Who?"

"Owen."

"What about him? Why don't you come out and tell me what's on your mind."

"You seem to like him. And you've both been working together, for my supposed benefit, for the past several days now. Long enough to get to know each other."

Frozen, she broke the stillness by casting a narrow-eyed glance over her shoulder.

"What impressed me most about Owen was how much he looked like you. I remembered when you came to the funeral home, you know. You were a younger man then. You looked just like him."

"Yeah, that must help," I said, and the words were bitter.

"Help what?"

"Don't fuck around. If you like him, don't pretend otherwise for my benefit. To spare my goddamn feelings. Pity the skeleton you should have buried. If I didn't know better, I'd think you kept me around to make you feel better about yourselves, like you're so fucking nice to always be thinking of me, bring me back from the dead when you should have left me to the maggots!"

I'd been holding it in like a writhing snake, but there was nothing left—no muscles, no flesh to bury the anger and jealousy in. It burst from my bones, words climbing out from behind my teeth without lips to snarl with. I invested the one asset I had, my blackened and shriveled lungs, with all the burning rage I could muster, and the words came out like hand slaps.

"I don't love him," she hissed. She held a scalpel in her hand. She'd been fiddling with it earlier and now her fingers became white-knuckled around the grip. Hollows beneath her eyes spoke of her long and sleepless nights. "And I don't love you, either."

My spine rattled, each knobby bone shuddering atop the other like a set of bricks. Was I really surprised?

"I'm not your lover, I'm not your guardian, and I'm certainly not your fucking mother, and it's about time you took care of yourself!" she snapped, throwing down the scalpel. It bounced once and rolled across the countertop in a flash of light. With a stomp of her feet, she kicked a gurney out of the way. It ricocheted against the wall, wheels spinning wildly like a broken shopping cart.

"Live and die as you please, Vitus."

She left me alone in the dark funeral home.

★

Niko was right; it was time I took care of myself.

I waited until night. Then I left the room, searching for signs of Owen. He had still not returned. Walking was difficult. All the joints were accounted for, many ligaments and tendons left intact, allowing me to move in herky-jerky motions. My fine motor skills were lacking, and I would never dance ballet. I took what I could get. I walked like a car without shocks.

I found a pile of my pus-smelling clothes by an incinerator. After a quick search I found my Glock buried inside. I emptied the weapon and broke it apart, examining it like a jeweler with a ring. Dirt in the barrel, faint smell of gun oil. It looked as pristine as the day I bought it so I put it back together, chambering a round. I fished a pack of cigarettes from the front pocket of the useless shirt left in the heap. I looked around the funeral home and half-started with a jump of fear when I met with the knight.

The empty armor struck me as even more sinister now. I leveled the firearm at the helmet, the black visor slit facing off with the hollow gun barrel. I imagined squeezing the trigger, the explosion of a bullet blowing shards of ancient metal apart. My finger bone pressed against the steel before stopping short. With a sigh, I let the gun fall away and set it behind the armor display. My intention was not to shoot, not yet. That would come later. For now I needed answers, not firearms.

I found a shovel in the closet by the door and I hesitated before leaving the building. The world was quiet in the darkness outside, but what would happen if someone saw me? A walking corpse was one thing, a skeleton walking around was a different animal entirely. Did that fall into the realm of indecent public exposure? Could I get ticketed for that? Corpse flesh is the sort of thing someone could explain away, could ignore, and people were adept at creating a hundred excuses to stretch reality back when I'd been sporting my gangrene chic. But a skeleton?

I pulled a cigarette from the pack and lit up with the butt clamped between my teeth. It didn't matter that the smoke wreathed up either side of my face without skin to hold it in. I flooded my lungs with bitter tobacco and, after a moment of deliberation, hoisted the shovel out the door with me and into the moonlight.

★

The family tombstones stood upright like doors in the light of the half moon. Cool coastal winds breathed in gusts over the land, brutal one second and calm the next. I could not feel the green grass against the bones that now made my feet; any onlooker would believe I was a skeleton ghost from an old folktale—stories they told in rural America about people who rose from the dead because they had unfinished business: lovers they never said goodbye to, wives they still wanted to be miserably married with, and stoves they had forgotten to turn off.

I, too, had unfinished business.

I thrust the shovel by the foot of the first grave: Clayton Adamson. The metal edge sank into the sod with gentle pressure, but the Jersey land was nothing but clay loam beneath, and underneath that, sugar sand. I smoked while I worked, long licks of cigarette fumes ringing my head as though I had risen from Hell itself, still singed from the visit. I inhaled deeply into my black and withered lungs, my teeth pressing into the butt with furious pressure.

It took hours. They don't dig graves by hand anymore; they hire a guy with a backhoe to rape the earth with noise and tearing. Not dignified, if you ask me, but little about our modern times has dignity anymore. Neither do I.

By the time I dug a hole hip-deep, the moon embedded a corona across the sky at a good pace. I finished my last cigarette with an hour's worth of digging to go, wondering how I was going to get a new pack of smokes in my condition. A mask? A hood? Perhaps I could scare a clerk into believing I was the Grim Reaper, and I would overlook his appointment with Death if he would keep me in good supply. As I pictured the scenario unfolding, I fell into the rhythm of my pumping skeleton arms until the shovel hit the lid of the casket, sending a shudder through my ulnar bones.

I stopped, setting the tool aside. The bone tips of my fingers trembled; I bowed down to touch the lid. The wood had rotted through and caved in on itself. I pulled away the intact slats, expecting to encounter a desiccated, rotted body beneath.

There was nothing.

I plunged my hands into the soil further. If there had been anything, any scraps left of my child, they were here no longer. Surely I had not eaten even his bones? I groaned, and suddenly my fingers met with hardness against rotted fabric. With a gasp, I pulled back my fist, my bony fingers closed around something, and opened them into the moonlight.

Dust.

Decayed, unrecognizable. The last evidence of the son I once had, a prophecy of my own future, once these bones could no longer hold together and time began to dismantle them at the molecular level. Was this my future, what awaited me? Is that what I was still living for?

I dismissed the mess and climbed out of the hole. Frustrated, I shoveled earth back in with long strokes of my skeleton arms, cursing under my breath.

Owen's likeness to myself was unbelievable, too unbelievable. From the blond roots of his hair to the coffee-mud of his eyes, what were the odds of such similarity? I barely had flesh left to offer for a paternity test, and I dared not alienate the boy by asking for a hair sample. Dust was hardly evidence of my dead little boy, but I refused to accept that Owen was my alternative.

Perhaps my suspicions were misplaced, and Owen was the genuine article. The dust in the child-sized casket six feet below me suggested it. Owen was ready to do anything for me, other than follow orders. How like me he was.

Suspicion continued to hound me. If Clayton survived the massacre, he would only be twelve years old today. Owen appeared to be eighteen, a man. The disparity could not be explained. I had been irrational, my foundations shaken in the basement when I finally confronted Jessica, withdrawing from the Atroxipine and surrounded with a hundred-fold images of little Clayton. I had allowed emotion to rule me, to sway my better judgment.

Here, in the cold graveyard surrounded by figures of stone I could reflect on my confused circumstances, my poor handling of the situation with Jessica. The only asset I truly possessed was my functioning mind, brain matter that refused to rot or decay, but transferred all my body's resources over to its smooth operation. My mind was the last great asset I possessed; it was time to use my strongest muscle.

Despite my fierce desire to penetrate the mystery, the answers would not come. In a rage, I threw the shovel and watched it roll away into the grass. I groaned and made bony fists of my hands. This is how it would be for the rest of my life—a barely functioning skeleton forced to roam the earth like a ghost.

Forever.

★

I found Niko coming in as the sun rose. I waited for her on the gurney as she swept through. She wore a long black coat fashioned after a nineteenth-century style. She looked like she stepped out of a Gothic music video, complete with sweaty rock stars and scantily clad extras. When she reached out to flick on the lights, carrying a scent of rose oil with her, I stopped her with my voice.

"Please—no lights."

Her arm fell away. Lips moist with gloss. She set her purse down on the counter and I remained seated on the gurney. She worked quickly, setting up the pump. The smell of formaldehyde permeated the air as the machinery whirred to life, and she put off the moment until she could do so no longer and reluctantly turned to face me for the first time.

"I wasn't sure if you'd be here," she spoke curtly.

I shrugged. Two knobs of bone lifted, then sagged.

She unwound the rubber tube, approaching my bones, and I lay back like a sedated animal while she pressed the tube into my viscera, winding through my rib cage, more slats of bone. The steady pulse of the machine began, pumping my heart in time. The sensation was like being tickled on the inside of my body. Drugs racing up the shreds of spinal tissue to circulate into my brain.

Suck. Thump. Suck. Thump.

"Niko," I said.

She looked up, waiting.

"When we're done with this dose, I need you to do something for me. It's the last thing I'll ever ask you to do, and you don't need to worry about me barging in on you in the middle of the night anymore. I want you to stay with Owen. He seems like a good kid."

Her mouth, pouty before, parted like a strawberry sliced in half—warm, red, ripe.

"Look at me, Niko. I've been limping through this life, and I don't know why. I thought it was noble, maybe, to keep on going when it would have been so much easier just to end it. A part of me didn't want to die. I was twenty when it happened. Is anyone ready to die at twenty?"

A silence spun out between us as I considered that, and then, taking a breath, I pushed on.

"I was young. I remembered being young, held it close to me. That kept me going, for a while. And then after the first couple of years, I forgot. I forgot what a heartbeat sounded like, or how to kiss, or those things that make life relevant, vital. After long enough, I'll forget everything all together, I imagine. I'll become like those zombies Jamie swears he'll never let me be.

"Look at me, Niko. Would you go on, like this? I barely have a body at all. Nothing but bones. I'm a shadow of a man. I want you to finish me, when the time is right. I'll be here, and promise me, when I say to do it, you'll do it. You'll take the scalpel and sever the spinal cord at the base of my skull—"

Unbelievably, she was crying. I didn't stop, even as I saw the wet tracks spill down her cheeks, wet mascara painting mouse feet at the dark corners of her eyes.

"—and when you're done, take the head and throw it in the incinerator. I don't want there to be any chances of coming back. Will you do that for me?"

She bit her lip, tasting salt tears across her wet lips. She remained mute, and I waited for her answer, not satisfied with silence. I needed her agreement.

"Do it, Niko. For me. Give me your word."

She gasped, like pulling a razor out of her skin, a sob shaking loose from her frame.

"Yes. If that's what you want, Vitus, I'll fucking kill you."

I tried to close my eyes, but then remembered there was nothing to close them with. How can one live like this? Forever staring, with no respite from the terrible images that we may look upon in one lifetime.

★

Empty.

I stared into the empty cigarette pack, white paper, crackling cellophane against my carpal bones. I could not acclimate to seeing my hands without flesh. Our identity is so much more than bones—skin and hair and blood and breath. Here I was without most of them.

And no cigarettes.

The final insult: I couldn't even smoke. I threw the empty pack, where it bounced against the baseboard wall. Bony fingers tapped frenetically against the counter.

Fuck that. I was going to have my cancer sticks.

I tapped my bony feet across the linoleum, to a pile of sheets on top of a gurney. Cursing, I attempted to untangle them from each other, pulling one out with questionable stains. I tried to sniff them, but without a nose, I failed miserably. Soldiers used to talk about the amputations, the persistent sensation of the limb even after the loss; but the feeling amplifies by the power of ten when you lose everything.

I wrapped the sheet around me as though I were a college boy at a frat party, putting on togas. Minus the alcohol and unnecessary hazing.

I left the room, the door slamming behind me. I would have my cigarettes, by God. I deserved a last meal before I died.

★

"Cigarettes, please."

Suburban areas always had an odd mix of teenagers desperate to be anything but suburban, aping the urban fashions of their favorite musical artist, or on the other extreme, desperate to align themselves with a southern country sensibility. This kid was the latter, wearing deer hunting camo over his flannel. He had a confederate flag on his belt, I noted with distaste. He could use a good scare.

The fluorescent lights were not doing me, or the kid, any favors. He was a ginger brat, with a ruddy, pocked complexion; the lights expanded my skull, enlarged it to titanic proportions. Every bone stood out in high relief, every craggy fracture, the deep, ivory lines where my teeth were embedded in my jawbone, the knobby sections of spine connecting from the back of my skull and all the way down like an eviscerated snake.

The kid had been reading a newspaper. At the first sight of me standing before his scratched and dirty counter, his hand clenched, tearing the paper with a snapping noise; a wad of tobacco he'd been nursing in his cheek came to a stop on the left side, frozen.

"You're a little young to be using chew, aren't you?" I asked. "And where are my cigarettes?"

He refused to move, staring. His eyes were vacant, which I suspect was no different from his usual expression, but in this case, they were vacant—so panicked he'd lost the ability to engage in logical thought. I suspected this was not a stretch for him.

I sighed and set a ten on the counter. The wadded bill sat on the surface like a curled worm and I leaned over to pluck a pack from behind the counter. The cellophane whispered between my bony fingers and filled me with a thrill of pleasure. Thank God for smokes. It was the only vice left to me. God took away everything else.

"Thanks, kid. Stop doing chew, that shit'll give you cancer."

A small shred of tobacco leaked from his open mouth, and he continued to stare after me as I left the shop. When I looked back, I saw him moving to the door to shift the sign from OPEN to CLOSED.

★

Back at the funeral home, I stood in front of the knight.

Picture, if you will, a collection of naked bones staring at an empty suit of armor. The visor a black, horizontal slit, a void evoking terror. The metal plates old and warped out of true; while they had been polished years ago, dust and particles had settled along the surface, giving it a mottled, stained appearance, blackened where metal met metal. I regarded it as nervous as a bridegroom on his wedding day, pacing the floor only to stop in front of it, contemplate it for a few moments, and then pace the floor anxiously again. The carpet in the lobby padded my bone-tapping feet, silencing my presence into a midnight hush.

It was down to me and the knight.

"There's only room for one of us," I muttered threateningly. A cigarette withdrawn from a pack, the hiss of the lighter against the tip, and I was inhaling fumes once more. My gaze never left the empty hollow of the helmet visor. Something about that emptiness shook me.

It's a metaphor, idiot. The knight is empty like you are.

Perhaps, I considered. I thought of the basement beneath the fortune teller's shop and Jessica within it. It was not difficult to recall those moments with her, when I had been oscillating between an animal self and a higher-functioning monster. I remembered my shadow-self, the Id Man, and my shuffling, pre-deceased corpse. All one, shattered person, a split consciousness.

Deep below the ground, Owen was descending to finish the job I had not been able to. I knew without being told and without having to ask that Owen should have been back by now. Would his better nature supersede him and cause him to fail at a critical moment? Did he have the courage to stare a child in the face and kill him if he had to? His fate could be determined by a wavering a gun, a missed target.

He could be dead already.

I considered all this with sober grimness.

I thought of the Id Man from the basement. But he was a part of me, wasn't he? The Id Man and I were one and the same, but he was buried deep inside my subconscious and sleeping now, pacified by Atroxipine.

Are you there?

Silence. I was alone inside myself, bones upon bones.

I could use your help right now, if you are.

In the silence, I sensed a rustling in the deep membranes of my gray matter and there was an answer. A snaking voice from a distant plane.

Rescue the kid, come back, and kiss it all goodbye, if dying makes you happy. But do it with a shred of conviction and integrity. You want the son you never had? Fuck the consequences and take it.

I bowed my head and the ember burned like a lodestone in the darkness and cast feeble light upon the armor itself. Up close,

I could see the armor was no reproduction; the metal was the real thing. Shoulder plates inlaid with swirling patterns and fine details. Exemplary craftsmanship that existed over hundreds of years but long forgotten in this new corrupt and modern age— along with the chivalry it once stood for, everything disposable and everything for sale and on credit, bought and sold and discarded like trash, people and objects alike.

Is this the world I belonged in, the one I wanted to continue living in?

No, I decided. My decision cemented, my certainty rigid and uncompromising. I flicked the cigarette away, extinguishing it with a grind of my bone-heel. "Not anymore," I whispered, and reached for the knight.

★

Niko made a habit of looking delicious; part of her charm was she didn't seem to know it—or she did and played upon it, turning perception to her advantage. Her hair gathered in generous black curls, except when she was working on a fresh corpse, and she would pull it up into a loose tie at the back of her head, letting raven-strands fall here and there. Her cheeks carved from the snowy mountain ranges of Nepal. Black clothes to frame her sapphire eyes as she strode through the front double doors and into the lobby and straight past the knight, trailing a sweet-smelling perfume through a path of putrid, acrid cigarette smoke. She never lost stride or even curled her nose, a veteran of unearthly gases and questionable aromas. If Pluto were embodied in a female form, Niko was its earthly manifestation.

"Niko," a voice called out.

She stopped and her fingers unclenched, nearly dropping her bag as she sank back into the shadows as though they offered her protection.

From the other side of the room, a man entered from a far door.

Taller and widened and filled with the weight of years. He looked down at Niko as he came around the circumference of the interior slowly, carrying with him an air of entitlement and bureaucracy. His face expressionless. His suit favored an appearance designed to be bland and bureaucratic, a brown number with the collar undone. His five o'clock shadow testified to unforgiving deadlines and his red-rimmed eyes suggested he had not slept in some time. Perhaps he had been a kinder-looking man in his younger days, but the years gave cruel edges to his face and made his aging body solid and immovable as a bull's. His hair was beginning to recede from the front.

"You didn't call," he accused her.

"I don't answer to you," she said.

"There was a time when you didn't answer to me, Niko. And it must be something you've gotten used to all these years, because we've never asked anything of you since you put Mrs. Adamson and Clayton Adamson in the ground. Your service doesn't end with a single job, Niko. You have not been released from duty. Do you understand?"

"I did my job. I prepare people for burial. I don't owe you a goddamn thing and you know it. You owe Vitus."

He sighed, annoyed. The slack flesh of his face shook with the clenching of his jaw and, with an angry spasm of his hands, he reached into an inner pocket to whip out a folded paper. It snapped in the air as he produced it and held it open for her to study the contents.

"Is that your signature, down here?" he asked, his voice terse as he tapped at the bottom with a finger.

"No one told me what I was signing. They said it was release form, that we couldn't talk about what we'd seen," she hissed.

"This appears to be a standard CIA recruitment form," he explained as might a bored professor, an unenthusiastic actor reciting a mediocre play. "This swears you to service when the country calls for it, to give us any information you might have on behalf of the United States government. Refusal to do so can result in undesirable repercussions."

She said nothing. He took a step forward and ceiling lights turned his face into the caricature of a skull with his eyes black sockets and the paper trembling in his hand. She took a step back until her spine met against the armor display. Metal plates jangling with the vibration.

I struggled to be motionless from inside the suit.

"There's nothing you can do to me that hasn't already been done," she seethed.

"Been to prison yet? Because I can assure you, we can do that. And if that doesn't terrify you, think of your family. It's not to suggest we would be so cruel as to hurt your family. We're not the mafia, after all. But nothing can compel us to continue to help and treat your ailing relatives on our good will if you refuse to do something for us in return. Is that so unreasonable?"

She said nothing. In that moment, she had the time to imagine any number of scenarios and with it the social shame attached to imprisonment, the loss of her job, her security, her home—and all of these could have been negotiable for the right reasons, but family, ah—how to justify and explain their increase in suffering? All this could be taken from her on the strength of a single piece of paper.

"It doesn't even have to be a federal prison, you know. We could pack you off to a Black Site. And all those high-end treatments at state of the art facilities your mother has been enjoying? All those prescriptions healing your loved ones, how do you think we developed those? If not pioneered off the largesse of Vitus's pain, than who? You owe Vitus. People all across this country owe him and may never know of it. But we can take it all away."

"I won't do it!"

"You *will* do it!" he yelled in return, and his booming voice filled the room and turned it into a thousand echoes that vibrated the plates of armor like strings of an instrument. "You will convince Vitus to do what is right, and this government authorizes you to use *whatever means necessary*. Make no mistake, Niko—I make every sacrifice required of me to repay the debt I owe to my brother. You make me out to be a monster, when all I have ever wanted to do is put an end to death, to stop this useless human suffering. With your help, it's not too late."

The silence spun out again, broken only by her ragged breathing.

"It will break his heart, Jamie," she whispered, her fist unfurling in a gesture of surrender.

"At least he will have one worth breaking, then," the man only responded, and with a flick of the paper, he disappeared it into his suit and faded away.

★

I held my breath as though I had one; the memory of lungs compelled me. I held and held, but I could hold my breath forever and I would not die, I would not expire; it is the humanity that lingers inside me, no matter how many times I try to drown it with a thousand cigarettes, with a thousand bullets and a thousand dead. It makes no difference. I held my breath like a man who has been stabbed and my ears boxed with Niko's words:

It will break his heart, Jamie.

And deep inside me, a raw and empty laughter from the other.

You're a fool, Vitus.

The silence stretched out long after she had left the lobby, turning down the sterile hall to her corpses on their gurneys, to tinker with their bones and flesh, to mold them into caricatures of living things for their viewings and their wakes. The silence lasted long after I knew Jamie was gone through the shadows and out the back door. I waited longer than reason to ponder this fresh agony I'd borne witness to.

I had no sooner managed to pull on the final plate of armor when I heard the lock turning in the door. Frozen, I allowed the drama to play out before me. At any moment, I could have put a stop to it, I could have cried out, made my presence known—and the desire had been there. To draw the sword. Pin Jamie against the wall. And was I really so surprised?

But who could I blame but myself? All I had to do was think about it; there had to be strings attached. The only reason Niko would have been allowed to see the bodies of my wife and child, to witness me there with Jamie, was because she had been taken into the ranks. Who knew better than I the dirty tricks of my father's meddling? I had time to wonder how much the hand of the old gray fox had been at work here. Counseling Jamie. Advising him. Whispering in his ear and pouring forth a multitude of poisons: *we can use him, Jamie, there's a lot of money in pharmaceuticals. Think of the people it would help. The diseases it would give relief to. Think of the money.*

And Jamie would have fallen into line as he always did. Obedient son. First for my father's love. Feeding me to the meat grinder for his approval. Perhaps Niko's greatest function for the government had been to provide a lie, both to me and to others who might ask too many questions about the dead soldiers they'd no doubt hired her to dispose of, to steer away uncomfortable questions about the remains.

They were old and dirty CIA tricks; I'd heard of it done through rumor and gossip but never met the proof of it. Popular on college campuses, the Central Intelligence Agency had been known to recruit students, persuade them into signing papers without realizing they were entering such dubious employment; once under the auspices of the CIA, they were little more than pawns, good for intelligence, but little else. It was my understanding that, as leverage, the CIA often threatened to "oust" the identities of the reluctantly recruited students, resulting in the claim that a portion of school suicides occur from the stress and fear of exposure as double agents.

And now, Niko was one of them.

Was he holding her hostage by threatening to expose her duplicity? Perhaps even by exposing her CIA status to me? What of her home, her people?

I chewed over the possibilities. Motive was the slippery issue—for what purpose was Jamie here, pulling Niko's strings? What was the end game? Was Owen involved as well? He was a helluva shot. Too good.

Had they hired him to kill me?

Now, that had a promising ring. It would be a lot easier to have Owen kill me than to have Jamie do it himself. Maybe I had used up my usefulness to Uncle Sam and the tab had been called due. The old gray fox bent before the firelight with a whiskey in one hand and a balance sheet in the other, and in that list of debits, crosses my name out. As simple as that. Jamie would arrange for someone else to kill me. For all I knew, Owen might be in the same boat as Niko.

Alone in the lobby at last, I stepped off the pedestal to the plush carpet. I plundered every conspiracy theory I could conjure from my head. The metal casing of the armor followed the command of my tired bones. I checked the firearm. The world reduced to a horizontal slit, and I missed the sensation of grinning, of a face that could express all that I was feeling inside, the tumult that electrified my neurons.

I didn't know why I hadn't thought of the armor sooner; it was like taking a Mustang for a ride. To think that I had feared the empty suit, registered sinister feeling in its presence. I had spent so long terrified of my unity with it, I had not stopped to think it could offer me something neither my rotting flesh or fragile bones could—restore strength where it had been stolen, integrity where it had been corrupted, and the opportunity, just maybe, to put things right. For once in my life, in the last hours I possessed it, I wanted to do the right thing—make this armor sing with purpose, absolve the blood of the crimes of the past.

"One way or another," I whispered, "I'm coming for you, Owen."

Jamie and Niko would have to wait. My son came first.

I turned on my heel and left, metal clanking emptily as I slammed the door closed behind me.

★

I boosted a car from the near-empty lot. An old Chevy Beretta. Aromatic with spilled beer and piss and cigarette burns dotting the fabric interior. The vehicle gurgled to life reluctantly. If knights were supposed to ride noble steeds, this was definitely not it.

You left the Thunderbird at Astra's fortune telling shop.

Gasoline hit the air as I turned the car onto the main drag. The visor cut down on my peripheral vision, but provided me with a soothing line of sight. Something about the metal structure of the armor gave comfort. Not quite as good as having skin and flesh and blood, but better than nothing but bare bones. I could at least not be reminded of my inhumanity by the unsettling sight of my skeletal structure as I went about my business. I wondered just how unnerving the experience was for Niko.

When I returned, I intended to put that all to rest; she wouldn't have to look at me or fix me anymore once I was out of the picture. We would all be better off for it. By taking myself off the chessboard, I could change the game in ways both dynamic and irrevocable. I imagined the old gray fox, gnashing his teeth and wailing—not in grief as a father for a son, but that I was no longer a useful pawn for his advancement.

Owen first, I reminded myself, and pressed the gas, burning rubber on the main road. The Glock remained in my shoulder holster, slung over the metal plates, while the shield lay against the tattered fabric car interior beside the sword. Fifteen bullets in the magazine, one chambered. Sixteen shots against a hundred kids are bad odds—and I hoped the sword would be sharp enough.

Call it a hunch, but I had a feeling the kids trapped in the basement weren't going to be singing show tunes and tap dancing on that stage by the time I got down there.

Ah, fatherhood, I thought grimly, and pressed on.

When I arrived at the shop, the moon was full and trekking across the sky with purpose. Niko would have noticed I had gone missing by now; I hoped and prayed Owen was still whole, still human. I had already decided that if he were not—if he had been turned, then I would do what Jamie should have done for me: I was going to kill him.

The shop was empty. Neon lights still advertised fortunes in brilliant, nightmarish color as I broke through the glass door with a metal fist. Glass flew and tinkled across the floor. Armor insulated the impact. Without the padding of flesh to protect my structure, I had to take into consideration how I moved and touched objects. Putting a bony fist through a window would have been out of the question before. The suit of armor changed everything.

I turned the knob from the inside and jerked open the door over the broken glass. Oddments and ornaments of crystals and tarot decks; pendulums and crystal balls shuddered on their shelves as I slammed the broken door behind me and marched toward the back. I took down the fabric strung from the corridors with a sweep of my armored hand. Jerked new age decorations from their supports and sent them cascading to the floor in reds, oranges, and burgundies.

I came to a stop in the stock room. A trace memory surfaced of Jessica leading me through these halls, through the black door, and down the steps to the waiting children. The moment sent a shiver through me and rattled me down to my metal. There would be no going through the door here; Owen had said they cemented it shut on the other side, and a brief attempt at breaking the lock and opening the door confirmed it. It budged half an inch inward, then stopped and could not be persuaded to move farther. I cursed, my breath icy against the underside of my metal helmet. I retreated to reassess my options.

Owen said he had used a ventilation shaft, and he had most likely used the same route to ferret us out when he rescued me and brought me back to the funeral home. I cast my eyes over the stock room. Empty boxes, dust bunnies waving in the faint wind. I watched their gray, frayed tendrils. Air flows close to here. I pulled at a set of industrial shelves, moving them away from the wall several inches. They scraped white lines across the dirty linoleum, squealing as empty boxes cascaded down, a set of tarot cards spilling across the floor. I stared at images of the Nine of Swords and the Knight of Wands exposed before me and, if it were possible, they inspired a deep unease, greater than the Death card itself. I dismissed them and continued until I was satisfied that I had enough clearance and stood back to examine what my efforts had uncovered.

A grate breathed air into the room from beyond the shelving and the covering to the ventilation shaft hung askew, marking the place Owen had used to penetrate the basement. I knelt before it, my metal knees scraping the concrete floor. This armor made enough racket to raise the dead—there was no way I was going to be able to quiet my approach. Owen had the advantage of soft material clothing, but in this suit, I was as clumsy as a zombie in a china shop.

A gap in the floor caught my eye. Half in and half out of the shadow of the shelves. I crawled closer and cut the distance until I was running a hand over the spot and then latching on with my fingers. The gap opened wide and gave way. A broken piece of concrete came away in my hand. I looked down into the hole in the ground and expected to see a secret chamber. A helpful flight of stairs to lead me to my destination.

Nothing in life goes so easy as that.

Instead, it was a cubby hole set into the floor that people had been traipsing across for years; Owen walked over it coming to and from this place without ever noticing that inside the deep and damp hole lay the curled and bound skeleton of a dead woman.

Beetles bred and reproduced in her old bones; shrouds of rotted fabric. I could make out the detail of the skeleton and the crack that spiderwebbed from the clean plane of her skull and illustrated how she ended up here. A blow to the head. Beside her skull, the glint of jewelry; silver baubles she had been lain to rest with and necklaces around her throat. One wrought in the shape of an astrological sign and I understood then, through the filaments of hair matted and tangled in the webs and used as nesting material for errant rats—this was the real Madam Astra.

Once upon a time, this had been a real functioning shop with a real functioning woman who told fortunes and believed in the fates. I saw the line of events with clarity—my wife in her tattered clothes, bloody with a set of my teeth marks—perhaps she hadn't turned yet. Did she come here for help? Saw the light on and came out of the darkness? And the real Madam Astra would have taken her in, served her tea and read her leaves and held her hand.

Right up until my wife turned and consumed the shopkeeper—dumping her in this place and then proceeding to consume and usurp everything else. The woman's identity and her place of business as an empty shell to shelter her while she began to build her empire.

I cursed and dropped the concrete square back into place. I regretted having discovered it and I sighed and resigned myself. This unknown grave must remain unknown for now. Forget all this, I told myself. There is more yet to do.

I withdrew the gun, confirmed that my sword remained in my scabbard. I was ready.

Zzzzt.

A lone fly crawled from between the grate slats, black body dull marcasite in the half-light. It took off, flying lazily into the stuffy, moldy air, and I jerked the grate from the wall, exposing the opening and letting it clatter overtop the hidden corpse in the floor.

"I'm coming, Owen," I whispered.

★

Moving silently was not an option.

The ventilation shaft was large enough to accommodate my size and width, and now that I was reduced to bones and metal plates, I was lighter than I had ever been in life; Owen was wiry and thin, allowing him to pass through the shaft with relative ease. There was no fear of falling through, but I sounded like a big brass band as I advanced, metal plates knocking against sheet metal.

When I was still alive, and even in death, I loved movie theaters. I loved being enveloped in the kind darkness, waiting for the screen to explode into color and light and reveal moving pictures of impossible fantasies, unrequited love, and bitter revenge. But in all the time I'd spent in movie theaters, never once have I seen a movie that showed me a dirty ventilation shaft.

In any spy movie where the hero risks his life to sneak his way into a fortified building, the ventilation shafts are clean and slick and sterile as ice; you can catch your own reflection in their smooth finish. The reality poses unexpected difficulties like dust and mouse turds and black mold.

I scoured clean trails behind me on the surface as I moved, angling my way through a stuffy, claustrophobic descent. I pushed irritated brown recluses and wood spiders ahead of me and cleared out their nests like a whale through a sewage pipe.

Puffs of particulate grit rose and swirled in my path. I felt packed into a vacuum bag, knocking and cursing all the way down and scrambling for purchase where the duct work graded too steeply. I could do nothing but slide down. At last, my metal plated feet hit an ornate grate at the bottom and, with vigorous kicking, I was rewarded with a clatter and then empty space beyond.

I squirmed through the opening to fall out onto the floor. Alone in the long, damp hallway, I froze in the darkness, convinced someone must have heard my raucous passage and were laying low, waiting to press their advantage. All my senses, dulled and damped as they were, strained for signs of life. I longed to call out Owen's name, but the words sputtered and extinguished. Cold concrete discouraged sound with the haunted austerity of a church—cold, impenetrable, and vastly unforgiving.

My eyes adjusted to the light, seeking forms and shapes through the narrow visor, passing over the dirty floor. In moments, I recognized the doors of the living quarters, where a young boy had shown me my room, and I had showed him my gun, coaxing information from him. The moment passed from me like old reels of a silent film, lost in time.

The orderly cleanliness of that hallway was gone. Doors once closed when I had first been ushered through the compound now stood open, and some hung askew from their hinges. Claw marks at the doorknobs and indentations in the wood. What few belongings the children had been allowed to have were flung every which way. Picture frames shattered and glass glistened like snow. Bed sheets and red robes strewn in tatters of fabric, blood stained, dirty, and in shreds. The scene filled the onlooker with a deep disquiet that the firearm in my hand could not dispel.

The silence was absolute.

I forged on, down the hallway. Beyond the furthest door was the main entrance leading to the altar room and the feast where

I had met my hundred children. Where were they now? Beyond the door? Were they little more than animated corpses, waiting for the benediction of my bullet?

I listened. No tell tale shuffling, no quiet shambling, no drooling zombie-gurgles from beyond.

I paused. I inhaled and closed my metal, armored hand over the doorknob. My fingers clicked with reptilian sound.

I opened the door.

★

Death lived in this room. I should know; we are well acquainted.

With the weapon drawn and steady, ready to aim and take fire, I let the firearm fall to my side, still clutched in my hand and the armor grating against bone. The dull black plastic barrel against stained metal plates.

I recognized the stage I once stood upon and stared at an ocean of children, all Clayton Adamson look-alikes; a slumped corpse lay upon the wooden boards now, as though the figure were only sleeping, waiting to arise and shamble to its feet. No sound, no movement, only silence prevailed. I approached the stage, my visor eye-level with the raised floor.

"Jessica," I whispered.

A pyramid of bones lay crumpled in the center with strands of blond hair clinging to the gypsy garb; if I had hoped to finish her off, I'd arrived too late. Nothing but bones remained. Her skull fractured by a shotgun blast. I studied the shards of her bone fragments and wondered how we began from those backseats in a cheap car on a high school night and called it love; all the way to this very moment.

I bowed my head and moved on.

Below the stage, amidst overturned chairs and broken tables, were the children. Their corpses could only have been dead for a day or so, though I had been gone longer than that while convalescing under Niko's care. Their bodies were emaciated, wrapped still in their religious robes, like monks fallen in combat; slumped here and there, some lay on top of the others, some by themselves. Their arrangement gave no clue to their demise. If they had been running, if something pursued them, if they had been afflicted by Virus X, there was no evidence of it. I expected zombies, and there were none; only dead bodies.

A hush remained, as though I had stepped into a desert landscape. Emboldened, I yelled.

"Owen!"

The silence persisted. I half-expected a corpse to stir and for them to arise as one and confirm my worst fears; to descend upon me with their gnashing teeth, to feed on . . . my bones. To crack me open and extract my marrow. After that, all that would be left was my soul, and surely there was hardly enough there to make a meal.

There was no sign of Owen. Through the helmet, I was desperate to pick out his form among the small children shapes but there was nothing. My horror at this carnage made it difficult to define my feelings—was I relieved *not* to see Owen here? Or did I dread that he met with a fate worse than the peaceful slumber these dead children enjoyed? Was I disappointed?

In an instant, they all seemed *my* children, children I should have been able to save. I was their father, and just like my son, I failed them each in their turn.

I cast my gaze down to my feet. Thought about that uncomfortable sensation of shame, of failure, of bitterness. A sensation that extended beyond flesh and deep scarlet blushes and downcast eyes.

I turned and left.

★

Down the hall I went.

I sought the far room of my final memories with Jessica where I had confronted my own Id; where Jessica feasted while I wrestled with myself to awaken and fall asleep all at once. I could not imagine there were any other places left in this wretched basement to search though and my steps quickened as I opened the first door into the chamber and then arrived at the last one.

The memory of Jessica was still fresh, vivid. The leash she pulled me along with, the dank cellar smells permeating every room and hall. The door loomed ahead and I set my hand to the knob to throw the lock.

"Owen," I called out, and opened it wide.

"Vitus!"

I stopped, my armored hand still extended over the knob; his voice resounding with every burning feeling in my heart to discover him still alive as the door yawned open. Yet, his voice projected from behind me just as the buzzing sound hit the air like a bass turned all the way up on a sound system and stitched out the rhythm of a pulse, insistent, angry, hungry. Caught between one motion and the other, I pirouetted on one heel so I stretched over the threshold to look behind me.

Owen materialized from blades of dark and shadow with his hand snaking out into the light for me. At first, I thought he was happy to see me, his hand open to touch me, to reaffirm our growing familial bond with an embrace. My skeletal teeth mimicked a smile of delight. Alive! Relief flooded through me to see him unhurt and whole, to acknowledge the healthy glow of his youth, his aching vitality of which I could never share.

I let go of the door.

His face twisted, like a rag between two fists. As much as he may have loved me, his cry had not been to greet me—it had been to warn me.

"Don't open the door!"

I turned back. Metal feet scraped the concrete in frantic response. Owen snapped out his firearm, cocked and ready. I lifted my weapon in pantomime of Owen's dark shadow, turning to face the blackness beyond.

ZZZZZZZZZZTTTTTTTTTTTT

★

Darkness.

Darkness defined by our desperate and fruitless searching, our attempts to make out shapes in the blackness. Side by side with

Owen, we peered into darkness, darkness buzzing and vibrating and trembling on a multiplicity of wings. A textured darkness.

A darkness stared back.

Flies.

Flies so thick they formed a dark swirling mass in the center of the concrete cell, blotting out the center bulb as an eclipse. The mass of flies formed like smoke and a shifting black cloud that moved as a living tornado with a gale force surge of howling wind. I registered the steady hum of their wings. So many of them occupying one space forced their notes to resonate with one another, deepening and expanding the sound. Owen's face became a flat sheet of paper smoothed of expression and color. The bulb chain in the center swayed with the force of the insects.

I lifted the Glock; the threat was implied, but what did I fire at? A million targets smaller than a penny? I had expected to be forced to kill a hundred monster children. With sixteen bullets, that goal had seemed absurd; now we had left absurd long ago and crossed over into the realm of surreal.

The fly mass hovered, buzzed, swirled, so thick they cast a shadow on the floor. I had never seen flies congregate in such a manner, as though they were all sharing a single purpose, a driving ambition without deviation of want or desire.

In the gust of sucking pressure with the opening of the door, the humming of their ceaseless wings dropped a note and changed direction. Each individual fly turned in symphony and the frenzy of their wings increased in pace as they faced us. The sensation of unnatural fear grew acute, and with it their focus, like a thousand lasers concentrated upon us as one; the Glock trembled, knocked against my metal hand in a senseless ticking.

Shooting was a foregone conclusion, and I did it anyway, as one whose panic trumps all reason into senseless action. I fired a single round into the black mass. My wrist snapped with recoil and I moved to stand in front of Owen. Heedless of his line of fire. The boy could save his bullets for when he truly needed them; for now, I was going to serve as his human shield.

The reaction was immediate. As though I had thrown a rock into a still lake, the bullet disappeared into the blackness as the seething flies absorbed it wholly and formed a great black mouth that rippled in response. The rhythm of their beating wings downshifted into a deeper tonal note.

Their queasy calm provided a prelude to the storm—in the next instant, they shattered apart.

A collapsing tornado deconstructed the dark column of their mass and suddenly flowed through the opened door in a mist of hairy bodies and beating wings. Their velocity was directed with purpose and undisturbed by our presence as they emptied out of the room. Owen's throat emitted a dry swallow, an audible click. I had not realized he had grabbed my arm and pushed me to the door to stand aside from the swarm while the last of a million flies seeped from the basement room.

"You shouldn't have done that," he whispered.

I cast a glance back down the hall where the flies had disappeared. "What is it?" I demanded.

"They're alive."

"Yes, I get that."

"No, I mean . . . they're single consciousness."

"Run that by me again?" I asked.

Perhaps the helmet was muffling my reason. I strained to hear his words, as though I could comprehend them better with the addition of volume.

He swallowed, his skin waxen under the feeble light. The lightbulb in the room swung emptily with the breeze of the passing horde. Each detail crowded in on me to impart a feeling of unreality too intense to be anything but real. I would parse these details later to fill my nightmares with the stained concrete and the howling noise of the swarm and marry each horror to my father's voice reading the words of Julius Caesar in my youth.

"I don't understand why—"

"Help me understand why, then!" I yelled, overwhelmed with a blind urgency. We needed to get out of here. I cast my gaze back in the direction where the flies had gone. I had no reason to believe that something worse wasn't building outside these doors and lying in wait for us every second we continued to debate our circumstances. This ominous lull was the world about to turn sideways.

"Her consciousness," he whispered. "It's *hers*. Look, there's theories that every cell has consciousness. Things like deep quantum chemistry having to do with quantum fields that give these cells a kind of consciousness. Maybe not identity, like you or I have identity . . . but just stick with me on this, okay?"

I made an impatient motion for him to hurry up and get to the punchline. He stared at the armor, his brow furrowed in confusion as he noticed it for the first time.

"Does it *look* like we have time to discuss my fashion choices? We'll talk about the armor later," I snapped. "Get to your point, boy."

"Look, if Jessica's cells have individual consciousness, just like all of ours are supposed to, that basic DNA that makes us uniquely us . . ."

"Yes?"

"All the maggots she kept inside her, that ate her . . . ."

He trailed off and looked aside, as though he could not meet my gaze. An awkwardness in his affect that inverted my thoughts until it seemed the room rocked and rollicked about me. I reached out to hold the wall to stop my relentless sway to and fro. Implications flooded in fast, one upon the other, until I was punch drunk.

The maggots from before had fed and slumbered in the basement depths. While I came to as a pile of bones on Niko's gurney, they awoke and sighed with the magical work of transformation from worm to imago to winged thing. They emerged sleek and new and hungry. Black and buzzing with the flavor of my wife wound through them.

They were all a part of . . . Jessica. Parts of her brain, her heart, her lungs, her flesh, all of the soft tissues that made my wife. Every little part of her amplified by the effects of the pre-deceased plague. If I had chopped her into little bits and buried her in a thousand boxes, she would still be alive, still trying to feed, even if all that was left of her was a finger. Even that would still claw for freedom, would remain hungry for flesh.

In this case, she'd been eaten into little bits and buried in a thousand flies.

Maybe more than a thousand flies. Maybe a million. All imbued and possessed with her force, her energy, her desire to feed and destroy. Zombie flies.

"But they're just house flies? I suppose that's a blessing. They can't bite and infect unless they lay larvae in dead tissue. Sweet Jesus," I wheezed out.

"He's not back, too, is he?"

I stared at Owen. His face was stern, leaving me to wonder if he was clever enough to be so deadpan.

"You'll be praying that he is by the time we're finished," I snapped.

★

I told Owen that I had a plan. My plan was to use my best talent: lie to Owen about having a plan. He took strength from it, and emboldened by my fearless-leader posturing, I told him to follow me and we began down the hallway.

My metal plated feet tapped along the concrete ground; in contrast, Owen brought with him a reassuring silence with an eye askew on the corridor behind us, his Mossberg at the ready. The sort of shotgun that puts holes in things at a 360-degree angle.

The corridor narrowed to the altar room ahead, the one I passed through only minutes ago. A knife's edge of weak light spilled through and cast more shadows than it dispelled.

I thought I had closed that door behind me when I passed through; I motioned for Owen to stop with a gauntlet fist raised in the air. Owen's footsteps halted behind me. I sensed his questions, his concerns, his building anxiety bubbling beneath his calm.

The door creaked in the draft.

Human nature desires flight in panic, often at the moment when it stands to help you the least. What I felt in the space of that silence was hard to define. I was so removed from humanity, reduced to nothing but bones, a human coat hanger for a suit of armor, that it was hard to express without taut muscle, sweating skin, heaving flesh, the taste and shape of my fear. Even without all the trappings of solid flesh, left with only my decayed eyes and my grinding teeth and the ghost of an infrastructure, the sensation of being observed and expected intensified.

I drew my gun. Owen's motions echoed behind me, dark with purpose.

I took a breath and led us through the inviting door.

★

Before, when I had first begun the long journey through the dark halls, through the destruction of the altar room, there had been nothing but bodies thrown about like dolls knocked from a display case, in different poses and wretched faces as they died and breathed their last on the stone floor. At first glance, it was impossible to say what had killed them.

Perhaps Jessica, sensing the end at hand, had poisoned them. Their communal feasting setup made distribution easy. The children had never had a chance—the end destination had always been this point in time, this pitiful destiny. They'd had a brief stay of execution from the moment Jessica had snatched them from the streets and raised them in her perverse network of Rogers followers, but after I'd left, the moment of truth had arrived. My coming heralded their personal End Times.

My greatest fear had been that the children would be infected; but in a strange moment of conscience, Jessica had refused to expose her surrogate children to the same disease that had destroyed her real child. I had to give her that much respect—she died a monster, but she had refused to make another in her place. There were no zombie children here.

Imagine our surprise then as we stood in the doorway and, one by one, each prostrate child on the floor slowly rose to his feet.

★

They were not alive.

"Vitus?" Owen whispered.

All over the room, the sounds of broken chairs being cast aside as bodies struggled to stand, groping for objects to assist them, filled the air, groans and whispering fabric, hands clenching and pulling at each other like children in the midst of delayed tantrums.

"Their eyes are empty, Vitus," Owen hissed, and I could hear the hysteria creeping into his voice as he bit panic back into his mouth and swallowed it down. "They're not zombies."

"They look like zombies."

"Flies infest and consume. They're inside their skin, Vitus! They're eaten-through with her!"

In an instant, I turned on him with the Glock in my hand, using the other to thrust against his chest and send him flying backward, Mossberg and all, back through the door and into the hall.

I couldn't allow him to risk himself.

"Vitus!"

I ignored him, slamming the door in his face and jamming the lock as he struggled to gain entrance. He pounded on the door with force until the wood shuddered, as though inhaling and exhaling beneath his fury. His muffled voice called my name and, as much as I regretted to leave him there, I turned back to face the room

"I can't talk right now, Owen. I've got to kill my children."

Sluggishly, they were still trying to find their feet. Their eyes remained empty and half-lidded, eaten through by maggots and decomposition; they trailed stains on the floor where their bodies had sat and marinated in the damp, leaking fluids onto the concrete and fermenting there. Fingers groped at the air and where there was no furniture they used each other to climb up, leaning against each other's bodies, dragging their red, stained robes along the floor. They were not zombies; their behavior was not so well-defined. They were a new breed of monster riddled through with maggot and worm and the howling grief of a woman scorned.

No sooner did I think it when their mouths opened, one by one, like blood flowers bursting in bloom, and from their open throats—

ZZZZZZZZZTTTTTTT

The buzzing persisted in a bone-deep electric hum, shaking down through my cartilage and every vertebrae that made my spine behind the metal. Blackness glimmered behind their lips. A thousand flies animating their shambling corpses and pulling at their strings like marionettes.

I assessed the situation in seconds, too busy with the business of murder to waste time on fear, on panic, on questions of right and wrong. In the back of my mind, the protests of my higher-functioning self became a gigahertz din—the part of me that cared about children, about desecrating the bodies, their most unholy murders. I did not think, however, that the flies would care so much about my tender sensibilities. Their intent was clear, in their open mouths, their bared teeth—

Kill Vitus.

And they had every intention of turning my bones to dust, armed only with child-size molars and incisors.

They outnumbered me by a hundred to one—all that stood between me and their outstretched hands was my suit of armor, a Glock, and a sword.

I dashed across the floor. Metal clanging as I rushed the stage at the center of the room. All the children turned in unison, their hair stained with droplets of congealed blood, to track me with needy clenchings and their outstretched hands like urchins begging for food. The humming reverberated from deep inside them where the flies frothed and foamed and worked through them with the force of an F5 twister.

"Oh Jessica, I never meant to hurt you so," I whispered as I turned to face the horde that threatened to close in on me from all sides. Indeed, the crystallization of her hate, her wounds distilled into one frozen moment of time I alone was responsible for, carried her forth even through the consciousness of a fly, never letting go, never giving up. A tenacity to be admired; a tragedy to be mourned; a consummation devoutly to be wished.

The humming increased in volume. How could I appeal to her consciousness, locked in the bodies of a thousand and one flies? If I spoke, might she hear me?

"Jessica," I called out.

The bodies, shambling from the outer reaches of the room toward the stage center, paused. The name registered, but then dismissed and fell out of memory as they continued forward with their greedy, open mouths full of writhing flies that nestled and ate at their tongues.

"Jessica, I'm sorry," I said.

Has there ever been so hated a word in the universe as *sorry*? What could sorry buy me now but time enough to regret that I ever been born, ever loved her, ever stood by her side, and at least, ever betrayed her?

The words had no effect.

"Fuck it," I hissed, and started firing.

★

One had managed to crawl onto the stage, pulling himself up with his raw fingers, the tips bloody and oozing pus as he wrenched his way to the surface. I kicked him back with an armored foot and he reeled in a flurry of awkward pinwheels as though he could gain purchase from the air itself. Metal jangled against my bones, from my toe to my spine, causing my breath to explode in a shudder. Flies ejected from his mouth, escaping their host and reforming with energy, searching for the next one.

A round fired, the gun disposing of an enterprising young undead lad who found the stairs and trudged up them, only to stumble back down, his head blowing out the back in a mass of brain matter and bug guts. Black flies swirled out of the starfish hole like cigarette smoke, ejecting from his body and seeking a haven in one of the other puppets, climbing greedily through their ears, their nostrils, licking at their eyes, maggots writhing in their flesh.

"Too many," I gasped, pushing against a child's chest with the muzzle of the gun. He had attempted to sneak up on me from my blind spot, where the horizontal slit failed to reveal the periphery, and he nearly made it before the sound of a footstep squelching blood alerted me. He fell off the edge of the stage with a disconsolate wail. I closed my eyes for a split second, processing a shudder of revulsion.

I would do whatever I had to do—though they were monsters, they were monsters in the bodies of children. Each blow, each gunshot, each strike was accompanied by a sympathetic pain response for flesh I no longer had, and a blind desire to comfort the children who had not brought this on themselves.

"They aren't children anymore," I said aloud between gritted teeth, and fired into the seething crowd forming below. Moments ago they had been scattered all across the room, but they were congregating quickly, swarming like their counterparts with one focus: tear me to shreds at any cost. I was their sole target, explaining why Owen was still intact after all this time here. As surrogate child, he was not the focus of their rage; he was but a misguided lost boy.

I felled one. The body collapsed with a slaughterhouse floor thump, opening the space up for his companion who trampled over him without hesitation, breaking bones with his eager steps. He opened his mouth, squirming with white larvae. Hair spiked and matted with blood. One open hand seized the air where he wanted me to be. I lifted the gun and squeezed the trigger.

Nothing happened.

I'd been waiting for this moment.

The Glock displayed the empty chamber, like a dealer at a casino holding his hands out. No luck there. I hooked the muzzle into my holster, because unlike in the movies, weapons are expensive. You don't just throw them away when you run out.

I unsheathed the sword.

★

I'll admit to a certain, boyish satisfaction in that moment alone. Amid the sound of their seething hatred, their churning saliva running down their jagged teeth and eye-fucking me with red-rimmed intensity, the metal divided the air and cut through the growling murmur.

Even the constant, maddening *buzzzzz* of the flies diminished for a split second before resonating once more with furious purpose. I felt the weight of the hilt, wrapping my hands around it the same way I would a gun, heel of my palm on the bottom, my guiding hand toward the top. I didn't know how to work this weapon, but I was ready for my on-the-job training.

I swept with a wide arc outward, kneeling so I could come in low enough to take the heads of the first two gathered at the lip of the stage. A wet separation of flesh and blood. The sword jangled against their spinal columns for an instant before slicing cleanly through the joints, exploding synovial fluid and cartilage in its passage. Their bodies fell like empty clothes and suddenly deflated and, without force, were reduced to broken dolls with the menace rooted out and cast aside from them.

Through their red-rimmed wounds the flies found egress, rose up into the air like frenzied smoke and flitted into the next host, through nostrils, mouth, and ears, crowding their faces until they were absorbed through their openings and left only the buzzing sound, the occasional flickering of their wings through their mouths.

Killing the children was one thing. How was I going to kill the flies?

★

Math class was in session.

I subtracted their numbers, graduating them to six feet under. I felled them like a lumberjack, heaving with each massive stroke of the sword. My bones trembled with the weight. I registered the breaking of my left hand when I struck a rib, the blade bouncing back into the air with rejection. The break echoed through the rest of my body, grinding against their defunct parts. Small pieces of bones escaped the main fracture like grains of sand inside a wet suit; they ground against the metal of the armor and fell into the main carriage to sprinkle across my ribs.

I cursed, my left hand falling useless. The tip of the sword fell to the stage and I struggled to lift it one-handed, where it wavered uncertainly in the hot, stinking air. I did not have the weight and the mass of a human man to drive the blows. Without my other hand to help guide and force the strike of the sword, it had all the utility of a butter knife. I could only swat at them, like . . . flies.

I backed away from the stage. Their vacant and ventilated eyes rested on the lowered sword and this sign of weakness reinforced their ambition. They surged forward, like fans at a concert where I was the main event, struggling to pull themselves to the top. Their brothers behind them helped to force them up so they could get their chance. I had reduced their numbers to half. It wasn't enough, I realized. They were going to have me.

Their bloody hands wavered in the air, overcoming the stage itself and standing upon the wooden boards. Remnants of the stage curtain rippled as they stumbled against the fabric, pulling at the old velvet and shredding it. They trailed their crimson robes behind them like pools of blood, the buzzing behind their eyes, in their flesh. I imagined that if I touched them, they would vibrate beneath my fingers like an engine beneath a car hood, powered by turbo-charged flies.

I backed farther away before their onslaught but I was running out of stage. I brandished the sword once more, hoping to buy myself an out, buy a little more time, buy a second chance, anything, please . . .

"Vitus!"

Through the narrow slit of the visor and the darkness of the altar room, I saw Owen. He'd found access through a side door, giving up on the main entrance once he knew I would never open it.

"Fucking kids," I snorted.

He stopped several feet in, staring open-mouthed at the seething horde. He did not take long to recover before reaching into his pockets like a man who could not recall where he kept his car keys, just at the moment he needed them the most. The expression on his face was near comical in its urgency.

"Get out of here!" I yelled. "Go, dammit!"

I turned away from him. I had nowhere left to run, and the kid closest to me had opened his mouth to reveal a great, black scribble of buzzing flies that oozed along his tongue. One nestled in the bone of his molar, tasting the tooth there with eagerness.

He hoped to taste me there, as well. He snapped his teeth and licked his fly swollen lips in anticipation.

"Vitus!" he cried again.

This time, instead of his first greeting call, there was a note of command, of urgency the first had lacked. Reluctantly, I turned away from the first several children who were closing the distance with their shuffling gait, mopping up blood and dust as they came. I did not even waste the time to reprimand Owen for the distraction. I hoped whatever he needed my attention for was well worth it.

A taser appeared in his hand. He met my gaze with fierce acknowledgment and lobbed it into the air in one great, underhand stroke, his mouth a thin line, his jaw set and his teeth grinding. He looked as I imagined my son might, the way I'd pictured days on a high school field, playing sports with his teammates or taking him camping. The sort of things I would have done with him if I could, the sort of things I wanted to carry on . . .

And it's not too late.

I raised my hand into the air, whistling a breath through my teeth. I felt a child's hand strike at my armor, hands against my back, weaving spidery fingers into the metal to tear the plates apart and get to the bones inside. In the next second, metal jangled up my arm with the connection of the taser against my leather palm plates, knocking against my skeleton.

I opened my fingers in disbelief and whirled on my heel to face the horde. They stumbled back and laughter issued from my mouth in long peals. I had lost my reason, my sense; had I lost it at the sight of Owen, at all those years of subdued desire for family and home and meaning, galvanizing me? Infected with the excitement of second chances? I rounded on the closest snot-nosed, fly-humming brat in my circle.

"Science class, children," I croaked.

I slapped the sword against his shoulder in an ineffectual blow, but the desire was not to stab or slice or dispel. The child snarled, a single angry fly dipping out of his mouth before entering again, and he reached for the tip with a child-chubby hand lacerated along the knuckles. He gripped the blade without feeling, while his hungry companions pushed up against him, extending their hands outward toward me.

I pushed the slotted nose of the taser gun against the blade of the sword and zapped it.

I cried out. Everything inside me seized as though a great fist had crushed me, then released me again. Somewhere in the guts and viscera of my rib cage, a remnant of my old heart remained, and it beat weakly against the electrical pulse, awakened before dying again. It was like having a star bloom inside your chest and then wink back into void.

I shook my head, dazed; electricity flowing back from the taser through every plate of metal that lined my arms, my legs, my chest, and my body, down through the sword, into the children beyond. They likewise struggled with it; but they were more parts flesh than I was. This was a force I had the power to withstand, but the children were not alive. They were puppets maneuvered by flies—and their small, black bodies could not suffer such a blow of energy without dire consequence.

The electricity jumped the sword and ate into the skin of the first child, and each one behind that one was linked by a touch to another, and his fellow in turn was touching another, and that one another, and so on. Blue veins of electrical fire encircled and then disappeared into their clothes, absorbed into their flesh while the sword vibrated and hummed with the energy.

And suddenly, the buzzing dimmed.

*ZZZZZZZZZZZZZZZ*zzzzzzzzzztttt.

The first child collapsed, weak muscles and red robes twitching to the floor, breaking the contact with his fellows. From his open mouth, dead flies rolled out like round beads of onyx, a broken necklace shattered apart into a thousand pieces and scattered over concrete.

There it is, I realized. *The last remains of Jessica. The last of her will, her love, her all-consuming suffering.*

The next child that had been linked to him fell to the floor, dragging another with him. Flies tumbled from their open mouths, their nostrils, and their ears, as though they were filled to overflowing with them, their dead bodies resting at last without the living insects to animate them. Children shambled behind them who had not been in contact with the electrical current, mindless and purpose-driven. I wondered if they could feel or sense their diminished numbers, that the divided soul of Jessica Adamson, carried in every fly, was dying by the thousands.

I lifted the sword again. My left hand flopped uselessly. I forced it up with a grunt, taser in hand, and held the sword tip out for the first eager child to lay his hand on it and clutch it with a straining fist, slicing skin against metal, before I lifted the taser and applied the shock.

I cried out again. My heart beat once, then fell dead. Leftover embalming fluid spurted from my vena cava like a disconnected garden hose with the water pressure cut; the muscle remembered ancient things, things like flesh and skin and capillaries and veins, things I no longer possessed but had been stolen from me, eaten away into a thousand small insects.

Some of those maggots ate you, *Vitus. Those flies are more than Jessica.* They are you.

I paused at the thought, waiting for the next line of children to advance upon me, stepping over the bodies of their comrades, trampling on their delicate toes, their fingers, even their faces. They looked like cherubs sent to sleep in the poor light, flies toppling and tumbling from their lips alongside maggots.

Perhaps my enemy had never been Jessica.

With each fly electrocuted and sent off to meet its maker, I was destroying a thousand pieces of myself animated in a thousand insects. After all—had Jessica truly hated me? Disappointed in me, rejected by me—but in all that time, she had only ever loved me, wanted me to stay by her side.

No one hated me as much as I did.

I cried out, a desperate wail from my blackened lungs. The sound shuddered the armor like chimes, plates vibrated against each other, and I waded into the fray with renewed energy, advancing on the last strand of children left. I was brutal in my purpose, connecting the sword to a child's cheek and lighting up his face with an explosion of blue electricity. Patterns jumped through the metal and into his flesh. For an instant, his eyes lit up with blue flame, and then turned dark again.

I killed the last of my children, the final humming *buzzzz* silenced in the altar room. They lay like spent roses in their red robes, the odd remnants of a strange cult, one that would never be found. These were all someone else's sons, someone else's children kidnapped and taken away. For a short time, Jessica had loved them in her damaged way, before poisoning them in the underground chamber. At least they did not live long enough to experience the indignity of their parasitic violation and, with resignation, I breathed out a small sound of regret. The sword tip hovered over the ground, the taser limp and useless at my side.

"Vitus."

I did not turn around. His voice was overwhelming in the silence. I had not realized how constant the hum had been, how it had filled and obscured every soft and quiet space. The emptiness that followed was like the silence in space.

"Let's get out of here. It's over. I've got lighter fluid. Get on your way and I'll follow. I'm going to raze this place. No one can ever know what happened here."

I thought about telling him about the flies. That Jessica was the force that animated them, that delivered this terrible onslaught; but it had also been me all along.

"Jessica—" I began.

"There was nothing left," he answered. "I found her skeleton."

There was a rustling of fabric, and his hand tapped a cylindrical object against my shoulder plate, a metallic *ting!*

I reached up and took it with clumsy fingers. The wedding ring suspended in my orange prescription bottle.

"Oh," I said simply. I turned and brushed past him, heading back for the ventilation shaft.

Zzzt.

I felt the hairy body, heard the buzz of the wings brush past my ear. In a second, my fingers closed over the fly. It beat itself against my bony fingers. Easy enough to kill it, but I hesitated. I have known many men given to destroying anything and everything in their path, but I have always hesitated for the lowly spider, the ugly beetle; it was the persistent feeling that this fly would be the last of its kind, the last to escape from this place. I pondered that, and with a grunt, I emptied the bottle of my wedding ring and shoved the fly into it, where it buzzed in outrage at its new captivity. A fraction of both myself and Jessica, in the body of a fly.

Before I left, I threw the ring into the shadows, where it bounced into concrete darkness, and then into nothingness.

★

Owen and I traveled back in silence.

The sun broke over the gray skyline, bursting into a half-light dawn known as the "blue hour," coaxing indigo shades from every shadow, bathing us in impressionist light. I watched the passing scenery through the slit in the metal, protected and enveloped in the elemental coldness of the armor. Pavement disappeared beneath us in a winding line of yellow, white, and black, comforting in its familiarity.

Owen smelled like lighter fluid and smoke. I smelled like metal, lead, and burnt blood. He had cast a final coating of accelerant over the toppled bodies of the children and the scattered flies before lighting a match and setting it ablaze. He made sure it was roaring before he headed to the ventilation shaft, and I helped him through the final passage with my good hand, pulling him up out of the dirty, dusty duct work.

I had stood there for an instant, with my metal hand pressed up against his forearm, until he turned to look at me and I at him. I observed the curve of his face, the clarity of his eyes. Something about him was so familiar, it was like staring at a ghost I couldn't identify. I wanted so badly to believe he was mine through and through, that my blood flowed through his veins and deep in his marrow, that we shared a fundamental bond. And he wanted to be my son; to fill the role. For what purpose? So he could replace his missing father? So we could lead each other deeper into a fantasy that did not exist?

A motion in his face, a twitch in his jaw revealed his discomfort.

"Does it matter?" he asked.

I said nothing, and we trudged out through the shop, past empty cardboard boxes and disused inventory, old spilled tarot cards and broken glass. The linoleum looked tired and worn, the gypsy garb an empty sham, a front for a woman who never existed. All the Rogers, the guardians and watchers, came here to receive instruction from their god-like mistress. I wondered what they would do now that she was gone. Like abandoned children, would they cry and mourn and weep before picking up their lives, or just elect a new damaged leader to replace the last?

I decided it didn't matter.

Owen silently took the driver's seat of the Thunderbird. I was glad to be in my own car again, this last familiar thing. I drew up the helmet visor so I could clamp a cigarette between my teeth. After a few minutes, Owen coughed, and I kept on smoking. He didn't ask me to stop, but I would have. I didn't ask where he was driving; but I knew at the end of the road, Niko would be waiting for me.

"Do you think she knew? I mean, do you think she understood anything that happened?" he asked after a moment.

Silence. The engine rumbled and I appreciated how the sound filled the void between us. The faint ticking of my bones vibrating with the car. He didn't say her name, but I knew he meant Jessica.

"Would it make you feel better if I said she didn't?"

"Do you think she had a choice?"

Now there was a question to ponder. I hoped he wasn't going to continue to ask these sorts of questions for the whole ride, like a caffeinated three-year-old in the midst of an existential crisis. Why? Why? Why?

"A choice in what?" I asked.

"To act the way she did. Do you think if she knew better, if she understood what was going on, she still would have . . ." he swallowed hard, and I could hear the sound it made in his throat. There was the ghost of stubble on his neck, and I was fascinated by the individual hairs making their way out of the flesh. I missed my flesh. I never knew a person could miss something so elemental, or even survive without it.

"Taken all the kids that she took? Still have brainwashed them, earned their love, then discarded them like trash?" I snorted. "A zombie is kinder than that, Owen. What she did took years. What I did to her took minutes . . ."

The observation hurt, but I made it anyway, hoping that, at least for his benefit, it meant something, mitigated the pain of having been stolen away like a changeling child and then forced to love another, only to be rejected once more. And watch the only mother he ever had reduced to a mass of flies. All come to this.

"If there was a way to fix it all, would you have wanted that? I mean, if there was a cure?"

"Atroxipine? That's no cure. I could have offered it to her, I suppose; for what purpose? To prolong her agony? No, I would have killed her, one way or another."

"No. I mean, a real cure. But it would have cost you your life?"

"I never knew you were philosophical, Owen."

I cast a glance over at him, and he was studying the rearview mirror with fixed intensity, as though the traffic patterns were a vexing puzzle he was determined to figure. I thought it was a strange question to ask, yet another in a long line of Why-Daddy-Why, right up there with Are-we-there-yet? Perhaps he'd ask me the meaning of life next.

I hoped to evade the question. It brought up conflicting emotions in me, and as each second passed, I found myself hating him for asking it, for refusing to meet my decomposing eyes. I hoped he would drop the subject all together as I blew out smoke through the armor's open faceplate and mashed the cigarette into the ashtray.

"I'm serious, Vitus. What would you do?"

I sighed. "There's no going back, Owen. You don't go back after . . ."

I shifted uncomfortably before continuing, almost desperate to make sure he understood.

"After . . . *after*. Your world is a divided between the way it was before . . . what happened, and what happens afterward. And you spend afterward dreaming of the time before. It's a fall from grace,

Owen. If I had the power to restore her, it wouldn't matter. She would forever only be half of what she was. A limping, damaged thing."

Like me, I thought, but did not say.

"Even so," I admitted, "if I had the opportunity, I think I would give it her. Yes, I think I would because, even as damaged as she was, she had the right to make the choice. And I would give my life to her out of gratitude."

"Even though you didn't love her?" he asked, sharply. I didn't think he had cared so much for these interior questions, these introspective leanings. Any other time, I would have told him to shut up and drive or ignored him; but I considered that this conversation could be our last, the last time I would have to tell him my story. His last connection with the only father he would ever have, my last connection with my only son.

"I didn't love her. But I owed her. She suffered greatly for what I did. And that alone would have been reason enough to forfeit my life. It's about being human."

Owen shifted gears as we slowed down and turned into the funeral home driveway. I flipped the visor down over my skeletal face, not desiring to be seen by anyone, even by Niko. I hated to think that this was the last thing she would see or know of me, this empty skeleton creature, as we rolled to a stop.

"Thank you," Owen said, and his face was drawn, his jaw flexing as I viewed him through the narrow visor. "Thank you for helping me understand."

I opened the door, a squeal of metal as I got to my feet and stepped outside the car. I looked back at him through the window as he stopped the engine. I wanted to ask him what he was going to do—I presumed he had no particular place to go. The Cult of the Flesh Eaters was all he knew, and then I realized he was waiting for me, of course. Waiting for me to talk to Niko, let her know we were all right, and then I was supposed to play my part, come back out and take us home, like a father with a son would.

I memorized the slanting blue light of the rising sun across his hard-angled features, casting us both in light and dark. It was all the more precious knowing this was the last time I could do this, watch him through the visor slit and keep him burned on the inside of my eyes just one last time. My patrimony would be made complete with my final abandonment.

I didn't tell him that I wouldn't be leaving the funeral home. And that's where I left him, waiting in the ticking of the cooling car engine, the warming pavement under the morning sun, waiting for a father who did not exist, and who had no intention of ever coming back.

★

I came in through the back door of the funeral home; I did not know the owner of the funeral home or its other employees. I had gotten the impression, considering the time she had kept me there while maggots were busy skeletonizing my body, that the owners were a hands-off bunch, and allowed her to oversee to the day-to-day operation of the intakes. All the same, I didn't want to run into anyone and have to explain why I was dressed in their decorative furnishings.

Silence was impossible. I clanked into the back, between the lines of empty gurneys. There were still no corpses. The room was stark and pulled me back in with the comforting smells of formaldehyde and menthol. The gurneys dressed in clean sheets, covered in foggy plastic, and I fondly remembered our brief make-out session with a thin barrier of polyurethane between us. If I had a mouth left, I would have been smiling, and just as quickly, that smile would have disappeared.

I was not here to remember her or to love her, though I would have liked to have lived long enough to know that sensation. To be a whole man, through and through, with blood and guts and a pumping heart.

I walked down the line of gurneys and chose the one closest to the door. I'd only just settled in with my legs dangling over the side, trying to figure out the best way to start taking off the armor, when the door swung open, and Niko stood there.

She looked paler than usual, and in disarray, as though she had not slept in a long time. Her hair was unkempt and out of place, lending her the atmosphere of a witch set loose with black magic, as though she had just come from a graveyard gathering ingredients for a cauldron. For all that gothic atmosphere, her exhaustion and stress did not lessen her; in fact, her distress intensified everything about her, her glittering eyes, and I could only sit back and watch her, mesmerized. She possessed so much life. I had not felt life in so long, and I felt it keenly now that I was approaching the end of my own.

This was what I remembered most about life, I thought. The rise and fall of my chest when I breathed out, and the accompanying beat of the heart. The pulse of blood through my veins, eating greasy fries at a greasy boardwalk burger joint. The smell on the ocean, the rank salt woven into your clothes and even on cold November days you could still taste it on the rain as though the ocean poured out of the sky. I watched a curl of her black hair resting against the delicate place where her neck and her shoulders met. I missed that tender anatomy, sweeping the hair away and touching it with the back of my hand.

I had none of that now.

I sighed and looked away. I listened to her footsteps as she approached, until she was standing before me. I waited for her protests, her outrage, even her tears; but there was nothing, and the silence terrified me the most. I turned back and stared at her from behind the visor, all the world reduced to a horizontal line.

She studied me with one plump lip caught in her teeth, as though in an agony of indecision. The moment passed. Her features smoothed. Finally, she reached out with both hands to touch my head and then she was lifting the helmet away, baring my skull before the surgical light.

"How can you stand it?" I whispered. "You look at beauty every day. And then you look at this."

"I work with corpses," she said, setting the helmet aside on the gurney beside us.

"But you wake up in the morning, and you look in the mirror. And every day, you wear that beautiful face."

She said nothing. There was nothing left to say.

I thought of all the things I could say as she knelt down and began to undo the metal plates that covered my feet, the calves, and on up to my thighs, exposing the sad bones that made my body, their porous, ossified surfaces, as though I had been picked clean by ravens and left to bleach in a desert sun. I wanted her with a fierce stab of desire. If I could not have her with my body, I wanted to take her with words, fuck her, saturate her with as much sex as I could violate my vocabulary with. But I did not have the words, only the silence. And it stretched out between us as thick as blood and tissue and membrane.

One by one, she shed me free of my metal casing. The bits of armor came away reluctantly as though they had found a monster worth calling master. I missed it in my own way, for the safety it afforded me, for the comfort it had provided against the harsh elements, shielding me from wind and light and fire. Even from the flies.

When the last plate of armor had yielded and she set it aside with the others on the gurney, she returned. Her jaw clenched as though that were the linchpin holding the rest of her face together. If she lost that, everything would collapse into a wound, a vulnerability that could not be repaired.

"Lay back," she whispered.

I struggled to do it, to brace myself with my skeletal arms, and she came to my aid, reaching behind me and taking my weight in measures until I lay flat against the gurney. I wished I could feel the warmth of her touch, as I would have with skin, but there was nothing but the hardness of bone, and it is unforgiving against her tenderness.

I listened to the sounds of her moving as she set up the pump beside me. I reached out suddenly, a desperate grab, and caught the thin material of her dress in my carpel finger bones, pulling her toward me.

"Let me listen," I croaked, pulling her down toward me. "Let me listen one last time."

She didn't understand right away. And then I had my skull pressed up against her chest, with her ample breasts fringing my vision, and I could have wept in gratitude that she suffered it, allowed a monster to kneel at her body, for the grace it could bestow.

And I heard it, deep in the hollow of her rib cage, that miracle that stops and starts and stops again, does it over and over, perfectly and without fail. The sound we come to life with, the sound we are ushered out with. I shuddered and felt her arms on my bones, registering as an insistent pressure.

"Vitus," she whispered. Then, again: "Vitus." Not a question. An assertion and a name.

"Yes," I whispered, and released her.

She pulled away, and then I felt her lifting my head and setting a pillow beneath me. I wondered if she had done this sort of thing at the Lazar House in Hawaii, that she did it with such patience, without revulsion, without shame. Had she done it for her mother?

I did not know, and I did not ask.

These were the last seconds. My life ebbing like a tide. I turned my skull to see the clock above the door, to note the time as I heard her delicate fingers rattle the scalpel against the tray: 9:36 in the morning. I had always thought I would have met a murderous end on a dark night. It pleased me to believe that I would die while the sunlight poured in from the small windows. I turned back and looked at the armor laid out on the gurney like the bones of an ancient dinosaur, waiting to be reconstructed.

"Are you ready?" she asked.

Her voice was flat. She covered it well, but I could see the glistening line of a single salt tear from her eye, down to her throat, where it disappeared beneath the collar of her jacket. I wished I could have followed it all the way to her warm center and become nothing, nothing at all, but a part of her.

"I'm ready," I whispered.

Goodbye to the world, goodbye to these bones; goodbye to Niko with her sad memories of the Lazar House in Hawaii, of palm trees and absent digits, empty spaces where fingers should be. Goodbye to the son I should have had, goodbye to the son I killed. Goodbye to bad memories and cancer sticks and criminals and betraying brothers and apathetic scientists and old gray foxes and forgotten mothers in nursing homes. Goodbye.

Vitus Adamson is finished with life and death, and at this last, I offer no prayers to Heaven and Hell, but one—that there be neither—and when I am dead, I may be nothing at all.

A syringe appeared in her hands, the needle a sliver of light dripping serum; I felt the pressure of the sharp tip penetrate between the vertebrae of my neck and skull, through the tender spinal nerves beneath.

And the world went dark.

PART 4

GOODBYE TO THE BONES

Thump-de-thump.
     Thump-de-thump.
     Thump-de-thump.
Heaven sounds like a heart.
Thump-de-thump.

My fingers moved. Cotton beneath their tips. For a long time there was no thought in my head, only the steady beat of a heart in the background of my thoughts. My ears filled with the ocean-sized sound of rushing blood. All these sensations so old they feel brand new. Sensations carried with us from the cradle to the grave, so common and shared and universal we fail to notice them. Not until they are gone from us.

Then, you notice. You notice the silence of your every wasting day and you feel the sensation of rot and corruption bloom from within to steadily consume and replace your heart. Filling it with darkness and mold.

But that was long ago and far away. Far away from the clean cotton beneath my fingers. Individual hairs that made up my eyelashes whispered over my cheek bones, and then they lifted and the darkness was gone. I stared at the ceiling, prostrate on a soft mattress, covered with clean sheets that smelled like baking soda and laundry detergent.

I smelled flowers. I turned my head and white roses were arranged in a vase beside me.

It's my funeral, I realized. *I'm in a coffin.*

I lifted my head to gaze down at myself, but there was no coffin. I lay in a bed dressed in a white shirt. No fluid stains, no mold decorated the surface.

Beneath the shirt, my chest rose and fell and hypnotized me with steady motion.

This is so strange, I thought. Slowly, I rose. My every motion measured and cautious, because I expected to render the moment asunder, that everything would fall apart to reveal the illusion, the joke. Am I dead, am I alive? Heaven or Hell, or a waiting room for either?

I reached for my Glock, but I wasn't wearing the holster. I glanced to the side of me, an end table. My wallet, my keys, spare change, and the gun with the holster. A pair of handcuffs. I picked them all up, stuffed the handcuffs into my back pocket, and felt the heavy weight of the weapon in my hand. I studied the lines of my fingers, the wrinkles in the peach-toned flesh of my skin against the cold metal.

It feels real, I thought, hefting the weight. *It feels real. More real than real.*

The thought carried with it a growing urgency. I strapped on the holster, and nearly stumbled out of the bed. The sensation of feet that don't squish or rattle with each step took me by surprise. I felt the muscles and tissues layered against the bone. I felt . . . healthy. Alive. Vital. *Cohesive.*

I felt *alive.*

I could hear my heart.

Thump-de-thump.

So long desensitized and dead, all my latent feelings coming to life, sending my nerve endings afire. Information processed through me with lightning speed, with no purpose or reason, overwhelming me with observations both trivial and immense.

Light poured in from the nearby window where the end table glowed with oaken warmth; hardwood under my toes, and my toes were naked. The nails at the end of my toes fascinated me, the grain of the surface where it layered over the skin, the coldness of the floor beneath. I shivered with the delight of the draft creeping through the building itself and the clean undershirt stretched over my carriage. My body felt proud and graceful as a lion rising from the Serengeti. I burst into laughter that bubbled up through me until I was effervescent with light and weightlessness. *My god, what is this, what is this feeling?*

I knew the truth, the revelation, before I thought it.

I am *alive.*

Thoughts of how, why, what, crowded in on me, but I worked with a paucity of facts. I did not even know where I was. I opened the door to my bedroom. *This is not my house,* I thought, but that's not true. Everything here is familiar but strange. My vision reported brighter images than I had seen since my eyes went dim ten years ago. Everything stood out in hyper-contrast. Someone had taken the time to insert brand new lightbulbs into all the sockets I had emptied when I first died so the world stood brand new and awash in light.

It is like standing in the middle of the sun.

I reached up and touched my face. Stubble beneath my palm. I gasped with the freshness of it, a grin spreading beneath my fingers as though I had never smiled in my life, as though I could hold it and keep it with me always. A supernova in my chest, a heaviness; I chased the breath, hyperventilating and falling back onto the bed with an arm outstretched as though I could hold the air itself for support.

This was my marriage bed. The whole room had been cleaned and stripped and old items of Jessica and Clay's packed and carted away. The sheets new, the mattress new. The place alive and transformed with the touch of someone who loves and cares for the man inside of it.

Maybe it's the past, I thought. *Maybe this is a flashback.*

But it's no distant memory come to life. I tasted wood fire on the air and lemon polish, the glass of water on the end table.

I got up again, thrilled with the sensations as they came and went and relentlessly continued. Every strand of hair on my body stood on end as though they could reach out and touch and feel the world around me. I looked for a mirror, but there was none. I passed out of the room and into the hallway. Closer to the heart of the house, I heard small sounds in the kitchen, and I recognized her figure, the clean lines of her back encased in a long, black dress. Trickles of her black curls ran down her back.

Niko.

I wanted to say her name, and my lips parted. I touched my face again to confirm that I was not a zombie, not a pre-deceased. I did not want her to know I watched her, only remain here and steal the moment in secret. She cleaned a dish in the sink. Water lapped against her hands as she lathered them with soap. The motion caused her hair to shimmer as it moved, the curves of her body like a fine instrument that invited to be played by an expert.

Barefooted, I stepped quietly over the hardwood floor, creeping up on her with military precision. My toes reported the chill surface, but I didn't care; the cold was delicious in this skin.

I touched her on the shoulder with my fingertips. She startled, raven hair falling over her side as her electric blue eyes met mine. Her expression fascinated me, the turn of her nose, the shape of her full mouth, but mostly the look behind her eyes, the look of assessment, judgment, consideration, and appreciation.

Attraction.

Yes, I thought, without hesitation, I cupped a palm to her cheek. Her hands were still wrist deep in dishwater, and I pulled her away. White suds fell from her fingertips in clumps like snow. She pressed a foamed hand against my chest, and the pressure delighted me, every nerve skin tight as a snare drum. My heart thudded against her palm.

I leaned in and kissed her.

She wanted more. Her mouth pressed insistently against me, her lathered hands pushing across my chest until she maneuvered me against the counter. If this was a dream, I liked where it was heading.

No words were exchanged. Her lips traced the slope of my neck to the shoulder, smearing red lipstick on the collar of my undershirt. I tore at the shoulder of her dress, revealing a bra strap that quickly followed suit. Her hands fumbled at the waistband of my pants and I lost my purpose as I felt the cold draft and her slick fingers take me in hand. Dish detergent and baking soda and soap bubbles.

God, I had forgotten. Ten years is too long.

"Now," I gasped, swallowing air and yanking her dress so hard it ripped with a squealing tear. I didn't care. I'd become an animal in my desire to recover all I had lost, to reclaim my right to the human race, to reassert my place, to satisfy this hunger. Our coupling was furious. I hoisted her onto the counter with a growl and I heard her gasp and felt her shudder, my insistent fingers digging into her shoulders to keep her steady as I thrust up and into her. We did it without thought, without consideration, though I imagined I would have stopped at her urging, but she pressed on me with as much force as I exerted on her.

She moaned into the ceiling with her hair snarled over my encircling, strangling arms. Sweat dripping down my temples, slicking my hair. I opened up the front of her dress to reveal a pair of perfectly formed breasts and bowed to anoint the center crease with tongue and saliva, taking a nipple into my mouth like the bud of a rose. I could not close my eyes, but watch her and shudder and tremble in time with her.

I tasted her skin and was not hungry.

I tasted outside wood fires and the soap she bathed with. She moved with helpless gasps, her eyes closed, her mouth open, her breath rushing like a bellows. I studied her face, transfixed by her flesh and all the ways that it moved, flesh I had once envied and coveted and wished for my own. Flesh I now had.

And I would never be hungry again.

The moment arrived, culminating in a climax that ached and hurt with its desperation. Just as swiftly the moment passed, her ragged breath intermixing with the sounds of my own. I

felt stunned and overwhelmed and drunk on the experience as
I pulled away from her, bare feet slipping against the floor. I
pulled my clothes back over my skin, mesmerized by the sight of
my own dick. I'd lost it years ago, signed it off and forgot about
it. Here it was, renewed, a fleshy beast of hungry dimensions.
I tucked it out of sight and braced myself against the cabinets,
every limb and cell inside me shaking.

She smoothed out the lines and wrinkles of her dress. I stared
without shame or care while she did it. She put herself back
together, piece by piece, pulling up underwear that had been
discarded across the burner in the heat of the moment, brushing
back hair matted with sweat. I cast my glance around the room,
and there were no mirrors.

That's odd, I thought. *I never liked them much, sure, but there
was at least one or two . . .*

I turned back and discovered Niko staring at me. Her eyes
were huge, frightened. We were both glassy eyed and coming
down from our climactic high with terminal velocity.

I cleared my throat. "Do you have a mirror?"

Niko bit her lower lip, and said nothing.

I tilted my head, and if the gesture was condescending, it was
meant to be, because after all, what girl doesn't carry a mirror
with her?

"Niko," I said.

"I don't have one," she insisted. Anxiety needled up my spine.
She didn't want me to see. And in an instant, a thousand images
detonated into my mind, like a two-ton weight impacting on my
skull, sending an information rampage cascading down every
nerve ending in my body. I remembered Jamie, Niko, Owen,
every small image and inconsequential moment magnified,
connections drawn between all of them and everywhere.

"Niko."

There was a darkness in my voice I thought I had left behind
with those useless bones I had once been. This was not a dream
anymore; it was turning in a nightmare, a nightmare propped
up on top of other nightmares, and Niko was hiding it from me.
Hiding everything she could reveal with a circle of mirror.

When she did not move, I was electrified with rage, a bitterness that I had forgotten in the brief minutes of this new life, all the old memories of my world before infecting and infesting me. I snatched her purse from the counter and with one swift motion upended it all over the kitchen, items scattering everywhere, tissues and receipts, makeup, movie tickets, her driver's license and crumpled bills. A makeup case with a vanity glass.

I snatched at it and she jumped as though she had thought to step in and take it from me. Her mouth opened, but she closed it and forced herself to stillness. She stared at me with an intensity I found unnerving.

I opened the case and looked at myself.

But I did not see myself.

I saw Owen.

✶

Owen. Self-proclaimed son of my flesh, my doppelgänger. My haunted eyes stared out from his flesh, my breath leaving my lungs in one explosive gasp. I strangled the urge to draw the Glock and shoot the mirror, blast it into smithereens all over the kitchen floor.

I looked up at Niko. My hand with the mirror in it trembled, and then went as steady as a flatline.

"This is not natural," I whispered. "This smells like Jamie. This smells military."

She flinched. Confirmed.

"Talk. Now. Explain this."

Her mouth opened, a round, empty hole, and then closed again. She lifted a hand to wipe at her lips as though she could nudge the words back inside her mouth.

"I'm not angry," I assured her, taking a deep breath to demonstrate my equanimity over the secret tumult inside. "But I think I deserve the truth, don't you, Agent?"

She hitched in a breath. "It's not like that, I didn't know—"

"Spare me the details. I'm waiting for your answer. I'm supposed to be dead. I asked you to kill me and that was the agreement we had, and yet, here I find myself alive, improved, and you're cooking in my kitchen. Hmmm? I'm waiting."

She tried again, a flush creeping into her cheeks.

"Jamie knew all along that Jessica had never died," she whispered. Her head hung, her chin leaning against her collarbone in her despondence. "They monitored her from afar, for a long time. Years."

I dared not interrupt her. Inside, a flood of protests stoppered within me. Why, Jamie, why? Why didn't you put her out of her misery? What motivation was there to let a zombie wander among society unchecked? And they had let her do it.

"He didn't tell me too much about that, only that they knew, and I guess because she was, y'know, different, they wanted to see how it would 'play out.' That's how he put it. Play, like something children do, you know? Medical research. Scientific data. You were the experiment for Atroxipine. Jessica . . . she was the control."

She shuffled her feet and crossed her arms, sneaking a glance at me from beneath the black fringe of her hair.

"Owen had been doing undercover work in the cult compound. Once the Rogers made their first visit to you, all the stops were pulled out and Jamie's been in town ever since, calling me into active duty. He said . . ."

I cut her off, sickened. "I know what he said."

Owen had been an operative all along. And yet, something uncanny about that connection stayed with me, knocking against my brain. Operative? Within the compound?

What operative starts at such a tender age? There was nothing legal about recruiting kids to serve . . . unless he'd been recruited after the fact, long after he'd been abducted by Jessica and then fled on his own. They could have approached him at any time after he'd cut his ties to the cult, and he'd have been a perfect person to use to infiltrate. As one of them, he could move among them easily, and report everything back.

And yet . . . the information hummed inside me, demanding my attention.

"Niko, where's Owen?"

Better yet, *who* was Owen?

Her eyes were wide and huge.

After a long moment, she began to tell me.

★

Owen left the Thunderbird in the parking lot to funeral home. From any distance, he might have been a high school kid waiting for friends before he ducked inside, scoping the empty tarmac with a level of penetration no high school kid possessed. When he was satisfied that he was alone, he slipped inside, past the lobby.

Static electricity built up beneath his feet as he stopped, feet away from the door that led to the intake room. Past the empty space where the knight would have been. He could see through a square of glass set in the door, a long line of gurneys. Vitus in his armor sat in the middle, with Niko bent down before him. Through the glass, Owen's eyes met Niko's, and the moment gave him the impetus he needed to hurry on past, over to the back room the funeral director used to balance the accounting and do paperwork and soothe the bereaved.

Niko entered a few moments later. She brought strange underworld scents of her funerary tasks with her, exhausted by the constant pressure of her many secrets. They rode her thin and ragged like wild horses, keeping her up at all hours, tossing and turning with all the things she wanted to do but could not, wanted to change but remained helpless to do so. She had been putting off this moment as long as possible, and now they were alone together in the room.

She stood at the door and stared at the wallpaper. A stain in the rug. Things that needed to be done and taken care of . . . until at last she looked at Owen.

"Have you decided yet?"

Owen nodded. She thought his eyes deepened a shade into a somber palette, infused with saturnine weight. His face young, heartbreakingly young for his wizening eyes.

"I'm going to go through with it," he said slowly.

"Why?" she whispered. "Bone marrow transplants are unpleasant. He needs more than that."

He shifted his feet as one does when buying time for an uncomfortable answer. Several chairs lined the small accounting room, a desk with papers spread over it, but neither could sit or relax. They were abuzz with nervous tension, not because of the company they kept—they were waiting for Jamie.

"Gratitude," he said simply.

Impatiently, she tapped her feet. Vitus was knocked out in the other room, and she told him so, but she feared to leave him there for long.

"Don't worry," Owen sighed. "I don't think it will be long at all."

He was right.

Jamie burst into the room, breathing heavy. The weight of middle age softened him and lent a latent innocence to his baby face completely absent in Vitus's. What Niko found repulsive about him was the personality underlying his sympathetic features; his need for control and bureaucracy repelled her. She could not bring herself to disguise her disdain, thinking it was men like this who would have left people like her mother in a Lazar House to die.

Left people like Vitus to die.

And hadn't he, in his own way? Abandoned his brother to a life he had shared responsibility in creating, and then gone about his own without a worry in the world?

She waited as Jamie took a seat behind the desk as though he owned the place, a man used to being deferred to on the basis of his high clearance level alone. He might not be CIA, but whatever his standing was within the various branches of military, it was enough to sway influence on levels she didn't care to think about. His smallest actions breathed entitlement.

When he was finally settled, he looked up and took his glasses off to set them aside on the desk.

"Debrief me, please," he motioned to Owen, tonelessly.

Owen's mouth turned into a bitter line, and he began with his return to the compound as Vitus recovered at the funeral home. He spoke of the shop, abandoned and dusty with age; the ventilation shaft, the dead bodies of the poisoned children. He found Jessica's body in the fray, recognizing it only by the wedding ring on her hand. She had been reduced to bones after the maggots were done with her.

"The ring?" Jamie asked, curious.

"I returned it to Vitus."

"Ah," he said, and gestured for Owen to continue.

He picked up as though he had not been interrupted. He had expected to do no more than make sure there were no survivors, and if there had been he would have assisted them. With no one left alive, he weighed his options and decided fire would be the best way to destroy any sign of their presence. While determining the best way to do this, he stumbled across a body, upsetting a host of flies that had been seething within it. Yet, this event was not unique to this singular disturbed body. Every corpse exploded with flies crawling and teeming beneath the flesh.

Ordinarily, flies would not have bothered him to such an extent; the whole thing struck him as silly, but—

"It was the way they moved," he explained, becoming animated with the fear of the moment. "They took form, one by one, they amassed themselves together, moving in concert. They displayed sentient intelligence and coordinated movement. I locked myself in a room and shoved a blanket beneath the door. The few flies that managed to follow me in I killed, but I was terrified to leave. I had no doubt in my mind that if the entity wanted to, it could form itself into a human."

"Do you believe it desired to kill you?"

He paused before answering. "At the time, I was convinced it could only be malignant, but in retrospect, I wonder if I had not been so overwhelmed by the fear and isolation, I would have thought differently. I couldn't say now for sure, no."

"But it's possible it may have been attempting to communicate?"

"It may have had that capability, but I didn't dare wait around to find out. I waited until I heard their buzzing fade, and even then I was reluctant to leave. I believed it was capable of setting a trap, and when it had been some time and still no sound, I left and kept to the shadows. I wanted to rethink my strategy and make sure I could eliminate the flies before I left."

Jamie nodded and Owen continued, recounting events until the moment he heard the clanking metal steps approaching down the hall, to the cellar room door where he hid in shadow, until low and behold, a knight in shining armor appeared.

"Sort of," Owen amended.

"He took the armor?" Jamie asked, incredulous.

"You did notice it was missing, right?" Niko said acidly, and he ignored the tone while she rolled her eyes. "What did you expect him to leave in? A suit and tie? Armor's not a bad idea when all you've been reduced to is a skeleton."

"I did not expect it, is all. It seems like . . ."

"Overkill?" Owen asked. He had been silent during Niko's brief comment, and expressionless despite Jamie's reaction, his retelling largely objective and likewise emotionless. Now, he allowed himself a vehement observation:

"I think you underestimate what it does to a man to look down at himself and discover everything that makes him human has been taken away. I do not know how he manages to keep his sanity."

Jamie sighed, displeased with this lapse in formality. He motioned to him to continue where he left off, and Owen did, without a change in expression. He described the events like a newscaster reading off a teleprompter. The fire in the basement, the escape through the ventilation shaft.

"Then we drove back here," he said without elaboration. "And that's where we stand now."

"I see," Jamie said only.

"I thought you were bringing back the cure?" Niko prompted. "Vitus is laid out right now, I thought I'd have it before I had to put him out."

Jamie waived a hand, exasperated. "He's been dead ten years, he can wait five more minutes."

Jamie dismissed her, and Niko swallowed back a curse. She did not like the way he waved away Vitus's fate, as though it were no more to him than a traffic weather report, his skeletal discomfort of no more concern than a rift in an ocean. He turned from her and stared hard at Owen.

"Well," he said, and his tone had changed, turned abrupt. "Amos, have you made your decision?"

Amos? Niko thought.

The words hung in the air, heavy.

It occurred to Niko that the words they spoke were laden with veiled meanings; that, in fact, all of the words they had spoken were suspect, a language designed so only Owen and Jamie would decipher it, leaving her to guess at what secrets they were exchanging under her nose.

Her hands clenched at her sides; the sensation of duplicity, of having missed something in their words, overwhelmed her.

Owen breathed out. "I'm ready."

"You willingly choose this? You insist upon this course? Think hard. I . . . I beg you to reconsider."

Jamie's last word broke, and in the silence, Owen made a fist and looked away.

"Do it."

Jamie's head sank.

His hand lifted from the desk; she thought perhaps he brought a pen up, but the object in his hand was a .45 of black steel and he shot it once, flame bursting from the end as his wrist snapped back and then all was still. She tasted lead on her lips. Her ears rang from the sound but she didn't move an inch, not even to jump; it had all happened so fast, she stood there, playing back the scene in her mind, waiting for her brain to catch up with her eyes.

Owen did not fall. He didn't rock back with the bullet, the way she thought they did in movies when people got shot. It sliced through him as easily as throwing a dart into a board in a sleazy bar, and he looked down at himself. A surgical hole in his black shirt. He touched it with a trembling hand, and then his mouth opened a little, his breath came in fast, unable to catch it. His blood-red finger curled into a loose fist.

He fell then, unable to support himself. Niko felt the wall meet her back, unaware that she had been retreating, ears ringing through a deep freeze. Their voices dwindling to a radio broadcast from a distant planet.

"Aren't you even going to ask why?" Owen whispered. Blood colored his lips and sprayed from his mouth as he spoke.

Jamie rose from the desk but did not move from behind it. He watched Owen, waiting for him to go on or die first. He did not speak but adjusted his tie.

"Because he's a better father than you ever were," Owen spat.

Niko thought people who were shot died fast. And while Owen didn't take his time, he didn't leave right away, either. His eyes dimmed and his face froze into a tragedy mask with the lips drawn back from his bloody teeth and gums as he strained to breathe. His hands clutched at his chest where the bullet had passed through before stopping in the wall behind him.

"I gave you everything," Jamie whispered as he stared at him. His voice broke at the last, a single tremor of emotion that betrayed everything he imprisoned behind his corrupt, bureaucratic facade, a man who traded away his integrity for advancement in his career in a desperate gamble to fix the mistakes of his past, to fix the brother he had destroyed, to be a better father to the son who did not love him. He had the look of man who could not grasp why everything he touches leaves a stain that no effort of science or good intention could wash away.

"You were but a child when you insisted that I put you to service. I broke rules for you. I bent a thousand laws and burned more red tape than you'll ever know over ethics and moral codes to set up your infiltration into Jessica's cult. You convinced your own mother that I should feed you to the wolves! You rejected schooling, you rejected all the playthings and luxuries that any seven-year-old would have given anything for. At thirteen you were uncontrollable. At fifteen, when I refused you, you would not eat, you went on a hunger strike, you forced me to relent and give you a place in the military no sane man would sacrifice his child, his son to. Everything you asked for—I gave it and more! And still, for all this, I will always be second place in your heart to Vitus."

Owen coughed, a bubble of blood emerging from his lips, his eyes glassy, rolling in their sockets. Through his labored breath, he smiled.

"You didn't even make it to second place," he heaved out with effort.

Jamie sent a fist to the surface of the desk. Wood buckled beneath it as he shoved stacks of papers and books to the floor in a rage, newspapers and forms fluttering to the ground, his face flushing red with an inarticulate cry of frustration and despair.

"Why?" Jamie whispered. "You would not let me rest until I gave you what you wanted. You wanted this! You chose this, against my every plea, against all my arguments! I signed your death warrant at *your* insistence, and it's not enough for your love, is it, son? What does it take to earn that place in your heart that my brother so effortlessly occupies? He killed his wife and child. Without me, he'd be nothing! *What does it take?*"

Owen grinned, red gums, teeth stark white against the blood. He opened his mouth to answer, to give Jamie the definitive reason he sought, a whistling inhale of breath as he prepared to speak . . . and then his arms fell away from his chest and his breathing stopped with his heart. His eyes were still alight, processing the last of the oxygen that was keeping his brain alive. Then, slowly, that too faded, and all that remained was the warmth of his body. What he struggled to say in his last moments remained unsaid.

Niko did not scream. She did not cry. She wanted it all to go back, to pull out the bullet and reverse the damage like a tape in rewind, but it wasn't a movie. Her swallow of panic made an audible click in her throat, and in an instant, she thought of their conversation when she had first come in—

Have you decided yet?

I'm going to go through with it.

Why?

Gratitude.

She gasped. She did not realize she was crying until she felt the tears. Salt burning on her skin. It had never been about surgery, about bone marrow transplants.

"Take him," Jamie said wearily. "Take him to Vitus. One of our people will show you what to do with him."

"What?" she hissed. "What am I supposed to do with a murdered body, you fuck?"

His look darkened, and she watched his hand on the .45. It did not move, but she had no doubt as he pursed his lips and stared at her that he entertained the possibility of making it two dead people instead of one.

"You're supposed to use it to cure Vitus," he said quietly. "The maggots were key. A happy accident. I should have thought of it. The one thing we hadn't thought of that could skeletonize him, deprive him of his infected tissue. That put Vitus in phase one and resolved our first problem for iatrogenic infection. Our second problem was identifying the genesis of infection in his body. It can spread through blood and skin, but Virus X doesn't breed in the brain tissue. It breeds in the marrow."

Niko's jaw dropped.

"No blood, no Virus . . ."

"Everything has to be replaced. A complete restoration."

"That can't be possible."

He laughed without mirth; stared down at his gun.

"We've done some trial runs since Vitus came back with the maggots. The problem is the bone marrow, you see. Blood cells come from bone marrow. The virus is bone-deep, Niko. We can change his skin, his muscle, his tissue . . . but his bone marrow can only come from a donor who matches his genetic typing. A blood relation."

Her breath caught in her mouth as she stared at Owen's crumpled figure on the floor.

"Why'd you let him do it?" she gasped. "You're related to him, too!"

"He wanted it! You think I didn't beg and plead with him every day? Damn you, Vitus," he hissed, slamming a fist against the table. "Amos—Owen—had it in his head ever since that funeral, when he watched Vitus's wife and child buried. He wanted to be just like him, wanted to save him. Wanted to replace the son Vitus lost."

"You could have been a donor instead."

"As much as it pains me to say it, Amos was a soldier in his heart. He could be replaced. But if I offered myself . . . who do you think was going to be left behind who would be smart enough to undo the damage? To clean the mess? To bring the genius of science to bear on the undead corpse that is my brother? Who, with what knowledge, was going to be able to pick up the pieces? Hm?"

"You didn't kill your son for Vitus. You killed him because you couldn't stand that he loved Vitus more than you. You wouldn't suffer it."

Jamie licked his lips and looked away.

"Go now," he urged, waving the gun to get her moving. "Wait with Vitus. The team will be in with what you need and they'll do the dirty work. Get him ready, Niko. Don't let my son's death be in vain."

A team of scientists and doctors encased in hazmat suits waited for her at the door. A phone rang and Jamie turned away with the receiver at his ear, speaking in hushed tones. Papers scattered on his makeshift desk. She made out her own damning recruitment form and beneath that, a shuffled paper with a presidential seal over an envelope and scrawled signatures, one signed with the name *Echo Inspector* and the other *Todd Adamson*. Then she was swept her away with the scientists and doctors, who gingerly danced around Vitus's skeleton as though a puff of air from his direction had the power to infect them all.

She laid out Owen on a gurney beside him. She had met Owen when he first arrived with Vitus, carrying him into the funeral home wrapped inside a blanket. She had not known him enough to truly mourn him; she grieved for different reasons. She grieved for what Vitus had to wake up to.

✱

And now, I was awake.

I stared at her as though I did not recognize her. I heard the words but could not seem to comprehend them. My flesh was alive and stinging with the aftermath of our sex, a musk lingered in the air. Sweat branded the small of my back in a trickle. I was alive and in love with every new sensation inside this flesh, and alternately disgusted, sickened and horrified by everything I heard.

"Owen was Amos. Amos was Jamie's," I whispered. My voice came out strangled. "Jamie's son."

Niko did not answer. I did not expect her to. I reeled in the moment, more isolated and alone than I had ever been before, even when I had been pre-deceased.

I held a hand to my forehead to stop the deluge of memories, but there could be no stopping it. I remembered the nephew in greater clarity—Jamie so proud over the phone, describing his newborn son from the hospital; the boy playing at my feet when I visited and my brother and I argued over Sarajevo and the old gray fox. The boy, always in the periphery, fading into the background. The boy with his head bent over his homework and his report cards. The boy, artfully invisible and studying espionage and war games at a fever pitch.

I pictured his birth certificate, the name writ bold: AMOS OWEN ADAMSON.

Fuck. In front of me all along.

But that was not quite the whole story, was it? Jamie pulled the trigger for any number of reasons corrupt and personal; but Amos gave up his life.

The second the thought manifested blood rushed out of my face.

"My boy," I gasped, and Niko reached out to steady me. "He knew. He had a choice, and he let it happen."

I could not process the event, as hard as I tried. It spoke volumes of devotion, of love, of the infinite size of Amos's heart. And he'd given it all to me, and why? Out of misplaced loyalty for a father? For me?

Gratitude.

Because he's a better father than you ever were.

Oh, dear god. The conversation from the car on our way back from the basement came back to me full force, every memory burning with new meaning, his veiled questions in his quiet voice, lulling me into answers I would never have given under different circumstances.

He felt he had owed me something. To pay for what his father had done. He gave his life to set right to a thousand and one wrongs, and the sacrifice of that decision made me want to cave into myself and cry until the crying itself killed me, stopped my heart like a broken clock and let me live to feel this no more. It seemed impossible while I slumped against the kitchen cabinets with my useless legs folded up, trembling as Niko struggled to hold me, that I should ever get up again, that I should continue to live, that anyone should have given me such a precious gift. Shame, hurt, love, bitterness, all these things and more swept through me like fire in the pines. Reduced all my ideas of self-worth into ashes.

And from deep inside, my old friend, my Id, had words to share:

This is a gift, he assented with urgency. *What do you intend to do with it, now that he has given so much in return?*

I turned and looked at Niko. Her eyes were dewy and threatened to spill over with tears. Perhaps it was the devastation on my face that moved her so, or the reasons were more elemental, the memories of that time and the murder itself.

"Niko," I whispered, and reinforced her embrace by lifting my own arms to clutch her close to me. She relaxed in my grip, all supple lines and soft flesh yielding to me. It aroused me to think I could take her again, here on the kitchen floor, and I had to suppress the desire. It still didn't help, and I hardened instantly, my mind touch-starved for ten long years and this body newly minted.

Click.

She stiffened as I locked the handcuff around her slight wrist.

"Vitus—" she began, and before she could struggle, I had her wrist enclosed in the second cuff like a bracelet, linked over the exposed plumbing pipes beneath the kitchen sink, leaving her other hand free as she protested with a cry. I didn't care.

"Vitus? What are you doing?"

I didn't answer, but left her on the floor as I rose, dust feathering patterns up her black dress as she curled against the cabinets, staring up at me with wide eyes, ossifying into marcasite. She did not waste her breath to beg or plead, to appeal to my better nature, or manipulate me with promises of love and devotion. Her tears were drying quickly.

She was no femme fatale. She didn't deserve this. But I was pissed, and hey—all relationships need work. And she could start by working on the handcuffs.

"Where are you going?" she asked, yanking at the cuff and busily examining the plumbing. I didn't answer her, turning on my bare feet and collecting my discarded undershirt, locating a button-down stuffed hastily in the closet from years ago. It was wrinkled and moth-eaten, but it would do. I slipped it on, found my shoes. In moments, I was dressed, and as I pulled my sleeve through my coat, I knocked over something on the end table.

The orange pill bottle. She had left it there for me. Niko's voice faded into the background as she cursed my name, and the bottle buzzed in return. It was the bottle Owen had given me as we were leaving the basement, a faint memory of the monster I used to be.

I'm human now, I realized. But I did not feel human.

Inside the pill bottle, the last reminder of a knight and his loyal son buzzed at the orange structure, defiantly beating his wings and his black, hairy body. He looked angry from the outside, desperate to get to me, to taste me, to tell his friends and make more friends inside the warmth of my flesh.

"I've got someone you can start on," I spoke to the fly, and shoved the bottle into my pocket. "His name is Jamie."

And I left Niko there on the floor, with a fly in my pocket and a loaded gun in my hand.